FALLEN

FALLING FROM HELL SERIES
BOOK ONE

SUSAN PERSON

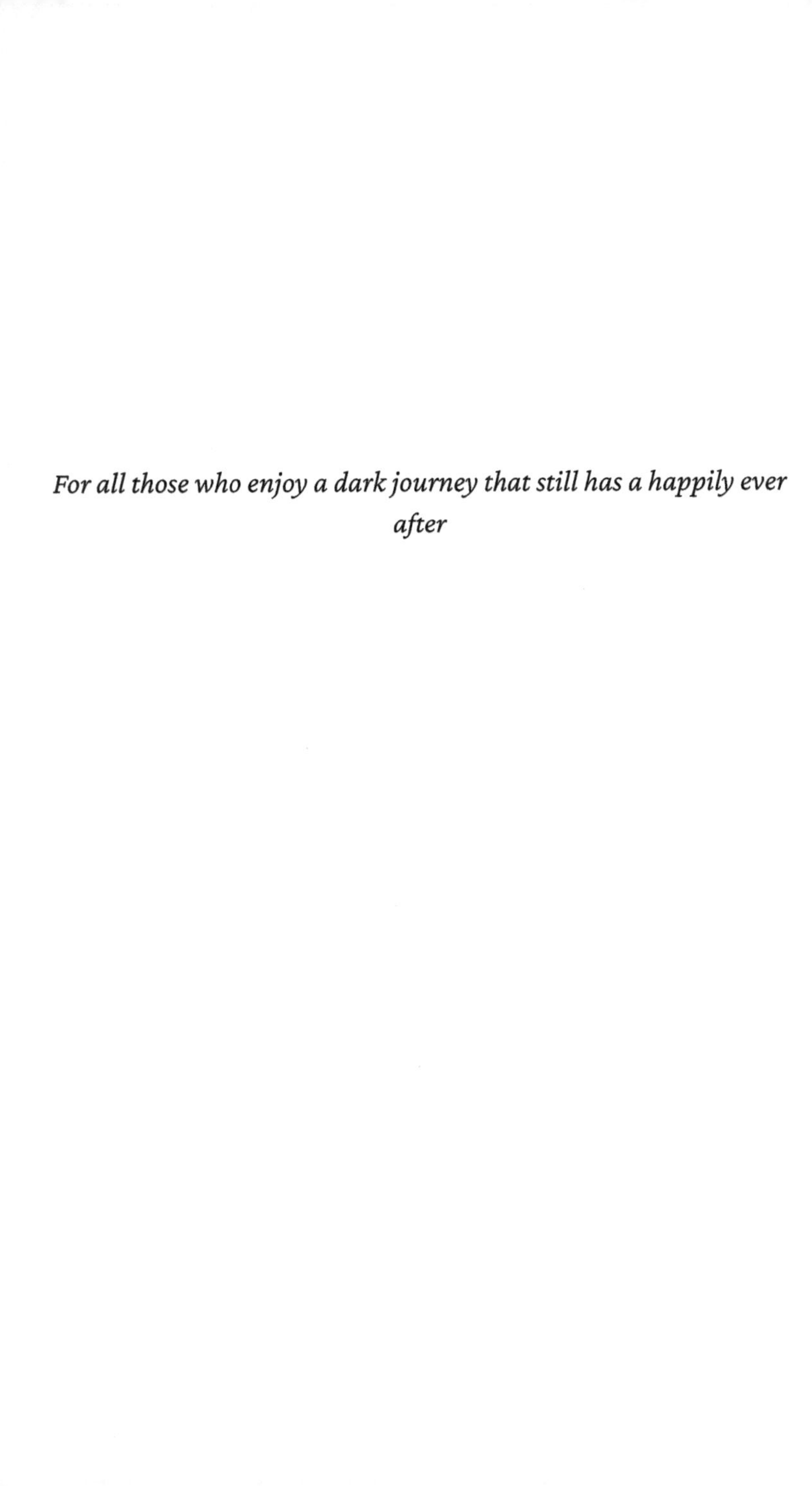

For all those who enjoy a dark journey that still has a happily ever after

FALLEN

CHAPTER 1
MORENA

"Morena," my father called to me as I walked past the door to his study. "Morena, we have a present for your trip." One year with humans. My mother and father granted me one year to live among the humans before I return to Hell with my decision. *When your parents are Lilith and Lucifer, negotiating is part of the daily.*

I peered into the expansive room to find Father seated at the conference table, expecting to see Uncle Amon with him, but he wasn't there. I glanced at the clock on the wall. This was his normal time to meet with Amon. *Strange.* Two demons I didn't know as well nodded their heads in my direction. I returned the gesture. Father waved his hand to dismiss them, and they exited without a word. *Bizarre even for Hell.*

Father smiled his Devil's smile and held his arms out to me. He hugged me to him.

"Your mother is very nervous about your trip, so I'm giving you this." He picked up a lacquered box with a pentagram carved into the top and held it open to me. His prized dagger with its black metal blade and red handle rested on a sea of blue velvet. This blade was one fashioned from the strongest metal and forged in Hell's own fires.

I glanced up at him shocked by what was in front of me. "But this is your favorite."

He lifted the dagger from the box and handed it to me. "And now it is yours. Draw it across your palm, and instead of summoning me to you, it will bring you home to me."

I gasped. This wasn't just any gift. Summoning Lucifer was no small feat, but this was different. This blade would transport me, wherever I was, to him. To do this required an object imbued with his power and was the ultimate protection my father could offer when not in his presence. "Thank you, Father. This is a very special birthday gift, and I will always keep it with me."

His smile grew until the skin around his eyes crinkled. He wrapped an arm around my shoulder and urged me forward. "That is not the only gift. Let's go find your mother."

My birthday was a big celebration in Hell each year, but I opted out of the big party this time in lieu of my request finally being granted. My twenty-first birthday would be spent in the Overworld. *Starting today.* So, I'd tuck my purplish-black wings in for the next year and live like those I will lure to Hell if I take my place as the future queen.

Father opened the hidden door that led to the shared meeting room between his and mother's private studies. The narrow passage had two guardians dressed in the red-and-black tunics required by those pledged to Lucifer and Lilith. They assumed their more humanlike forms as many who served my parents did, but even in the candlelight, their eyes glowed red like the fires in the lower levels. Father preferred the dimmer candles over the electric light, but there was no shortage of power. He had brought many items from the human world to Hell for Mother. Electricity was one of those.

"Lilith," he sang out to her as we entered the room.

"Here, darling." She walked forward, flanked by two guardians and another figure shrouded and silhouetted in grey.

Jax.

My heart flipped and burned in my chest with a mix of happiness and anger at the sight of him. He pulled the shadows to him like I wouldn't know him anywhere from his earthy rich scent and warmth or his dark hair. His hand pushed the mass of black waves away from his face as if he knew.

We hadn't spoken in the last year. *Why is he here?*

"I don't understand." I looked back and forth between my parents, confused as to why Jax was here and what this had to do with my trip.

"Jax is going to accompany you for the year," Father said.

Not a gift. That's a curse.

"He's half demon. He'll age among humans," I blurted out. It was shitty of me and the only weak argument I could think of in his presence. It was, also, the one thing that stung him. The one thing I would never say out loud to him. At a time when we still spoke, he'd confided in me how the full-blooded demons taunted him about his ancestry, and now I used it. I was no better than those assholes, but it would be torture to be stuck with him for a year knowing he would never be mine.

"It's only a year," my mother said, dismissing my plea.

Sweet angel's ass. Did she not have a clue how estranged Jax and I have been?

Jax brooded behind her. He didn't look any happier than me.

"Why do I need a babysitter? I'm an adult in both the Underworld and Overworld."

"He's not a babysitter. He's a travel companion." Mother pushed him toward me like we were little kids and should play nice together. He didn't resist her, but his body stiffened.

It was wasteful to argue with Mother and Father. I shook my head. I was their only child together. The only one born to them in the human way at least. Yet, I was not like either of them. They often called me their 'glorious creation' as if I were divine and not Hell born, and that was why they over-planned the protection I would need. I'd have to find a way to ditch Jax or at least ignore him in the Overworld.

I glanced at my father. He gave one single shake of his head to tell me I would not win this argument. I met my mother's gaze. "Fine. Whatever."

Jax's shoulders slumped, and he winced. *Nope. He doesn't want to be part of this trip any more than I want him there.* In the times I traveled with Mother, he'd never gone, and I'd gone out in the Overworld with the younger demons with little protection. *Why now?*

"Your father and I have set up a home for you to use, and it's stocked with blood should you get injured and need to heal." I knew to expect this. The city was chosen by me, but they made the arrangements to make sure I was best protected. Not that there was much to fear. No one really knew who I was in the human world, which was one of the most appealing things about the trip.

"I'm not one of your Night Children, Mother." I didn't like the taste of blood, but I healed faster with it. Jax would need it to sustain his demon side. They must have planned to send Jax all along.

"No, but the alternative is to eat human flesh like me," Father said. He didn't have to consume human flesh. He liked doing it as an intimidation tactic, but I'd never seen him eat an entire human unlike some of the lower-level demons who had far less control of themselves.

I cringed inwardly. "Pass." I swallowed. "Hard pass on the flesh."

"If you just stayed in the Underworld, we wouldn't need to have this conversation," Mother said.

Not a chance. She didn't act this way toward Alessia, the one she referred to as my sister in the Overworld. I opened my mouth, but Father cut in, keeping his tone light.

"Lilith, you've spent time among the humans, and so have I. You know the allure it holds. Let her enjoy her youth."

It clicked. Jax wasn't my babysitter. They thought I would be undisciplined without one of them there and needed a clean-up crew of one. Who better to send than a demon like Jax who needs status to hold rank? My parents didn't trust me because of one incident five years ago. *One. My first encounter alone with humans.* The lack of confidence dug into my chest like I was gored by a horn from one of the least powerful demons who couldn't shift into a human form. I wasn't the inexperienced, naïve demon I was then, but Mother and Father still saw me as that angry girl.

I studied Jax. Outwardly, he looked much the same, but he was a little leaner and more muscular. The training agreed with him. I cleared my throat against the nervousness his presence created. "And you're okay with this?"

Jax raised his gaze to meet mine. His hazel eyes locked on me. His flashed from goldish brown to demon red. "Yes."

My stomach fluttered. *What had they promised him in return?*

We had barely seen each other this past year and hadn't engaged when our paths did cross while he had trained with Father's elite guards. As a year older than me, he was eligible to decide on his own, and he decided to join the most trusted forces despite my protests. At the end of training, the elite guard drank a mix of Father's and Mother's blood to swear their allegiance. It made it difficult if not impossible to deny them a request, and that was a fate I couldn't watch happen to my friend.

Yet, it would, if it hadn't already.

"I'm ready." I slung my bag over my shoulder and turned to face Mother. Her long, dark hair fell over her shoulders and framed her ageless face. Her features were tight. She was far less comfortable with my trip than Father. Her Night Children provided plenty of examples of bad behavior, and, unlike Father, she had once been human.

"No one is ever ready for the fall." Mother kissed my cheek.

The fall was like cutting an invisible umbilical cord. I

would no longer be bound to her when I traveled from the Underworld. She wouldn't be able to sense if I'd been summoned either. All demon children had this rite of passage, and I was several years older than most when they did it. *Autonomy awaited me.*

Mother raised her hand and mumbled some ancient words under her breath. "Take her hand, Jax."

He extended his hand to me, and I glimpsed his double-fighting swords strapped to his sides under his cloak. *Where is he going to put those while we're out among the humans?* He slipped his hand into my sweaty palm. Electricity webbed out and up my arm from his touch. I ignored the sensation in my belly the closeness caused.

"Do you remember the ritual that will call me to pull you back?" Father asked.

I nodded. The dagger was sheathed at my back.

Mother's palm struck my forehead with the force of darkness. Pain split my skull, and I fell backward. And I kept falling through the fires of Hell. A summons pulled a demon through a portal, but this was different. The fall felt like... freedom.

Jax's hand slipped to my fingertips, and his free hand grasped my wrist so tight I was sure my bones would break. Perspiration beaded over my body from the intense heat. Hell was a strange place. I'd never noticed the heat while there.

A rush of cool air brushed against my skin, and chills ran through my extremities. My back struck the ground hard, and a crushing weight pinned me down. Fear spiked in me. *Calm down, Morena. You're fine. Assess the situation. It's just...*

Jax.

I shoved him until I was able to roll him off of me. His chest rose and fell, so he was alive. His color was good in his normal sun-kissed hue. There were no injuries visible, but he was out cold.

I unfurled my wings and fanned him while I patted his face. "Jax?"

His eyes blinked open, focused, and widened. He flipped me on my back so he was positioned over me again. This was different from when we landed. Awareness of how close his body was to mine skittered over my skin. I pressed my hands against his chest.

"Let me up," I said, eager to end the contact.

"What are you doing? You can't show your wings here."

My stomach plummeted. "Shit."

He was right. Part of the deal was I would keep my demonic powers hidden... including my wings. I reined them into my body and took in the area around us. I didn't see or sense anyone near.

Jax pushed up and extended a hand to me. I grasped it and let him help me to my feet.

"Be careful, Morena. Your parents can't protect you here like they can in Hell."

"I'm not an idiot," I said. Although I certainly felt stupid for my mistake. I did appreciate Jax's warning, but I suspected it was more due to duty to my parents than our former friendship. *Friendship.* That chilled my insides. My plan to tell him I wanted more was thwarted by his announcement to train with the elite guards.

"I know the risks in being in the human world. Can we just get to the house?"

Jax pointed over my shoulder.

I turned to view a massive lawn and manicured shrubbery placed in perfect precision around the outer perimeter. While the lot must have been cleared for the monstrosity of a home, several large trees were preserved to provide shade. A swimming pool was just outside the backdoor of the giant mansion in front of us. There were no other houses visible from here. This was isolation. *Ugh!*

"How are we supposed to blend in with that? That's not how the average human lives." I slapped my forehead with my palm. It throbbed in response, still sore from where my mother pushed me out of Hell.

"You're still the heir to Hell, and you can't expect them to let you live like a common human. You need certain protections."

The freedom I thought I would get on Earth suddenly seemed out of reach. The opportunity to spread my wings, metaphorically, of course, disappeared with each step we took toward the house.

"Let me guess. They covered it in protections to prevent anyone from scribing my location, didn't they?"

I expected them to do it, but I'd hoped they hadn't. Stassi wouldn't know I was in the Overworld as long as we were in this house unlike when I traveled with Mother. The medallion I'd given her wouldn't cut through that kind of spell.

"Among other things, yes."

"I'm not my parents," I said under my breath. I'd trained to fight Nephilim, the half-angel half-humans who walked the Earth. My parents led forces and survived hundreds of wars. We were not the same. If they wanted an heir worthy of the task, they needed to let me experience things and not shelter me from them.

"No, but we don't want a repeat of what happened when those humans did a random summoning spell."

The sting of regret wound around my spine and squeezed. "Trust me. I can't forget killing them. I'm not proud of it, Jax."

Father never held it over me, which is probably why he granted my twenty-first birthday wish to live here for a year.

"Lucifer had to release four souls to make amends." He placed a hand on my arm.

My skin warmed where his fingers touched. I stepped back and narrowed my eyes. "I'm well aware of what my father had to sacrifice for me."

I marched toward the house. The weight of the protections cast a heaviness over me. I twisted my head around until my neck cracked.

"You'll need to enter through the front door the first time," Jax called from behind me.

I rolled my eyes and didn't look back. Everyone knew when a location is sanctified, it could only be entered one way without setting off the wards ... or worse. More often than not, the front door was the entry point, and the system linked up like a biological alarm system. Jax must think I'm an absolute moron for him to have said it. "Thanks," I muttered my response.

Ignoring the lush vegetation that covered either side of the walkway, I wound around to the front. The white brick and stone façade stood out against the greenery, and the beauty didn't escape me. I grasped the door handle, and it opened.

No key needed except me.

The entryway was marble and flanked by a winding double staircase. A chandelier dangled down like stars floating at various distances. *Breathtaking.*

I moved forward to the hallway and was startled at my image. My blonde hair shimmered with a silver cast in the light here. I glanced up at the chandelier. *It must be the white light from it.*

"Don't recognize yourself?" Jax asked, the corners of his lips turned up.

"My hair is so shiny. I've never seen that happen," I whispered.

"It's always like that, Rena." Jax grasped a tendril between his fingers and ran them down the length to my waist.

Rena. I missed that nickname.

My breath hitched in my throat. A soft current buzzed in the surrounding air. His eyes drew up to mine, and he let go of the hair.

"Sorry," he mumbled and walked through the foyer to the kitchen.

My skin warmed and betrayed me. If Jax blushed, he left the room before I could see.

Did he feel that same electricity between us?

I wanted to unfurl my wings to drive a breeze to cool my skin, but I shouldn't do it even inside my own temporary home. The more I used them, the harder it would be to break the habit, and I didn't want to be lax and slip again where my wings could be seen. Best to keep them tucked away for the rest of the year. *Damn, it's hot here. Maybe Jax crawled into the cooler.*

I made the corner at the end of the hall into the kitchen in time to see Jax polish off a glass of ice water. His lips were damp, and he ran his tongue across them. I ignored the urge to taste him for myself and shook my head.

Contrary to what humans liked to say, there was ice water in Hell.

"Thirsty much?" I leaned against the doorframe.

"Want some?" He shook the glass. The ice clinked against the side. A smirk broke across his face.

I smiled back and shook my head. "I'm good."

His eyes raked over me in a slow movement like he was memorizing me, and an uncomfortable urge to squirm formed in my belly. I focused my gaze out the windows behind the breakfast area.

"You might want to change your clothes before we go into town. They don't usually wear black leather during the summer here."

I looked down at my clothes. I'd showered and changed clothes before we left. "This is one of my favorite outfits."

He shrugged and refilled his glass with water. "Suit yourself. Texas is almost as hot as Hell during the summer."

The last thing I wanted was to look like I didn't belong. The goal was to fit into a life in the Overworld, not stand out. I sighed. "Fine. I'll change."

"Wait, Morena."

"Mmm. Hmm." I turned back to face him.

His shoulders tensed. "Which do you think you will choose?"

"I don't know. I haven't seen what's in the closet." It wasn't the answer to the question he asked.

He looked away and his Adam's apple bobbed when he swallowed. "Will you take your mother's place here, or will you choose to live in Hell?"

I inhaled and let it out slowly. "I don't know, Jax."

CHAPTER 2

RENA

I threw open the door to the walk-in closet and scanned through the clothes Mother's followers placed in the room. Most of the choices looked more like something Mother would wear during her visits. Lots of long, dark-colored dresses filled the space. She lived in various shades of black whether here or in Hell. Relieved to find a section more in line with my taste, the outfit I selected consisted of a pair of jeans with shredded knees and a silver halter top held together in the back by a single tie. These items were not anything my mother would wear, so they must have been selected specifically for me.

I pulled out my cell phone that only got reception when I was actually in the Overworld. Stassi's number stared back at me. She was one of the few humans who didn't have to speculate if we existed. Her education in the occult had led her to the clubs demons and Night Children frequented, and I found myself spending more and more time with her on each trip I made. We'd parted on harsh circumstances the last time I saw her, and I wasn't convinced she would come tonight. I typed out a quick message with my plans and tossed the phone on the tufted bench against the wall of the closet.

My leather jacket made a thud when it hit the floor in front of the mirror. I trailed my finger across the pentagram-shaped birthmark just below my clavicle. It sizzled and turned the color of embers. I stared at my reflection until it returned to black. The symbol marked me forever as Lilith and Lucifer's child. I would never be less, and I would never be more. My parents warned me from an early age a choice awaited in my future. *To rule Hell. To rule the Night Children. I had to choose one world to rule. A place where the bulk of my time would be spent.* As the years went on, I'd often wondered if there was more to the decision.

I changed clothes and ran my hand across the shoes on the shelf in front of me. There were boots on the lower shelves and sneakers on the highest one, not that Mother would ever wear sneakers. At eye level, there were stilettos and evening shoes for every occasion. I selected a pair of silver strappy heels.

A soft knock rapped on the bedroom door.

"Come in, Jax." I watched for him to enter.

The door opened, and he leaned against the frame. "Your mother's other children are here to escort us."

I smoothed my hair down in the mirror. These escorts were different from the ones I usually had assigned when I visited with Mother. They were designated for the duration of my stay. It annoyed me to have so many guardians. "Of course, they are."

"Can you ask them not to feed while we are there?"

I met his gaze in the reflection and saw concern. "You're part demon. Why does it bother you?"

He shrugged and averted his eyes from mine in the mirror. "It doesn't. I just don't want to draw attention."

Liar. I headed toward the hallway, excited to start my year of somewhat freedom and hopeful to see Stassi. *And avoid Jax.* "Let's go see what this city has to offer."

"You sure you want to go out in this?" His hand pressed against my exposed back.

The contact set my skin on fire. I stiffened and froze.

Jax's hand lingered. His palm flattened against the small of my back.

My breath quickened, and I teetered on my feet. "Can you remove your hand?" I hoped he could move because I couldn't.

"S-sorry," he said and brushed passed me. Footsteps echoed down the stairs.

I took a few deep breaths and followed.

At the bottom, four of Mother's children waited. They inclined their heads toward me.

I forced a smile. "We can skip all that. I'm Morena, and you can call me that." I turned to the Night Child that looked my age but with golden-blond hair brushing his shoulders. "I believe you were with me during the last trip." I immediately blushed remembering the huge fight Stassi and I had because she wanted me to stay in the Overworld instead of returning to Hell with my Mother.

The Night Child nodded. "Alec is my name."

"Yes, it's good to see a familiar face."

"This is Helena, Erik, and Lana," Alec said. Each inclined their head as he introduced them. The others all appeared to be slightly older but still close to my age. Looks deceived often among the Night Children though.

"It's nice to meet you all. I'm sorry you have to waste a year with me. We can have fun tonight, but do not make it obvious you are there with me."

LIKE MOST OF the joint demon and vampire hangouts I'd visited on other trips, the entrance was in an alley. It was a ridiculously bold show of power against the Nephilim to be so close to the city center. The alleyway location hadn't deterred humans, demons, or vampires judging by the line that wrapped around onto the sidewalk of the Dallas street. The sweat from the humans swathed the air in a tangy, salty scent.

Music pounded from the club. A pentagram emblazoned the area over the large metal door. The symbol was hidden from human eyes but visible to demons and Night Children. My birthmark responded in recognition. The eagerness from the four vampires guarding me rolled off. Their thirst was palpable.

I glanced at them, annoyed I had to have guards at all, but it wasn't their choice either. "No feeding tonight. It's my first real night on Earth. I don't want to have to cover your tracks."

"We cover our own," said Erik.

I bit back a smile at his brazen attitude. He was brave because he knew who I was but had no idea of the power within me.

Jax rounded to face the bold Night Child. I stepped between them. The only respect given in the shadows was earned through blood and brawn.

"Do not test me," I said, looking up into his dark eyes. My hand closed around the Night Child's neck, and I lifted him off the ground. My nails sunk into the tissue.

His throat bobbed under my grasp. "Yes, Morena."

I dropped him. He landed on his feet to my disappointment.

His crimson blood darkened my nails. "Look what you made me do." I wiped the blood on his shirt. "Do we all understand no feeding tonight?" I met the eyes of each one. Each one nodded in agreement. Their faces showed no emotion, except for Alec. His eyes danced with fear, and I wasn't sure if it was of me or something else.

"Now, let's have a good night." I walked down the sidewalk to the doorman and smiled. He was big, taller than average. A stern look set on his face, but the corners of his lips turned up when he met my gaze. His scent hit me. *Demon.*

He was a Keeper. They were charged with containing any situations within the area. The less the human police or news media or any media, for that fact, was privy to the better. Father said controlling the narrative was increasingly harder to do.

"Morena, we were told to expect you." He unhitched the rope and waved us through.

Next time, we would have to visit a club not run by Father's minions. When the clubs have more notice to expect me, I'm escorted to a more selective entry. I wanted a more authentic experience.

While we had social times in Hell, there were no clubs in the Underworld. That was a unique adventure to the Overworld, and the clubs I'd been to on Earth before had limited human interaction. Here the scents of humans mixed with Night Children and demons. Mostly human though, and the aroma was delicious. *No wonder Mother's other children were so pissed. I denied them open dining.*

A small amount of guilt beaded like pebbles in my stomach, but I pushed it away. This was my experience, and I wanted to make the most of it. Music vibrated through me, and I watched the patrons move in time with it. I glanced at my phone, and Stassi hadn't answered. The music thrummed on, and the idea of losing myself in it beckoned me. I cut my eyes in Jax's direction. He scanned the room like the predators we were.

"Let's dance." I grabbed Jax's hand and led him toward the dance floor. Warmth, similar to when Jax touched my back, built from our contact. Perspiration gathered in my palm. I let go as we reached the center of the floor.

Jax's gaze skittered across the room and came back to me. His eyes were filled with concern.

"Loosen up and have fun like we used to." I found the beat of the music and swayed to it, lost in the sea of people and otherworldlies like myself. "Remember dancing to the music my mother would bring for us?"

He started to move then. "You. She brought it for you. I

was just lucky enough to be your friend." He smiled. The first real smile I'd seen on his face in a long time. The times I'd passed him in the hall or dining room after he entered training he'd barely acknowledged my existence.

I turned my back to him, and he inched closer. His body pressed against mine, and we moved together as one. A tingling sensation swept up my middle from the contact, and I didn't try to stop it this time. Jax's arm curled around my waist like it belonged there. The want for him I'd denied existed for the last year shuffled to the top.

The beat of the music slowed, and half the people scattered while the others paired up. I looked over my shoulder and met Jax's eyes. A little flash of demon red passed across them. My stomach did flip-flops. I wrapped my arms around his neck half expecting him to pull away.

He slid his hands around my waist and pulled me close. The now familiar heat expanded across my lower back.

His mouth came close to my ear, and the gust of breath from him tickled. "Your mother's children are watching every move you make."

"Not surprising." I'm sure she gave them precise orders on what to allow. "You're the son of a powerful demon. You could take them and more."

"Half demon." His voice dropped, and his grip on me loosened.

The proclamation was a sharp reminder I'd used the knowledge for my benefit before, and I needed to let him know what I really thought of him. "Yes, but you've always been more."

Jax focused his gaze on me. Demon red glowed in his eyes.

My breath quickened. *Why do I feel nervous? This is Jax!*

"More than just half-demon," I added quickly.

He pulled me closer. His breath brushed against my ear. "Rena." My name sounded rough on his lips. "We shouldn't."

The music changed to a quicker pace. "I know," I said, very aware of how closely Mother's other children watched us.

I took a small step away to create distance between us. My back chilled from the lack of contact, but the desire was harder to quench. I danced further away from him and into the mob. I didn't have to turn to know he followed but maintained the space.

The dance floor crowded with people once more, and I surveyed the floor for someone else to dance with... anyone but Jax. I couldn't take the contact or the questions that would come later.

A mass of dark curls swung back and forth in front of me. My heart quickened. *Stassi.*

She pressed up against me, resting her hands on my hips. "Hey, devil woman," she whispered in my ear.

Pleased to see her, I smiled. "Hey, sexy human woman."

Her lips brushed across mine. While I couldn't see Jax nearby anymore, I could feel his gaze on me. Guilt spiked up my spine. Stassi and I flirted around each other for years, even messed around a little this last year, but I'd never flaunted it in front of Jax. He hadn't been in my life the last year, though, and while we weren't a couple, Stassi and I had been intimate but open. She liked being free with the men and women she counted as partners. Stassi and I had even brought a guy she knew back to her place once. I'd engaged in foreplay with them, but I'd never given myself fully. I'd always thought that my first dick-in-vagina sex would be with Jax and with love between us, but maybe it was time to give up on that idea. He wasn't the same Jax he'd been. That much was clear. He might play along on the dance floor, but his actions this last year proved I wasn't important to him. Stassi had made it clear on more than one occasion she wanted a relationship whenever I was ready.

"Uurrrgh." I pressed my hand to my upper chest and scanned the room. My tattoo blazed, not the ember from earlier, but a warning. *Nephilim.* I didn't see them, but they were here.

"We need to go." I pulled away and waved at the four guards. Jax came to my side. "Nephilim," I whispered to him. I grabbed Stassi's hand on one side and Jax's on the other and headed for the door. The crowd danced on as we pushed through.

A white light exploded in front of us. I stumbled and threw my body in front to shield Stassi. I shoved her down to the ground as the bulk of the blast blew me backward. *Thunk.* My head connected to something hard. I slid down and looked up. A metal pole was the culprit. Screams cut through the air.

Jax pulled me back to my feet. "Are you okay?" he shouted over the roar.

Chaos erupted all around us, mainly from the humans. The demons and Night Children prepared to fight.

"I'm okay," I said, rubbing the knot on my head. "Where's Stassi?"

"I'm here."

I held my hand out. Her hand shook as she took mine, and I helped her to her feet.

"We need to get you out of here," I said to her and turned to Jax. "It looks like we have a fight on our hands."

"This isn't our fight." His face set in a hard grimace. He guided me toward the back, and it was like swimming upstream in the crowd. I grasped Stassi's hand firmly in mine. Only two of our guards were with us. Either the other two remained to fight, or they had fallen to the Nephilim.

White light speared demons and Night Children around us. They fell to the ground and slowly dissolved into fiery ash. I'd seen it in other fights, but not with this many Nephilim and not so organized. The gruesome sight of so many deaths at once turned my stomach.

I tried to pull free of Jax's grip to fight, but the two remaining guards formed tight ranks around me, and I lost my grip on Stassi's hand. I was caged in between the three of them. "Stop," I said. "We're not leaving our people to die." I dug my heels in, but the narrow stiletto broke on one shoe. I missed a step, stumbling forward.

Jax reached down to the other shoe and yanked the remaining heel off. I looked over at Stassi, and Jax yanked her hand to his.

"It's a Nephilim attack, Morena," he said. His eyes were a deep, dark red. *Anger.* "We are evacuating you per the protocol of this visit."

"I know what it is, Jax. I'm not leaving our people to be

extinguished like a campfire." Whether I knew them personally or not, these were the people who served my parents,
and they didn't deserve to die like this. I pushed Jax away
from me, but a sting at my wrist grabbed my attention.

A bloodcuff. One ring sat firmly around my wrist and one
around his. Rage turned my vision red. *Are you kidding me?
I'm a trained and skilled fighter, and this is what he is doing. I'm
the daughter of two of the most feared beings in this world, and
I'm being treated like a prisoner.*

"You're an asshole." I narrowed my eyes at him as he
pushed me forward. Only an incantation by the one who
placed the bloodcuff could remove it.

"Blame your parents," he muttered as we left out a side
door.

Few lights shone in the alleyway. Rotted food and trash
polluted the air. *Not one Nephilim.* "Jax, cut me loose."

"Not a chance."

"Jax, this is a trap. Cut me..." *Zing.* An arrow flew in front
of my face and landed in the heart of a guard, Lana. "Stassi,
get down on the ground." She flattened herself against the
ground. *Zing.* Another arrow zipped by my head. My demon
voice rumbled around us. "Now, Jax. Release me, or we're all
going to die."

CHAPTER 3
RENA

Jax formed the words to release the binding. I watched the metal fall to the ground at our feet and melt into a puddle. The blood cuff blocked my senses, but they returned with a sizzle on my shoulder. My birthmark came to life, and I gazed up to the rooftops.

White light streaked down in front of us. Nephilim trapped us in the narrow area. Six of them stood on either side of the alley. Their half-angel side gave them an ethereal look. A human eye would miss the diaphanous cues and probably think the man or woman was beautiful, but to my demon eyes, it was the angelic look regardless of face shape, skin tone, or hair color. They were all tall though. That trait was common. Their swords were drawn as they circled us. The heavenly glow rippled around the sharp edges.

I grinned at Jax. "They should have sent more."

"Don't do it, Morena. We can beat them without it," Jax said through gritted teeth.

"Where's the fun in that?" I rolled my shoulders, not that

I needed to loosen up. "Stassi, scoot close to my feet but stay low." I glanced at Jax and Alec, the remaining guard with us. "You two might want to come closer." Alec moved to put his back against mine, and Jax was shoulder to shoulder with me.

I inhaled a deep breath and held out my hands. "Ignis Infernus," I said, my demon voice reverberated off the buildings and shook them like an earthquake.

A ring of fire rose and encircled us but took the path I willed it. *To our enemy.* The Nephilim shrieked and howled as it engulfed them with zero chance to run. Their bodies charred and turned black until a pile of ash made up the circumference. Burnt flesh scented the air, and I held my breath. The flames receded to Hell having completed their task.

Satisfaction settled over me for the retribution their deaths brought. They killed many, including at least one of my guards, Lana. *Hopefully, Helena and mouthy Erik fared better.*

"There will be more. We need to get out of here," Jax said. He formed his hands through the symbols to call a portal. I checked Stassi over, and other than being stunned, dirty, and missing her shoes, she appeared uninjured. Jax's hand found mine and mine found Stassi's. He pulled us through the gateway with him.

I landed on my feet in the living room of the mansion. Stassi landed on her feet next to me, and I was surprised at how well she did for her first time. I stared at Jax, stunned by his ability more than the Nephilim attack. "Since when can you call a portal?"

"Those selected to train for your father's personal guard learn. You know this," he said, his tone even.

"Train, yes. Very few can actually do it, though, which factors into his final decision. Have you taken the oath?" I narrowed my eyes at him. Sending an oathbound guard here with me wouldn't make sense whether it was Jax or not. The timing was right, especially if he had mastered portaling. Father coveted that skill almost as much as he did a talented fighter. My worst fear was that if he had sworn to my parents, they would have tasked him with giving his life to save mine. I would not allow that, but trying to stop an oath-bound warrior was like trying to tell a new Night Child not to drink blood. The act would be futile.

"We don't have time for this. You need to summon Lucifer to pull you back." He took my wrist and pulled me toward the stairs. I tugged my arm, but he had a strong grip.

"We need to get Stassi home safe before I do anything." *Why is he rushing me back to Hell?* I pried his fingers from the narrow part of my arm. If I went home, there was no way Mother would let me return without her, tether severed or not. "And I'm not leaving because of a few Nephilim."

He turned to face me and stood silent for a moment. Worry creased his brow along with something that looked like fear. It couldn't be fear. Jax didn't fear anything. "Alec, can you see Stassi home?"

"I'm not going anywhere." Stassi lifted her chin, her voice strong and bold. "Without Morena."

I smiled inwardly, but I knew the look on Jax's face, which meant I knew he wouldn't speak the truth he had to share in front of her or Alec. "It's fine, Stassi. I'll text you later. Okay?"

She studied my face, and I tried to make it look serene. Stassi slid her fingers into my hair and pulled my face to hers. "You better text me, devil woman."

"I will," I murmured against her mouth.

She pressed her lips to mine in a soft kiss. "I mean it, Morena."

"I know," I whispered as she pulled away.

Alec led her out of the room in the direction of the garage. A reinforced Range Rover would be waiting there as was standard for our visits. At least she would be safe on the ride home.

"Will he wipe her memory of the entire night?" I asked, knowing the answer. A human wouldn't be allowed to have the knowledge that I wielded Hell's fire in the Overworld. It was already pushing the boundaries that she knew who I was. *What* I was.

"Rena..." The softness of his tone was kinder than I expected.

I turned to face him and met his golden-brown eyes. The worry there deepened, and his forehead wrinkled. I lost myself in the depths of his eyes. If things were different, Stassi wouldn't have been the one I was kissing tonight. It would have been him. But he made his decision. My heart threatened to shatter in my chest, because as much as I cared for Stassi, what I felt for Jax was so much more. I swallowed down my pain.

"So, tell me what you didn't want to say in front of Stassi

even though Alec is going to wipe her memory," I said, keeping my voice even despite my own inner turmoil.

"I couldn't repeat it in front of Alec either," Jax said, his tone solemn. "We heard rumors the archangel Gabriel is amassing forces against your father."

That's what he's freaking out about? I shook my head from side to side. "Gabriel is an ass, but he still loves Father."

"Think about it, Morena. That was more than a regular attack."

He was right. The number of Nephilim in this incursion exceeded any I'd heard of recently, and they seemed organized. *Very organized. Almost like they had a specific target.* I shifted my gaze to the picture hung above the high-backed chair. I hadn't paid any attention to it earlier, eager to enjoy my freedom outside of these walls. The old painting depicted a triumphant angel over a battle. *Strange to be hanging in the house.* I looked back at Jax. He'd noticed it too.

"Whose house is this, Jax?"

"We were told there were items in the home to keep up pretenses in case humans came over for the customary welcome. I don't think it's anything to worry about." The slight waver in his proclamation gave away the concern he tried to hide.

"I wouldn't have thought a demon club would be ground zero for a Nephilim strike either. They usually go after small groups. Tonight was planned. There was something there they thought was worth the risk." The only organized attacks I'd seen in the past were artifact related or to rescue a prisoner.

The same look crossed his face, and I knew for sure it was fear this time.

"Me," I said, my voice strong as the realization sank in that I was the object of the raid. *The Nephilim knew I was there.*

"We have to go to a safe house." Jax formed portal symbols in the air.

We can't just bounce around without a plan. I covered his hands with mine. "Unless you have seen the location, that's not wise." The location must be known to the one creating the portal. Only the most experienced and gifted could portal from images and schematics.

He looked away like he was hiding from me or ashamed. "I have."

While I'd been hurt by Jax this last year, I'd thought I could trust him, but his behavior had me questioning if I should. "Jax, do you know why they would want me? How do they even know I am here already?"

"We knew the Nephilim had been organizing. While we couldn't see the source, we could see the activities. Ambushes on demons have been increasing," he said, sounding remorseful.

I wanted to believe he hadn't had a chance to tell me, but he could have told me about this upstairs in the bedroom before we left for the club. I slipped into my heir to Hell mode. It was the diplomatic demeanor I used when Father asked me to sit in on various sessions. "And Father thinks Gabriel is behind it?"

"He is an archangel, Morena." He sounded annoyed.

If anyone has the right to be agitated, it's me, not him.

"Michael is the one who is the warrior. Gabriel is a messenger. Why would anyone, especially Father, think it is Gabriel?"

"Gabriel has tried to contact Lucifer and Lilith."

Both of them. Why would an archangel reach out to the Devil and the Mother of Night Children? Understanding sank into the pit of my stomach.

"He has a message for them." My vision was unfocused. Jax blurred into the room. "Something is out of balance."

Of all his siblings, Gabriel was the only one Father would mention with deep fondness. Father missed the close relationship they'd once had. Gabriel couldn't visit Hell without repercussions, but on the rare occasions Father walked on Earth, Gabriel would find him. *Had Gabriel sensed I was here? Had he sent Nephilim after me? That wasn't Gabriel's style though. He preferred one-on-one meetings.*

"Let's go to the safe house," I said. "We need to get some answers."

My pentagram birthmark flared, the pain sharp enough I hissed between my teeth. *They're here.* I covered the mark with my hand.

"We have company," I said, keeping my voice low.

Jax formed the symbols, and we jumped through our second portal of the night.

I recognized the chat piles of mill sand and remnants of buildings in the once prosperous town of Picher, Oklahoma. Mother had brought me along on more than one occasion to check on the Night Children here.

Years of mining had turned the small but bustling town into a toxic land... for humans. The US government bought the land and relocated most of the residents. A tornado swept through several years ago and destroyed many of the structures left. Mother's Night Children found a place to retreat while nature reclaimed the area. The Night Children mostly hid in the tunnels which ran all the way from Picher into Joplin, Missouri. I doubted any human brave enough to traverse deep in the tunnels made it out alive.

"Why here, Jax? This isn't a demon safe house."

"It's where your parents insisted I take you if you were in danger."

"And when were you here?"

"With your Mother during the last full moon."

Her last trip to cull the numbers. It left little question in my mind, but I asked anyway. "Have you performed the final ceremony? Are you sworn to Mother and Father?"

He looked up at the waning moon. "You don't know what it's like, Morena." He paused. "To have been spared but not belong anywhere."

"Answer me, Jax." My demon voice threatened and now wasn't the time, so I tempered my tone.

He turned to me, and those dark eyes flashed red. "Yes, I'm sworn to my leader."

It crushed me inside. My body folded in on itself, and my blood rushed like a flood in my ears. I let my eyes close and breathed in the stale air of the dead town around me. It required several breaths to compose myself enough to respond without my demon voice.

"So, volunteering for this journey had nothing to do with me and was in service to my parents."

"Morena, I—"

"It wasn't a question." I turned and walked toward one of the old buildings. In my trips with Mother, she showed me where to find hidden blood banks her other children kept fresh. I don't know if my anger at Jax caused it or just the events of the night, but I craved human flesh to the point my mouth watered at the thought. Still, if a human appeared in front of me right now, I wouldn't give in to the desire. *Blood though. Blood I could drink right now.*

The decayed building had faded red dots spray painted next to the handle. They were in the shape of the star in a pentagram without actually making the symbol. I found the doorknob and twisted it open. The room was pitch black. The electricity was cut long ago to the external source. My inhuman eyes pierced the darkness and noted the hidden door where my hearing pinpointed the hum of the alternate power source. I pushed open the door to the small room and lights powered on as I stepped through the doorway. A sterile scent covered the smell of rot from the outer shell. Several refrigerator units lined the walls of the tiny space. I opened one that was empty. The second one was empty as well, but the next one had enough blood in bags for two people.

"Looks like someone robbed the blood center." I tossed a bag to Jax and took one for myself. He looked at the bag like it was poison. "Just drink it. We need to be ready." I didn't tell him I was so mad it made me hungry. My anger rushed back to me, and I ripped open the bag and tipped it into my mouth.

As soon as the metallic taste hit my tongue, I remembered why I didn't like it. The weird twang of it caused me to pucker.

"Why drink it if it doesn't appeal to you?" Jax asked.

"Why do you?"

"Because you told me to," he said as if all his answers were plain and obvious.

"You're not bound to me like you are to my parents."

He crossed the room and put one hand on my cheek. "Morena, whether because of an oath or not, I would have come for you."

I stepped away from his hand. "I guess there is no way we can prove that."

A shadow over Jax's shoulder caught my attention. My heart quickened, and I moved into a battle stance. The dark figure moved into the light.

CHAPTER 4
RENA

The silhouetted figure stepped into the light. I relaxed out of my battle stance.

"Uncle Amon!" I ran to him and threw my arms around him. "What are you doing here?"

"Your Father thought my services might be needed." The tall, ancient demon hugged me in a warm embrace. He spent less time in Hell these days, but the distinct charcoal scent clung to him. His arms were like a fortress of protection, strong and close to impenetrable.

Amon held the position of general in Father's army. *Strange that Father would dispatch one of his most senior demons to meet us.*

"I'm so glad to see you," I said. Uncle Amon hugged me to his side. "Do you know Jax?"

Jax studied Amon, but he said nothing. He fixated on Amon like he was ready to pounce. *Not like him to be rude. Especially to a high-ranking demon.*

I stepped away and toward Jax, but maybe he didn't recognize him. My uncle left the training to other demons and focused on strategic dealings with Father. Still... most demons knew exactly who he was. "Amon is Father's second-in-command."

"Yes, I've seen you occasionally during my training," Jax said, his tone even, but his jaw ticked. The vein on the side of his head protruded.

"Yes, yes," Amon gave him a tight smile. "You're Lucifer's prize student. He talks of you often."

My eyebrows shot up that Amon would take such an interest in one of Father's favored students as to know him by name. His focus leaned toward strategy, specifically on how to keep the Nephilim scattered. A task that appeared to need greater focus considering the attack tonight. If Father and Mother entrusted Jax with my safety, Amon wasn't the right person to meet us at a safe house. *So why is he here?*

"You are too kind. I am one of many." Jax gave a short half-bow to Amon. The forced respect in Jax's actions caught me off guard. Most demons found Amon intimidating. He'd been an enforcer demon before he rose through the ranks. Not many who crossed his path lived on to speak of it.

"Demons are not usually so modest, even when they are only half." Amon's verbal jab was typical for someone of his rank, but it surprised me. He had several half-demon children himself, both in Hell and in the Overworld, who he hadn't claimed yet. A sour burn formed in the back of my throat.

Jax's eyes glowed red. Not just a flash. Demon tempers

only knew release through brawling or at Lucifer's command. If I didn't stop this now, it would get bad fast. Amon was almost as old as Father himself and had a strength nearly as great. He would rip Jax apart.

I slapped Amon's arm. "Uncle Amon, don't be cruel." He might taunt Jax, but he wouldn't risk crossing the heir to Hell.

He shifted his gaze to me. "I'm sorry, Morena. I don't understand why your parents would send a half demon to protect you."

Jax lunged at Amon. I thrust my arm out, and his demon reflexes stopped him within a split second. My forearm hovered in front of him. He was stronger than me, but I hoped his bond to my parents would halt his actions here too. For him to strike Amon would be certain death, and there would be nothing I could do to prevent it. *He had to know that.* His nostrils flared with wild breaths. Amon stood still and statue-like. *Why was he provoking Jax?*

With my arm still out, I looked over my shoulder at Amon. The rage on Jax's face left only one option. I had to put distance between them. "As you can see, Uncle, your services are not needed."

"I cannot leave you here," he said, reaching for me. "The sun will be up soon, and your mother's other children will not be able to protect you."

Jax stilled. I hoped his training took over, but I shifted closer to Jax, keeping myself between them in case I misread his body language.

My birthmark itched. *Strange. I didn't see a pentagram*

inside the room. Jax's hot breath came in steady currents behind me, and his hand pressed into my back. His touch was a momentary comfort as I scratched the mark next to my collarbone. The birthmark seared to life in an intense burn.

"Aagh," The chances half angels surrounded us outnumbered the odds it was something else. *How did they get so close without us knowing? It was like at the club.* "Nephilim," I ground out.

A firm hand around my waist pulled me through another portal. I landed hard against the ground. *Amon. Even he can't stand against that many.* I scrambled to my feet, but Jax, already on his, formed the symbols to close the portal. It equated to the slamming of the door.

"No!" I reached for Jax's hand to stop him, but he'd finished the ritual. The portal closed in front of us.

"He'll be fine, Morena." Jax guided me away from the spot where the portal once opened.

I shoved against him. Not only was Uncle Amon fighting Nephilim on his own, but Father would likely end Jax's life for the treasonous act. "There were more Nephilim there than I have felt anywhere. We need to go back."

His arms held me firm but loose. "No, Morena. We can't." He released his grip and rubbed my arms.

Tears formed in my eyes. I might be the daughter of two powerful beings, but my power did no good in this situation. "This is a stupid way to get revenge. I hope you know Father will punish you."

"He's a traitor," Jax said, his voice low.

No way. My hand slid to my throat as I recalled Amon's absence from his standing meeting with Father.

"What?" I looked up into hazel human eyes. "What do you mean he's a traitor?"

Jax created space between us like he prepared for me to strike. "Or at least your father suspects he is. He hasn't reported back to Hell in weeks."

"That's not unusual when a demon is on a mission." I paused. For a demon of Amon's ranking, it was not the norm. My mind swirled, swallowed in the betrayal. I'd noticed he missed meetings, and if I had, others had too. But unlike my father, I'd dismissed it. "Why wasn't I told about this?"

Jax added more distance, at least an arm's length away. "Your father didn't want to tip him off, so only a few know."

And he'd trusted Jax with this knowledge. Who else had he told? "Does my mother know?"

"Yes." He lifted his foot like he would take a step forward but dropped it back into place.

My heart sank deep into the recesses of my chest. *Had they used me? My effort to convince them to let me take this trip served as a charade.* "So, I was bait for Amon?"

"No," he said. "That's why your mother had so many protections on the house and property. They wanted to shield your arrival here."

"It's not like we were going to stay in the house, Jax," I said, my tone flat. "And the house wasn't exactly safe if you'll recall. I was the lure. I don't know whether to be more pissed at Amon or my parents. Why was no one there to take him?"

"I didn't have time to send word, and my orders were to keep you safe above all else." His eyes were sad like they were when those shitty demon boys teased him. The edges of his mouth turned down. I'm not sure if it was guilt or failure, but it wasn't relief, which was what I felt. I should have some gratitude, but it was stuck behind the anger that boiled in my gut.

"You mean without me seeing." My words wavered close to my demon voice.

He had saved me, and he sent Stassi to safety with Alec. I took one step forward, undecided whether I owed him a hug or a punch.

"No, I didn't know if it was him or Gabriel and didn't have time to message Hell." Jax reached for me, taking my motions as an acquiescence, but I stepped back, not ready for what contact with him would bring.

I took in my surroundings with great recognition. The modernized old space was one I'd been to many times with Mother. Her apartment atop the most loyal subject's dwelling.

"Why are we in New York? And why are we at Gothica? It can't be a coincidence we keep using Night Children haunts versus demon safe houses." The blood aroma thickened the air and made it hard to breathe. The old church made up the largest of the Night Children's covens in the world, but even those numbers could not stand against a demon like Amon if he had a legion on his side.

I believed what Jax told me, and we'd have to leave. Mother's children would die to protect me, but that price was too high. *Too much to ask of Mother.*

Night Children rustled below as they returned and settled in for the day. Dawn approached. The soft sounds drifted up to the top where we hid in Mother's apartment. I yawned. My first day on Earth wasn't what I thought it would be.

The point of this trip was for me to have freedom, but also to prove I could be a leader. It might have started rocky with secrets, but I knew the truth now. And I refused to go back to Hell as failed bait.

CHAPTER 5

RENA

I paced the length of the living room and contemplated my options. Jax sat on the couch and watched every step I took. The Night Children rested on the floors below us, but they would not dare disturb Mother's rooms without imminent danger or permission.

"Your mother's children are loyal to her in a way demons never will be. Archangels are closer to demons than Night Children." He took a long pause. "Whatever the threat, your mother thought this was the best option."

I paused in front of the stained-glass window. It depicted the union of Mother and Father. *Although not in the usual way humans saw them.* Humans usually saw them in some cartoonish form like him with a forked tail and her as some kind of succubus. But this piece of art in the window was true to who they really were — more humanlike than most cared to believe. The sunrise cast an array of colors like a prism across the wood floor. I followed the lines right to Jax.

He reclined back on the couch. Darkness bloomed under his eyes and represented the toll his human side took while in the Overworld. In the Underworld, he could go days, maybe weeks, without sleep. Here he grew older and required regular rest. He gave up the safety of Hell to come here whether at the behest of my parents or not.

My anger dissipated. I crossed the room and sat next to him. I needed to know more before I left Gothica. I needed to know what Jax knew. "So, I'm just supposed to summon Father to take us back to Hell?"

"That's the idea." He studied me. "For you."

The urge to squirm under his intense gaze made it difficult to sit still. I had to concentrate. "Me? He'd take both of us."

"No, I'll stay and continue to track the activities of Amon and the Nephilim." His heavy eyelids drooped.

"What's really going on, Jax?"

"You're safer in…" His voice trailed off into a soft snore. My heart swelled. It shouldn't given he'd likely sworn himself to my parents, but I couldn't stop the sweetness blossoming in my chest. He'd exhausted himself with so many portals close together. It would have taken a toll on even the most powerful demon. He must feel safe here in my presence to give in to it.

The bedroom was the obvious choice for me, but I couldn't bring myself to separate from Jax. His face relaxed as he slept, and his features looked more like a twenty-two-year-old human than a demon. My heart sputtered around, and I pushed back on the warmth spreading across my chest.

He made his choice for my parents. His life would never be of his choosing now.

I pulled one of the throw pillows from behind me and tossed it to the opposite end of the couch.

Jax stirred and mumbled. "Rena…" The rest of the words came out too low and garbled for me to understand.

I wondered if he dreamed of me half as often as he visited my dreams. In the state between deep sleep and wake, everything remained like it was before he left to train. Most every meal eaten together, sparring together, sneaking off to play pranks together. Somewhere along the way, the feelings had become more than friendship for me, but I guessed they hadn't for him. I missed those innocent days.

Jax's hand slid off his knee and rested on mine. The palm faced up, and I could slip my own into his. He'd taken the oath to my parents, and that was a choice I couldn't reverse with love or power. Demons who refused orders under the oath died if they fought too long, most bursting into flames. Nausea hit me hard in the gut. I lifted his hand in both of mine and sat it in a gentle motion back on his leg.

The pillow at the other end looked less than comfortable, but sleep called for me too. I leaned over and tried to find a position to relax.

THE WELCOMING AROMA of bacon and eggs woke me. I blinked my eyes open. It had to be midday by the position of the sun.

I sat up and noticed Jax no longer slept next to me. Panic twinged in my gut, but it subsided as soon as I found him standing in front of the stove.

"You're awake." He smiled. The dark circles were gone from under his eyes. His face lit up as though he'd rested well.

"Hard to sleep through the smell of bacon," I said, watching him scramble eggs.

"Your mother's followers keep the place stocked." He gestured with a spatula to the refrigerator across the kitchen. "I didn't think she ate this kind of food."

"Unlike most of the Night Children, she still has a taste for human food. She doesn't need it, but she enjoys it." She was the original. None of the rules applied to her that bound the rest of them. It might be the reason she practiced immense patience and kindness with them.

"That is fortunate," he said, flipping a piece of bacon in a cast-iron skillet. "Because I woke up starving. What about you?"

My stomach growled. Unlike my parents, human food could nourish me along with blood and other things that made me gag to think about. "Apparently so."

He handed me a plate, and I took a seat at the breakfast bar. A glass full of orange liquid sat in front of each spot, along with a napkin and fork.

"Is this orange juice? I haven't had that in years."

"Yep. It's freshly squeezed. There was a bowl of oranges." He sat in the seat next to me with his plate.

"You squeezed the oranges?" I laughed. "Who are you?"

"Demon strength makes it a quick job." He forked some eggs and studied me. "Eat." He took a bite.

A tingle slid down my spine. I turned to my plate and shoveled a forkful into my mouth. *Why am I so nervous around him?*

I swallowed hard and searched for something to say. "Since when do you cook?"

"I'm half-human. We have to eat, so we learn to cook."

"Mmm," I said, taking a bite of bacon. "You're pretty good at it."

Jax laughed. "Is that a compliment from the Devil's daughter?" He patted my knee.

The same knee his hand had fallen on last night while he slept. My stomach quivered. I could kiss him. Just lean forward and press my lips to his. I grabbed another slice of bacon and chomped it. *What is wrong with me? He's sworn to my parents.*

"Rena?"

I looked over to see Jax's gaze fixed on me. *Had he said something I missed? Must have.*

"I'm sorry. What?" I asked.

"Don't pretend like you didn't hear me. You have the dagger to summon your father."

Oh. A piece of me hurt. He sought to send me back so soon.

"Yes, I have it. Are you ready to get rid of me?" I pushed the food around on my plate.

He sighed. "It's not that. My duty is to keep you safe, and that's the safest place for you."

"Why don't you just create a portal then?" My fork clanked against my plate. I pushed it away.

His voice softened. "It doesn't work like that. You know this. It's like a muscle, and I haven't exercised it enough to portal that far." He squeezed my knee.

Electricity radiated over my leg and shot through my body. I stood up and turned my back to him to break the contact.

"I don't want to go back yet. I'm supposed to have a year." It sounded selfish and bratty, but I didn't care. My whole life existed in the shadow of my parents. The Mother of Night Children and the Father of demons. At least in the Overworld, some autonomy could be mine. I could prove I was worthy of whatever choice I made and not just destined by birth to assume it. This situation might put a damper on the hell-raising I'd planned, but it might get me to where I wanted to be at the end of the year. Stronger. Worthy. And a decision was made.

I cleared my throat. "Jax, I need to stay. If that means we go our separate ways in order for you to keep your oath and track Amon, then so be it." I faced him.

His face fell, and his eyes flared demon red. "No."

"No, what?"

"No, you are not going out there on your own," he said, his voice close to a growl.

"Then buckle up, because this ride will not be Devil smooth. I'm not Father."

He wound his fingers through mine and looked into my eyes. "I'm always here for you, Rena."

Sparks like when he touched my leg spread across my

hand. His eyes flared red again, and he dropped my hand. *Did he feel it too? Dare I even think?*

No. I folded the thought up and buried it in the recesses of my heart. He had sworn the oath, and I understood its power.

CHAPTER 6
RENA

I found some tennis shoes and clothes to change into from Mother's closet. *I'd have to ask her about those shoes. She'd never be caught in them.* I worried about what would happen when Jax's oath to my parents conflicted with my decision to stay here. Cellphones didn't work in Hell. Other than traveling back to Hell, his only option to communicate was to summon a lesser demon to carry the message to Father. The simple summons worked almost as fast as a call. My thoughts flashed to Jax fighting his orders. I shuddered at the images and shoved the thoughts away. Jax couldn't end with that fate. I'd navigate that lava pit when we came to it.

The Nephilim concerned me more at the moment. I could return to Hell where I'd be safe and sound, but Father and Mother weren't known to run from a fight. Neither would I. The Nephilim would disclose their plan to me. *And Uncle Amon's role in it.* I wouldn't stop until I knew exactly why they needed me and put an end to it.

"Jax, you said Uncle Amon hadn't reported to Hell for weeks. How long have you known about Uncle Amon's betrayal?" Pain expanded through my heart, causing the rhythm to beat off the normal cadence.

"A while." He shoved his hands in the pockets of his jeans.

I focused on his eyes and waited, careful not to go to the Devil stare inherited from Father.

He sighed. "We've been monitoring him for a few months."

My anger at my parents for using me as bait subsided. We'd agreed on my trip to the Overworld a year ago. The distress for Amon's disloyalty replaced the space in my chest.

"Tell me everything you know."

"It's not much, but I'll tell you." He took my hand.

My fingers tingled. I tried to pull away, but his grip tightened.

"Come sit with me, Rena." He led me to the couch.

"There is no way Gabriel would be a part of taking over Hell or trying to eradicate demons," I said, unable to believe Father's brother would even try that. They'd buried their grievances long ago. None of the angels wanted to go anywhere near Hell unless it was for a family visit, and those had become fewer over the years.

Jax rubbed his hands over his face and met my gaze. His eyes were a soft brown. He wasn't angry at me. Not at all.

"You didn't think Amon would betray your father either. Things aren't always so simple. I do know Gabriel cut off communication with both of your parents. Wasn't he in love with your mother?"

I leaned back against the couch. Gabriel was the one closest to my father. *Amon's absence. Gabriel's withdrawal. Their* actions were independent. They had to be. Amon wouldn't work with an angel any more than Gabriel a demon. "That was two thousand years ago when he was in love with her. They have been passed that for a millennium at least. Besides, she's not human anymore. That was part of the deal."

"Yet she had a daughter, which shouldn't have been possible."

"I know you're not suggesting Gabriel is my bio dad. I have a demon voice and other things ... " *Other things were a bit of an understatement. I had power like Father's. He'd even told me my abilities were unique.* A shiver ran through my body.

Jax rubbed my arm in light, feather strokes that caused goosebumps to form. "Of course not. I'm just saying that archangels are vengeful. He might want payback."

I took a deep breath and forced it out. "I guess it's possible." *Gabriel and Father were close, but could Gabriel have kept it that way for a reason? Was it an ulterior motive?* Sadness crept into my chest and joined with the gnawing hurt already there. "How does Father ever trust anyone?"

"I don't know, Rena." His gaze searched mine like he thought he'd find the answer I wanted there. "I know your father has never lied to me, and that's all I need to know."

The oath. It's already seeded in him. No, Father didn't lie, but he could spin the truth into a web so tight there was no escape.

Jax stood and held his arms open. "Need a hug?"

I hesitated. *I do. Damn the oath.* I took his hands and stepped into the safe space his arms provided.

He rubbed his hands over my back and pressed me tight against him. His head leaned against mine.

The tension in my body lessened. I sank into the embrace and closed my eyes. My body heated. I inhaled his warm demon scent, like a campfire on an autumn day. The closeness created a refuge I hadn't realized I'd missed.

"Rena," Jax whispered into my hair.

The way he said my name fluttered over me like a gentle flap of wings and caressed my skin. I lifted my head and gazed into his eyes. Demon red flared back. My own red eyes reflected from his pupils. He'd looked at me like that before but never followed through with the promise his stare held. I wouldn't miss this chance. This was my birthday trip, and I wanted this. Even if it was only one time, I wanted to taste him. I ran a hand into the hair at the base of his neck and tilted my head toward him.

He inclined his. Our lips met in a soft dance. The electrical current coursed between us, stronger this time as it transformed into something bigger. His kiss deepened, and my mouth parted to accept it.

I tasted and teased as urgency grew. My hands roamed over his arms and back. I wanted more. I wanted him. *The oath. Fuck.* My heart thudded, pounding in my ears. He would never be free to be with me.

I pressed my hands against his chest, and I savored the

taste of his mouth for a moment longer. When I pushed away and broke the kiss, my heart crumbled.

Jax's gaze met mine. I took a step back. His life would belong to my parents. Every single bit of it. Tears burned my eyes, and I blinked them away.

"I'm sorry," he said. "I didn't—"

I pressed a finger over his lips. "Don't. I'm not." *I'm only sorry you took that damn oath.*

He took a step back, equal to the distance I created. The space between us doubled.

I cleared my throat. "Mother's children will rouse soon. We should figure out where we need to go to get answers."

"We could start at the mansion. I'm curious how the Nephilim could discover it with the protections," Jax said, his voice rough.

The Nephilim could be watching the house, but they weren't that organized. *Normally.* If it were normal, we wouldn't be having this conversation. "I'm interested in figuring that out, too, but what if they are there? Then what?"

"It should be safe to go back. They wouldn't expect that."

No, they shouldn't expect it. Nothing about last night was an average attack though. We needed distance. Jumping straight into the house was a bad idea. There could be incantations to trap us. Things we could sense if we approached versus landing in the middle of it.

"Can you teleport us into the field where we landed when we fell? That would give us an advantage in case there are guards or confinement spells. It should be close enough for my birthmark to alert us." I ran a finger across the mark, and it responded with a gentle burn. The tiny tinge of pain comforted me.

Jax's gaze followed my finger. His eyes roamed up my neck to my gaze. "Yes, I can get us to the spot."

I tilted my head to one side, waiting for the crack and the tension to subside. "Okay. Let's hope there is something to go on ... like that stupid painting."

"I've been thinking about that painting too. We were told to expect items there as cover, but did you see anything else?"

"No, the painting was it." I looked at the stained glass window. *There were always hidden meanings in celestial renderings.* "Which angel was depicted in that painting?"

"I didn't look close enough to see."

I had to go. I needed to know if it was Gabriel. If it was, then I'd summon him myself to deal with this mess before it required Father's attention.

"Well," I said. "Spin up a portal for us already."

His expression was tight. He nodded and formed the symbols. I stepped through the portal and for the first time, I was nervous about doing so, but my next step was into the field. The clean scent of a fresh rain shower greeted me. The wet grass stuck to my shoes.

"Smells good." Jax inhaled a deep breath behind me.

"It does." I ignored the urge to lean back against him. "These grass stains will never come out of Mother's white shoes." I lifted one foot and inspected it.

He moved to my side and chuckled. "I've never seen your mother in athletic shoes."

I laughed. "Me either. It's almost like she knew."

"She's gifted. It's no wonder you are too." He winked at me. "Any tingles?"

Very aware my mouth gaped open, I forced myself to close it. *Do I say yes? Do I tell him? Yes, Jax, you give me lots of tingles.* A flush filled my cheeks.

"I mean..." He paused, and his Adam's apple bobbed up and down. "Is your birthmark burning?"

Ooooh. I trained my sights forward on the house. "No. No Nephilim detected."

"Good. We'll go around the back. It gives us the most cover should we need to run."

"After you." I gestured forward, hoping we had the house to ourselves without a Nephilim interruption.

Jax took the lead. The only sound as we passed the guest house was the waterfall for the pool. There were no signs of the Nephilim we avoided last night. I paused when we reached one of the back doors.

Concern etched Jax's otherwise perfect face. He whispered. "Anything?"

"No, nothing."

He opened the door, and I followed close behind him.

"It doesn't look like anyone has been here since we left," I said, surprised to find the house undisturbed.

"They must have known what they wanted and already left. We should check out the painting." He reached for my hand, but I didn't take his. My heart dropped. The less we touched, the better, given the ultimate way he would serve Father.

An acetic odor burned my nostrils. "Does it smell weird in here?"

"Like what?"

I sniffed the air. "Like vinegar."

"Yes, I smell it. Did you use a hairbrush while we were here?"

"Um, yeah," I said and touched my hair. "I used one in the apartments at Gothica too. What does that have to do with vinegar?"

"Nephilim have a way to track, and vinegar is an ingredient for the spell." He grabbed my wrist, and I didn't pull away this time. "Are you sure you're not sensing any Nephilim?"

I ran my fingers over my pentagram birthmark. *Nothing.* "Definitely not."

We stood in front of the painting, and Jax grabbed my arm. His eyes widened. "Fuck."

The pungent vinegar odor filled the room.

"Guess we know what they used the vinegar for." Jax shook his head.

"We know two things."

Jax looked at me and wrinkled his forehead. "What two things?"

"We are smart, and this was a clue."

Jax chuckled. "Unfortunately, neither of those points does us any good at this moment."

I sucked in a breath, and a rotten egg odor assaulted my nose. The vinegar was mixed with it. The scent was almost impossible to smell over the acetic vinegar. *Is it... No. Maybe.* "Gas. I smell gas."

"I don't." Jax spun around, smelling the air with each turn.

"We need to get out of here." I grabbed his hand and ran for the door.

I tugged him into the kitchen and around the massive marble island, cursing the size of it. Jax didn't resist, and I headed out the way we came. The sulfur odor smothered everything else.

I crossed the threshold. Jax's hand slipped from mine, but I heard his footsteps with a slight smoosh noise on the damp sod.

The wet grass caused me to slip when I tried to stop at the spot in the field where we arrived a short time ago. Jax skidded into place next to me with far more control and turned to look at the house. I stared at his profile. His jaw tightened. Even worried, he was handsome.

A short rumble shook the ground. An explosion deafened the space around me. I flew backward and slammed into the surface. Stars spiraled out across my vision. A thud came from beside me. I rolled over onto my side against the hot pain in my back. Jax was next to me. His eyes closed. Panic spiraled out through my body, and my muscles strained against the movement.

I shook him. "Jax?" I shook him a little harder. Fear worked through my limbs and left me weak. My hand slid on his temple. Blood coated it. *Damn his oath and damn the expectation my parents set for him.* I kissed him hard on the mouth. "Wake up, Jax. Wake up. We have so much more to do."

CHAPTER 7
RENA

Jax's eyes opened. "I'm fine, Rena." His hand went to the bloody spot on his head. "Ouch."

I released a breath I hadn't realized I held. *He needs to heal.* "We'll go back to Gothica. They'll have some blood to fix you."

"I'm okay. Better once we get off the wet ground though."

I pushed up off the damp earth and helped him to his feet. My hands were covered in mud and grass. I swiped them across each other to knock the debris off.

The air expanded around us in a loud clap of thunder. *Sweet angel's ass. What in Hell's fury was that?*

"Rena?" Jax said, his tone confused.

"It wasn't me." Lightning cracked across the sky and lit it up with golden-white hues.

Not normal thunder and lightning. Angel's ass was right.

I spun around in the direction of the sound.

Gabriel, Father's brother, dropped in front of me. *Fucking archangel's ass to be more accurate.* It'd been him. Jax's intel was right.

"Morena." Gabriel nodded. He tucked his glowing white wings to his back but didn't conceal them. His light-colored feathers contrasted with his wavy, dark hair and sun-kissed skin. I craned my head to look him in the eyes.

"Uncle." I squared my shoulders. "Is this your doing?"

"I do not wish to fight you," he said. "I saw you were on Earth and wanted to talk."

"Conveniently, after the house I was to stay in blew up. I have nothing to say to you." *I did though.* There were lots of questions I wanted to ask him, but there was no way I would be able to defeat an angel as powerful as Gabriel. He deserved any torment I could inflict, and I knew just what to say to do it. "You might be Father's favorite sibling, but you are the reason he cannot return to Heaven. You are the reason he was cast out."

He unfurled his wings, and the white feathers dripped with Heaven's fire. The light was so bright it made the sun appear dim.

"I assure you that was at your father's own doing," he said, his voice confusingly calm compared to his powerful stance.

I prepared for a battle I had no chance to win. My training was vast, especially for my age, but an archangel's strength had few matches. I called to the fires of Hell and allowed my wings to spread to their full span. They dripped with molten sparks. Gabriel's were brilliant in their light, but the beauty lied and hid the agony they would inflict. Mine gave a pure promise of pain without a deceptive dance. And they shielded Jax from Gabriel's view.

"Listen to me, child." Gabriel's voice echoed with the lyrical angel cadence.

"I'm not your child." My demon voice was invoked by his word choice, but I reined it in. "But I'm listening." Jax stepped around my wings. I shot him a piercing gaze. *Why couldn't he just stay behind me for once? The oath. It would always be the answer.*

"You think you are soulless because of your parentage, but you are not. There is good in you."

"I'm born of two soulless beings who rule Hell. How could I have a soul?" A soul meant passage to Heaven and entering those gates was something I'd never entertained. My place was to rule Hell or Mother's other children if I chose. I fought back the tremble trying to rattle my body. I didn't belong in Heaven. Ever. *Did I? Could I have a soul? How? I'd killed humans. There is no redeeming me. Why is he doing this now?*

"Your father, like me, is angelic, and as such, there is no soul for him."

So, no soul. That's not news. "This I know."

His hands formed a prayer position, and he rested his lips against the tops of his fingertips. He paused for a long moment. So long dread filled my gut like acid.

He let out a breath as he readied himself to deliver a message. "Lilith was once human before her power grew. She believes her soul was traded, but it was not. It is why she cannot reside permanently in Hell and must return to Earth with regularity."

Mother? A soul? I could no longer control the tremors. My body shook hard enough that my teeth threatened to chatter. The fire on the tips of my wings grew brighter with every rapid heartbeat in my chest.

"How—" My voice cracked against the tightness in my throat. I swallowed and tried again. "How could this be true, Gabriel? She is the mother to the Night Children. I'm half of her and half of Father."

"I can show you." He unsheathed his sword, and Heaven's light radiated from it. "Hold out your hand."

I hesitated. A slice to the palm with my Father's dagger would summon me back to Hell. *Would Gabriel's sword send me to Heaven? Would I be trapped there if it did?*

"It will only show you the truth," he said.

Did I trust Gabriel? Whether I did or didn't, he had the answers to my questions, and I'd allow him to show me. I opened my shaky palm up to him. "Did you send the Nephilim after us?"

"No, I deliver my own messages." He lowered the sword in slow motion.

The truth of his words rang clear. I trusted him and held my palm out steady and strong.

A blur of darkness spun in front of me. *Father? No. Jax!* Panic snaked down my spine. Gabriel's sword, already in motion, couldn't stop. Jax stumbled back into my arms. The sword nicked Jax's forearm. One scratch was lethal for a demon. There was no air around me. I sucked in a breath trying to fill my lungs.

"Jax?" I lowered him to the ground. "You idiot. What were you doing?"

"Saving you." His voice weakened with each syllable. I took his hand in mine and squeezed, willing my strength to him. But I was no healer. A sour taste formed in my mouth as my mind caught up with the realization of what would come next. An excruciating death. *No. I have to do something.*

"Gabriel, fix him." I couldn't look away from Jax. His normally tanned skin paled to a grey like a mourning dove. His grip on my hand loosened, and I watched him slipping away with each labored breath.

Gabriel squeezed my shoulder. "I'm sorry. I can't, Morena."

"Then get the hell away from me." I shoved his hand from my shoulder and reached for the dagger strapped to my lower back.

I drew the blade across my palm. Blood pooled, darker than the liquid in the veins of Night Children but not black like a demon's.

"Looks like I'm saving you." I dripped some of my blood into Jax's mouth as the portal to Hell pulled us through. *Please let it sustain him until we get to Mother.*

I hit hard against the floor of the private study. Jax's body landed on top of me. I flipped him over.

Father knelt beside me. Relieved to be back in Hell, I looked up at him. Unease marred his face and stole my momentary reprieve. I turned back to Jax and held his way-too-lax face in my hands.

"Morena, are you hurt?" The disquiet in Father's voice unsettled me more.

Water dripped on Jax's face. The liquid belonged to me. My tears. "Help him, Dad."

"What happened?"

"Gabriel," I sobbed. "Gabriel touched him with a heavenly artifact. I gave Jax some of my blood, but he's still unconscious."

"Lilith!" Father's voice carried through the halls of Hell like an alarm.

Mother materialized almost on command. "You don't have to..." Her voice trailed off.

"Help him," I said. Tears streamed down my cheeks and onto Jax's face. Desperation drowned me. I met my mother's gaze. "Mom, help him."

A deep frown formed on Mother's face as she took in the sight. She looked to my father. "What happened?"

"Gabriel's sword," Father said, his voice resolute.

She dropped to the floor across from me. "Morena, the only thing I can do to save him is to turn him into a Night Child. Do you understand?"

The one thing he wouldn't want to be. He would hate me, but I'd have to accept that to save him. He took an archangel's sword for me, and this decision would be mine to make for him. In time, I hoped he would forgive me. I nodded. "Save him."

Mother drew a long fingernail from the base of her palm up her arm several inches. The same crimson blood that ran through her Night Children gathered along the open wound. She angled her arm so the blood dripped into Jax's mouth. Her wound closed.

"Now what?" I looked at her. *He'd be okay.* That's what mattered most even if he never spoke to me again.

"We take him back to the Overworld. He'll need to feed

when he wakes up." She moved over to the same side as me and rested a hand on my cheek. "I'll go with you."

I leaned against her shoulder. *What have I done? I don't think someone with a soul could have made the decision I made.* Gabriel was wrong. I had no soul. Jax was a proud demon, but he'd struggled with being half-human. He'd be all Night Child when he woke up, but I didn't believe he would appreciate that or me. Wh*y did Mother make me decide? He's sworn to them, not me.* The question I longed to ask burned on my tongue and demanded an answer. "Will he forgive me?"

Mother sighed and smoothed the hair away from my face. "It might take some time, but he's an idiot if he doesn't."

A hiccupped sob escaped my lips. "I called him an idiot for jumping between Gabriel and me, so I guess that answers the question."

She squeezed my arm and patted it. "Oh, honey. Men do stupid things for love."

Did she say...love? My stomach fluttered.

"Heh. Hmm." Father cleared his throat behind us.

"You're an angel, dear," Mother called over her shoulder.

"Love? You think he loves me?" My heart pounded like a drum.

"I can't imagine he would have volunteered to go with you if he wasn't."

"Volunteered? You didn't order him? I didn't know." I covered my mouth with my hand to stifle another sob.

Father kissed the top of my head. "Just be gentle with his heart."

Will his heart even want me when he realizes what I chose for him? But at least he will be here to hate me.

Mother looked up at Father. "I'll be home tomorrow," she said. "After I get him settled at Gothica."

"Take your time, my love. This is important." Father bent to kiss her. "Do you want me to call someone for a portal?"

"No need." She smiled up at him. "I love you, Luce."

Only she could get away with calling him Luce. He'd strike down anyone else who did. That was their love.

"I love you too."

Mother took my hand and placed it in Jax's. She positioned our joined palms over his chest. "You'll need to hold on tight. I'll hold his other one"

She pounded her free palm onto our pile of hands. And we fell from Hell. Again.

CHAPTER 8
RENA

The three of us landed on the floor of Mother's apartment at the top of Gothica. Her guidance made it a softer arrival than mine, and I was thankful given Jax's condition. His eyes were closed, and he made no movements. He looked peaceful and his color was better, but that wouldn't last. He'd take on the translucence of a Night Child by the time the transformation was done.

"Help me get him into a more comfortable place," Mother said.

She and I moved him onto the couch in as gentle a motion as we could. I sat on the edge next to him. While his color had improved, he was too still.

I'd seen plenty of humans turn, and they writhed in agony as their human selves died during the transition. Dread coiled around me like a vice. "Shouldn't he be jerking or something?"

"Demon transition is different than human," she said, her tone soft. The care in her voice gave me some comfort.

"But he is half-human." I pressed a hand to his cheek. It was warm. "He feels hot."

"His human side is fighting, but his demon side is calm." She wrapped an arm around my shoulder. "It's normal, Morena."

"How long will it take?"

"It's different for everyone," she said. "It could be minutes. It could be hours or even days."

Days... "But he will survive?"

"Because the transition is from me, yes," she said.

Her blood was the original and more powerful. He'd be like Alessia, Mother's second-in-command, stronger than the others. *Shouldn't I be happy about that? I should. He'll have stature and a place of his own. So why is my heart shredding?* I focused on what would come next. "And how will he feed?"

"There is blood here he can consume, but..." She paused. "He will have the desire to feed as all Night Children do. He'll want blood from the source, and the yearn will be powerful. Possibly too powerful to resist."

"He's going to hate me." My heart twisted in my chest. I'd have done it a hundred times over to save him. If living with him never wanting to see me again was the result, at least he would live.

"Morena, Jax has loved you since you two became friends. I've watched his love grow over the years. He's exercised great patience over the last year in preparation for your trip. It's your turn to show him the same patience."

"But he is sworn to you and Father. How can he love me with that oath in place?" My words came out bitter, and I regretted them, especially after what Mother had done for him.

She lifted my chin and looked me straight in the eyes. "His oath is to you, my daughter. It always has been."

"What do you mean?" *To me? I'm not the leader of the Underworld or the consort.*

"Your father did not accept his oath to us. He told him that the heir needed his oath more than we did. While many have been offered a choice, there has been only one not to choose us. Jax did not hesitate to swear to you."

Fresh tears pooled in my eyes. "He swore to me? And no one told me?"

"He asked that we keep it between us, and your father agreed. I think Jax wanted you to see him and not the oath."

My breath hung in my chest. He wanted me to see him, and I wanted him to see me. *We are both idiots.*

"Sweet angel's ass, Mother. I knew he'd taken an oath and assumed it was to you and Father," I said, barely able to form the words. "Does being a Night Child break that oath?"

"I've never turned a demon who has sworn the oath, so I can't say," she said. "But he might be different from who he was before. You need to prepare for that."

If he were to forgive me, I wondered what that would look like for us. The transition changed everyone and some significantly more than others. Even if he gave me absolution on the act, his feelings for me could be different. *Love.* Mother had said he loved me. I'd cared about him for longer than I would admit. *But did I love him?* With the blood of the original, he would be able to come to Hell, but like Mother, he wouldn't be able to stay. If he did find a way to move past what I did and if he still loved me, would he be content with an existence like theirs?

His hand moved closer to me, and I slipped mine into it. A current sizzled to life between our hands, and I closed my eyes, thankful it was still intact. He squeezed my fingers so tight it was painful, but I grasped his cold fingers in the same manner. A single tear formed at the corner of his right eye, and I wiped it away.

"I'm here, Jax," I whispered against his ear. "I'm here, and I'm not going anywhere."

Hours passed, and Jax didn't move. I stayed at his side holding his hand and waited for him to squeeze mine again. The stillness unnerved me. I'd never seen Jax so motionless. Of course, I'd never asked my mother to make him a Night Child before either.

Mother's hand on my shoulder drew my attention. "Are you hungry? I can fix you something."

The memory of Jax cooking breakfast earlier landed heavily on my chest. I met her gaze. "No, I don't want anything to eat."

"Eat," Jax said, his voice strained.

I sat up straight and glanced at Mother, not sure I hadn't imagined it. I rested my hand against Jax's face. "Hey, are you awake? Are you hungry?"

His eyes stayed closed, but his mouth opened, fangs exposed. Demons drank blood and ate flesh, so this really wasn't that different. Except it was. He'd see the world through an altered lens. Everyone in Hell would look at him in a different way. *And those assholes who'd taunted him...* It was my fault. All of this.

"I'll get some blood." Mother headed toward the kitchen.

"We've got food for you." I rubbed his arm. "It's coming."

Mother returned with sealed bags. "These have a tube. You can tilt it up to drip in his mouth, and he can suck on it like a straw when he gets some strength."

I did as she instructed and positioned the bag with the tube in his mouth. The first drop of blood hit his tongue, and he clamped down on the tube. The contents of the bag were drained in moments. I stared at the empty bag in disbelief. *Was it normal?*

"Here." Mother handed me another full one and took the one Jax had sucked dry.

Jax's eyes remained closed, but he drank another bag down.

"Why isn't he waking up?" I looked up at her.

She handed me a third bag. "It is different for everyone. Sometimes it just takes time, Morena. Be patient. He will wake up."

Patience had never been something I was good at in my life. *Wake up, Jax.*

As selfish as it was, I needed to see he was okay. To know he was still Jax. To find out if he would still look at me the same way.

He went through five bags before he lost interest. It was about the same as a demon would need to heal if significantly injured. I sat beside him and took his hand again. He maneuvered so his fingers laced through mine. I let out a breath to ease my tension and watched for any movement.

His eyes shifted under his lids. My mouth went dry. He was all right. The color in his cheeks was rosy, which they weren't as a demon, but he appeared to be past the transition.

I leaned in next to his ear. "Open them, Jax. Open your eyes."

He blinked a few times and red eyes met mine. Not demon red, but Night Child red like blood.

The tension in me released, and I felt lighter at the sight of him awake. "Hey."

"Hey." He stared at me. His expression looked blank, but he reached up and cupped my cheek. I leaned into it and relished the sparks. "What happened? How am I here?"

He pulled his hand back and studied it. Sensations would be different as a Night Child. From what Mother had told me, everything was intensified, especially in the beginning.

"We can talk about that later," I said, not sure how to tell him he was a vampire, and he had me to blame for it. "How do you feel? Are you hungry?"

"I feel... different. I don't feel like me," he said. "Not hungry but... not satisfied." He sat up at Night Children's speed and put his hands on either side of my face. His gaze locked on mine, and all I could see was him. Nothing else mattered in that moment of shared existence. His lips hovered over mine, and he claimed me. It wasn't like the gentle kiss from earlier. It was full of need and desire. I leaned into him.

"Maybe that should be done when I'm not here," Mother said.

I pulled away from Jax and looked at her. My cheeks burned as a blush formed. "Sorry."

"I was young once." She smiled, but it was forced. Concern was written in the creases on her forehead.

Jax moved off the couch and knelt in front of my mother. He looked up at her and then to me in confusion.

Fuck. Was that what Mother's blood did? I'd never been there when she created one of her own. Alessia was older than me, and the others were scattered across the world representing her. *Jax is going to kill me. I should have told him the moment he sat up.*

"It's the sire bond," she said. "Rise, and we need to discuss what you are experiencing."

She sat in a chair while I sat next to Jax on the couch.

"Because you have consumed my blood and I am the original, you will feel that bond when I am near," she said, her voice gentle but firm.

He glanced at me. His hand went to the base of his neck. I expected to see hatred in his gaze, but that wasn't what was there. Confusion and desperation looked back at me, and as the one who caused all of this with my stupid trip, I owed him an explanation. It was my debt to pay him with the truth. All of it. No matter the outcome. I braced myself and turned to face him on the couch.

"Gabriel's sword struck you. It was just a scratch, but that's all it takes from a heavenly artifact to end a demon's life in the most excruciating way. I'm sure you have heard stories of this from the wars when Father fell from grace. If

Mother hadn't given you her blood, you would have died. There wasn't anything Father could do or that could be done in the demon realm." I squeezed his hand, but he jerked it away.

"I'm a vampire?" His voice was rough, and he grabbed his throat.

"Yes, you are," I said. "It was the only way, and I made the decision, Jax. Not Father. Not Mother. Me."

His forehead wrinkled. "I'm neither human nor demon anymore." He stood up and walked across the room and turned to face me. "Am I?"

"No," I said, keeping my voice soft and even. I shook on the inside, fearing the worst as he drew his own conclusions.

Jax looked between my mother and me and settled on my mother. He ran a hand through his hair and let it rest at the back of his neck. "I will not be able to live in the Underworld?"

My mother shook her head. "Not permanently," Her tone was solemn. "You will be able to stay as I do, but you will have to leave periodically-"

"To feed on human blood," he said, moving back to the seat beside me.

"Yes," Mother said.

Jax's tortured gaze settled on me. He blinked a few times like he was trying to reason out something.

I scooted closer to him and pressed my hand against the side of his face. "You are still you. The Jax I grew up with. The Jax who has been my friend. The Jax who was brave enough to put a bloodcuff on me. The Jax who took an archangel's blade for me."

He shuffled on the cushion away from me. His face hardened.

My heart slowed and twisted. *Please don't.* I let my hand drop to my side and braced myself for his hate. I deserved it. I made a decision for him that wasn't mine to make because I didn't want to lose him. Anything he said to me I earned, and I'd have to take it.

"Morena, I don't want to hurt you," Jax said.

Morena. Not Rena. The use of my formal name from him stung worse than anything else he could say, but I didn't miss his fear. He was afraid he would attack me, and that wasn't Jax.

"You won't hurt me, Jax," I said.

"Maybe if Lilith compels me not to, but you can never be sure." His bitter tone sliced through me.

"Jax, she's a demon. Her blood will not appeal to you," Mother said.

"I can't take that chance." He inched further away on the couch. "I swore to protect her, and I can no longer do that as a vampire."

"Jax..." His name rolled off my lips with almost no sound.

"I'm not the same person as you said. I'll never be again. This is what I'll be forever." Disgust passed across his face.

Shattered slivers of my heart broke away.

"I can help you adjust," Mother said. "I'll arrange for my second-in-command to help you. In time, you will understand your new world and find your place."

"And I can help too," I said, but my voice no longer held the confidence from earlier. The look on his face broke me in two. "I've been around the Night Children enough to understand."

Jax let out a long sigh. "I can't force you to leave Gothica. It's your mother's house, but I don't want your help."

My insides folded in on each other. I closed my lids to hold in the hurt and pushed it down deep. When I reopened my eyes, I was cold to the bone. *If he didn't want me here, then why should I stay?* I would always be a constant reminder of how he became vampire, and the disgust on his face would be what I'd see when he looked back at me. This was his new life, and I was his old life. He wasn't asking for space. He didn't want me here. He didn't want me. I would be the constant memory of why he was no longer a demon.

"Then I'll leave," I said.

He met my gaze with his Night Children's red orbs and a look as cold as I felt. I pulled out Father's dagger.

"Morena, calm down," Mother said.

"I'm calm," I said. *On the outside.* On the inside, my heart gave into the fractures, and if there was a soul there, it shattered too. Jax looked away. My throat tightened and plunged into my chest. "I wish you the best, Jax."

I slid the dagger across my palm, watching the thin line of blood bead, waiting for the summons to pull me through. The yank was welcomed.

"Goodbye, Rena," Jax said.

Tears sprung to my eyes at my nickname from him. I blinked back the hot dampness and dove through to Hell.

CHAPTER 9

JAX

I sent her away. The person I cared about the most. The one person I knew cared about me. I didn't want Rena to see me satisfy this unending hunger. The constant craving ached inside me like a wound that wouldn't heal. *How could I fulfill my oath to her when the only thing I could think about was blood? Human blood. It was all I wanted.*

Except I missed Rena.

It had only been two days, less than forty-eight hours, a blink of time by demon standards, but I missed being in the same world as her. I'd known when she was close and far, and she hadn't been close since I told her to leave. My selfishness to have her here wasn't the best thing for her. *I know this, so why will the ache in my chest not go away? Why do I see her every time I close my eyes?*

"Jax," Lilith said. "Are you ready to practice? Alessia has a volunteer for you."

Rena's mother stayed, and as much as I appreciated her, she was a constant reminder of Rena. The Mother of Night

Children taught me their ways, and I should be grateful. She had others like Alessia who could take over my ... education. I wasn't sure why she did, especially when I refused fresh blood every time she brought a human into the room. My fear was I would turn one or kill one, and I didn't want to damn anyone else to this existence.

"I don't need the volunteer. I'm fine," I said, my tone free of emotion, but the insatiable burn in my throat gnawed at my resolve. I'd stuck my finger down there in an attempt to scratch it, and the itch was worse with a human this close.

Alessia, Lilith's second-in-command, was far less patient. She shoved several humans in my face. It was harder to resist them each time. The vein on their necks throbbed in a hypnotizing rhythm, expanding and contracting in a staccato. I crossed the apartment and closed the door to the room designated as mine.

I wanted the blood of those humans more than I wanted to live. *Live.* I snorted. I was dead. *Undead. Vampire.* Not that I'd been alive in the human sense before, but I'd been half demon and half-human. I'd felt alive then and had a chance to earn my place by Rena's side. But now, I was a vampire, and it would never happen. Lilith could reign in Hell with Lucifer because she was powerful. *The original.* I didn't possess any power to make myself worthy of a position with Rena.

A soft knock echoed on the bedroom door. "Jax, can I come in?"

Who turns down the Mother of Night Children? My creator. I couldn't if I wanted to. "Yes."

She entered the room as the presence she was. Lilith was

Lucifer's heart. The reason his beat even though hers didn't. *And my heart no longer beats. No quickening when I see Rena, even though I worried she would hear the rapid thump every time.*

Lilith sat on the bed next to me. "I know you think resistance makes you strong, but it doesn't. Refusal will only make you weaker, which makes you vulnerable."

"I'll drink from the bags." Consumption from the containers was closer to normal. *I can do that to survive. No, not survive. To exist.*

"That can sustain you, but it will never give you rest from the craving." Lilith's voice was softer than usual.

"I don't want to satisfy the craving." The hunger was the prompt that kept me grounded in what I was and would always be.

"It doesn't make you brave to not consume." Lilith's tone became more commanding. "It will be your undoing and make you a risk. A Night Child will feed when the urge is uncontrollable, and the results can be dangerous if you aren't trained."

I heard her, but I didn't want to live in a world where Rena wasn't an option. The admission to myself settled in my stomach like a volcano of rage, ready to explode.

"Why are you so concerned for me, Lilith?" I asked. "Why not just let me become weak prey for others?"

"Because Morena chose for you to live. I made you myself. There are love and responsibility in those promises, whether spoken or unspoken," she said, her voice soft again.

Rena. The spot in my chest where my heart was constricted. No rapid beats at the sound of her name.

"No, I'll not drink from a human today." *Not today. Not ever.*

"Very well."

Lilith left me alone in the room, but she wouldn't allow me to leave. I couldn't exit Gothica, and I assumed I no longer had the ability to call portals to Hell. Nothing stopped me from trying but myself. And the risk of another disappointment.

I reclined back on the bed and remembered the kiss Rena and I shared. The warmth of it ignited me, and I wanted to repeat it over and over. But that would never happen again.

CHAPTER 10

RENA

I hit the mat on my back hard. "Again."

"Morena, you are distracted," Jess said, his voice harsh. "You need to focus."

Father planned to send a group after Uncle Amon, and I asked to be part of it. He hadn't said yes or no, so I trained while he considered it.

I narrowed my focus on Jess's movements. He moved like a cat around the square surface. His actions were fluid but predictable if I paid attention. The pattern appeared to me. I lunged in the air and landed a kick square in his chest. He landed flat on the padded surface.

The satisfaction of the takedown was one of the few things I enjoyed in the days since I returned to Hell. I laughed. "You are too predictable, Jess."

He shook his head. "Better."

I held out my hand for him. He grasped it. His foot planted in my hip and flipped me over his head.

The wind knocked out of me, I gasped but chuckled. It

was the first time since I'd returned to Hell that I had. For about two seconds it felt good, then the reminder of why I hadn't laughed took hold.

"But not good enough," he said.

The door opened and shut. I prepared for Jess's next move, but he stood and took a bowed position.

I looked toward the door and then scrambled to my feet. "Mother."

"Morena," she said, wringing her hands. "I need to speak with you."

"Of course." I walked toward her. Rumors would spread, but we'd managed to keep Jax's change a secret to give him time to adjust. The last shard of my heart that was left held hope he would want to visit Hell again one day. Eventually, his transition would come out.

"My study," she said. I didn't challenge or ask questions on the walk there. She was serious, and uneasiness churned in my gut. *Jax is fine. He's fine. I'd know if he wasn't.*

She shut the door behind us, and I leaned against a chair.

"Sit, dear."

"I'm good, Mother."

"Sit, Morena." Mother sat on the couch.

I did as she asked and took the chair closest to me. "How is he?" Guilt squeezed my heart. "Who is with him?"

"Alessia is watching over him." Sorrow seeped out of her words. "But he refuses to leave the bedroom and will only drink blood from bags."

Alessia wasn't my favorite of Mother's children. She was cold and hateful, and she was the last person I wanted near Jax.

"And if he doesn't drink from a human?"

"He will be confined to Gothica until he does." Her tone came out frustrated, which was not like her.

It has only been a week. He just needs more time. But I had been with Mother when we had to end a Night Child who waited too long and was lost to bloodlust. She couldn't let that happen to Jax. Why hadn't she made him drink?

"You need to come back with me, Morena. His oath to you might still be intact, and you might be able to convince him to drink from a volunteer. He needs to do it without compulsion, but your bond might be able to reach him."

I blew my breath out through my lips to calm the tsunami in me. "I made a choice for him that he wouldn't have made for himself. He doesn't want me there, Mother. He's not going to listen to me. Bond or no bond."

Her tone softened. "You are the only one he is going to listen to, my daughter. He might be confused and struggling, but he still loves you."

Her words knocked the wind out of me. If I thought there was a chance Jax would listen to me or even talk to me, I would go, but he made it clear he didn't want me. Revenge was all that remained for me, and I would have it. "I'm going after Uncle Amon and Gabriel too."

She took my hand in hers. "Your father has plenty of help to tend to them. Jax only has you."

My chest tightened, and my heart pounded against it. "He made his wishes known that I was not welcome."

Mother touched my face and gave me a sad smile. "He's trying to protect you. Don't you see that? He doesn't want to hurt you, so he's hurting himself."

Her thumb ran under my eye. *Tears.* I was crying and hadn't realized it until then. She spoke to the tiny piece of hope in me, and I couldn't say no to that possibility no matter how small. "I'll go. I just need to tell Father."

"He already knows," she said, her voice strained. "We can go."

She took my hand, and I fell from Hell for the third time in a week.

I landed on my feet in her apartment in Gothica. The first thing I thought of was the breakfast Jax had cooked. My gut ached with sadness.

"Where is he?" I asked.

Alessia sat on the couch and met my gaze. "Still in the bedroom. He refuses to come out like a coward."

I leaped at her and the couch scraped along the floor. I pinned her against the frame. The anger dragged my demon voice out. "He is no coward. Don't say that again, or I will wipe your existence from the Overworld."

"Rena." His voice sounded gravelly, but it was him, and he used my nickname. My heart danced in my chest. He wrapped his hands around my waist and hauled me off of Alessia.

I turned in his arms and hugged him tight to me. "Jax."

He pulled my arms away and met my gaze. His eyes were full of pain. "What are you doing here?"

I glanced at my mother. She had her arms crossed over her chest and a half smile on her face like she knew she was right.

"Alessia, come with me. You and I shall have a talk about your manners," Mother said.

I waited until they left. The door shut quietly behind them.

"Mother was worried about you," I said, unsure what to say.

"Oh." He stepped back.

"And I was too."

He looked up with his red eyes meeting mine. "There is no need to worry. I've got it under control."

Sweet angel's ass he is stubborn.

"Jaxon, you might fool some people, but you cannot fool me," I said.

He smiled, but it didn't reach his eyes. "You haven't called me Jaxon since we were kids."

"When you start acting like the responsible and wise Jax, then I'll call you Jax again," I said.

He chuckled. "You've never called me responsible or wise."

I laughed. "Well, I couldn't give you a big head. Could I?"

He peered at the ceiling as if what he wanted to say next was written there. His gaze found mine, and the seriousness in his eyes tapped into my guilt. I buried it for later. He needed me to fight for him because he wasn't fighting for himself.

"Rena, I'll never be the Jax you knew again." The pain in his eyes was almost more than I could take. If I gave into his hurt, he wouldn't move forward.

"So what?" I shrugged, remaining steadfast in my argument. "We all change through our lives. Yours might have been a little quicker than some, but it's just another change to work through."

"I'll never be accepted back in Hell." He winced.

What he said could be true, but there wasn't a way to know until he tried. His confidence needed restoration. "Mother is accepted. You will be too."

He leaned back against the breakfast counter, the same one we'd eaten at a week ago, and shoved his hands in his pockets. "No, I won't. I'm the son of a demon, and I can't even claim that now. She is the powerful Mother of Night Children. We are not the same." His tone was resolved. I studied him and saw defeat in his eyes that had not once been there while he was a demon.

"Mother and Father will not allow you to be rejected."

"And that will only work while in their presence or yours. I'll never be able to walk the halls on my own." The loss in his voice damn near broke me, but he needed my strength right now.

I wanted to argue, but he was right. It was unlikely the demons would accept him without us there.

"We'll tackle that another time. Today, we need to get you to consume some warm blood so you can regain your freedom." I tried not to sound repulsed because the irony that I didn't like drinking it either was not lost in the moment.

His nose wrinkled like the thought disgusted him worse than me.

Same. But I didn't say it. He already knew, and it wouldn't help the situation.

"Aren't you hungry?"

"Starving," he said. "But I don't want to drink from a human. How about I make us breakfast?"

"Human food isn't going to satisfy you," I said, unable to keep the mixture of sadness and frustration out of my tone.

"But it sounds better to me than blood. How about you?" He smiled. This was my Jax. The one that was the fixer and cared for me above everything else. I read what he needed, and that was something familiar. I'd do this with him, and I'd drink blood with him later if that's what it took. *Gag.*

CHAPTER 11
JAX

I cooked the same meal for Rena I had the day everything changed. I pointed to a barstool at the counter. "Sit."

"You're ordering me?" She raised an eyebrow. A smile as bright as the sun spread across her face. "No one does that. I kind of like it."

My insides were like slow-moving molten lava. The urge to press my lips against hers and devour her was hard to ignore. Lilith was right in that I didn't crave Rena's blood, but I did crave her. Every inch of her.

I smiled back. She'd been my universe for so long, but I didn't think there was a chance. *And there wouldn't be now that I'm a Night Child.* My anger killed the desire in me. I wasn't angry with her. I might have even done the same thing if the situation had been reversed, but I'd always be a vampire and not worthy to sit beside her in her kingdom. I placed a plate in front of her.

"Eat." I forced another smile.

"Where's yours?" she asked.

I had said it sounded better than blood. *Why did I say that?* The bacon aroma scenting the air was strong. It didn't smell repulsive like the volunteers Alessia had brought to me, but I wasn't hungry for it.

"Making it now." I put some of the food on a plate and took the seat beside her. *I'll take a bite and scoot it around on the plate if it tastes bad.* "How is it?"

"Better than we get in Hell." Rena took a bite of bacon.

I bit into a slice, and it tasted...good. Much better than the humans smelled. My stomach growled.

Rena gave me the side-eye. "You need to eat more."

"So I've been told," I said, hearing the bitterness in my own tone. I took a bigger bite.

Rena's eyes narrowed on me, dissecting me like she was so good at doing.

She sighed. The exhale of her breath was like a warm breeze over my body. The hairs on my arms stood up, and my dick twitched.

"I miss you, Jax," she said. "I know it's only been a week, but I want..." She turned her head away, and her voice trailed off into the air. I reached out for her hair to run my fingers through the softness of it, but I dropped my hand. She wasn't mine to touch, and she never would be.

"I can't go back," I whispered. "Not like this." As a half-human and half-demon, I'd worked twice as hard to achieve the same respect as other demons. Demons saw vampires as lower than the lowest ranking demon. Even if I did return to Hell, I'd never be allowed in her circle.

"Then I'll stay," Rena whispered, turning back toward me. Her eyes held unshed tears, and it nearly sent me to my knees to beg her to stay. To apologize for sending her away. She slid her hand over my knee.

I wrapped my fingers around hers. "I can't ask you to do that. This is my life now. Not yours."

"You're not asking. I want to be here."

Does she? Or is it pity for what I am now? Is it guilt for my sacrifice to save her from Gabriel? And I'm not even sure I did save her. Hell was her home. She couldn't stay here. She was the heir to the throne of Hell. "You have duties."

"And I still have a year to live in the Overworld for my birthday," she said.

It would be great to have her here, but her life, her training, everything was in the Underworld. Lucifer and Lilith couldn't possibly let her stay a year after what happened last week. I didn't trust myself to be able to protect her from the Nephilim, and Lucifer would make them pay for the attempts on her.

"I don't want to hurt you, Rena." My voice cracked. "You are too important." I left off 'to me.' I didn't need to add that and confuse her.

"There is nothing more important to me right now than you," Her eyes flitted up to mine. The tears were gone, replaced with demon red, the color they became when something impassioned her.

The impulse to kiss her slammed into me. My cock hardened. I gave in and leaned toward her. *A goodbye kiss.*

Rena's fingers entwined in my hair. She pulled me closer. Her lips crashed against mine. I stood and pulled her tight against me. My hardness pressed against her. The nearness of her body made me insane. I ran my tongue over the seam of her lips, and her mouth parted to invite me in. She moaned, and it almost undid me.

I pushed her up against the counter and reached behind to move the dishes aside. She put her hands on either side of my face and held my gaze. The desire in her eyes spurred me forward. I lifted her onto the counter and stood between her legs.

"Rena," I rasped out against her cheek as I trailed kisses down her neck. Her head fell to the side opening up the space for me. I licked behind her ear and down to her collarbone. Another moan, a deep sound from her gut, passed over her lips.

The vein on her neck throbbed back and forth. My fangs extended down. I opened my mouth and leaned into her neck. *What am I doing?* I jumped back away from her. My teeth ground together. *I almost bit. Almost bit Rena. Her blood doesn't even appeal to me, and I barely stopped myself.* "Rena, you need to leave."

"Wh..what?" She stammered.

I met her gaze. The hurt on her face told me I'd done exactly what I didn't want to do. Wound her. Damage our relationship more. *Fuck.*

"I can't control myself around you. I almost drank from you." I forced myself to keep my voice even, but inside it ripped me apart. Gutted me to the core.

"I understand how vampires have sex, Jax. Drinking blood is part of it," she said, her tone offended.

She understands... I refused to let it go further. I ran my hands over my face while I composed myself.

"It's not right for me to drink from you." I looked out the window. This was what Lilith and Alessia warned me about. If I didn't drink human blood, I would lose complete control, and I forbade myself from being near Rena when it happened. The ache in my pants protested. "You should go."

"Look at me." Rena's tone was full of strength but she didn't use her demon voice.

I faced her. There was pain in her unshed tears, but the warrior spirit that earned her respect in Hell took over. She wouldn't give up without the truth. "I need to figure out what it means for me to be a vampire now. I can't do anything else until I understand what I am."

She nodded. "I'll help you. However you need me to."

"It's not that I don't want you here," I said. *I want you under me and on the couch and in the bedroom.* "But I don't trust myself around you. Look what I almost did."

The reality sunk in on me, and all my desire faded away. Ice filled my veins.

"We'll figure it out together," she said.

"No, Morena," I said, making my tone formal. "I am a servant of your mother, and I need to learn what that means. I can't do that with you at my side. I'll use you as a crutch like I always have."

Her eyes reddened. The tears edged closer to falling. My chest tightened. My resolve threatened. I had to look away.

"It's time for you to go. Go enjoy your year of Earth." I turned my back on her, unable to take the rejection in her eyes. *It's the right thing to do. I'm not what she needs.*

The door to the apartment slammed, and the room

emptied of life. The heaviness of her absence blanketed me. I went back to the bedroom and crawled into bed.

CHAPTER 12
JAX

"Jax, wake up," Lilith's voice drifted to me, her urgent tone almost like a shake.

I sat up in bed, not realizing vampires slept so deeply. "I don't want any blood."

"It's not about blood, Jax," Lilith said, flustered. "Do you know where Morena is?"

I leaped off the bed. "What's happened?"

"Do you know where she went?" Lilith's face held concern.

"No, I thought she went to find you." I walked out to the living room looking around like she would materialize there. Fear found the place where my heart was with ferocity.

"She didn't say where she was going?"

"No..." I averted eye contact. She'd brought Rena here to talk to me, and I'd sent her away after I almost bit her and almost fucked her. I forced myself to look at Lilith.

She crossed her arms. "Tell me everything, Jax."

"I made us breakfast," I said, skipping the make-out

session. "Then I told her she needed to go live her year in the Overworld while I figured out how to be a vampire."

"And she left?" Her mouth hung open like she was stunned Rena would leave on her own.

"Yes." I didn't know what to say the Lilith, but I had to find Rena. The thought consumed me more than the starving ache for blood. *I have to go find her.* The need to locate her grew in me with laser focus.

"Did you have a fight with her?" Lilith tapped her foot.

"I wouldn't call it a fight, but we disagreed," I said, pulling on my shoes. "I'll head out now to find her."

"No, you can't leave Gothica until you consume human blood, and we know you can control yourself. I'll go look for her."

"Then bring me a damn human, and I'll drink," I said, my voice coming out in a roar. It was a commanding tone that I shouldn't be using with the Mother of Night Children and Queen of Hell, but she might as well end me if she expected me to stay here while Rena was missing.

Lilith raised an eyebrow at me the same way Rena did. "I'll have Alessia bring a volunteer up."

"Don't leave without me," I said, pleading instead of demanding this time.

"I'll ask Lucifer to send out a search crew. I'll be with them." She tossed a medallion to me. "Hold this in your hand and say my name once Alessia has given you a pass. It will bring you to me."

The search crew consisted of the bloodhounds of Hell. They had no empathy or compassion. I didn't want them anywhere near Rena. If they found her first, they would corner her, and with her in pain, she would come out in full fight mode. *I can't let them find her first.* But I had to consume blood, human blood, to get out of here. The thought disgusted me, but I'd do it for Rena. I'd do anything to get to her.

Lilith exited with the quickness of a vampire and left the door open. I inched toward it. Before I could step into the hallway, Alessia appeared with a blonde woman dressed for the club. Her top was low with most of her breasts exposed. She wanted the bite more than I wanted blood.

"Dinner is served," Alessia said with a smile that was more of a snarl. "This is Talia. She's done this before, and be forewarned, she's a moaner."

I gulped. There was no appeal for me to this woman, but I wanted to find Rena. This was required of me.

"Don't look so excited," Alessia said.

Talia walked over to me. She tilted her head and moved her hair to the side to expose her neck. It didn't invite me the way Rena's had, but it was the only way I'd be allowed out of here. *Do it, dumbass. You need to find Rena. Just do it.*

I stood close but not too close and leaned over. I concentrated on the vein in her neck until my fangs dropped. A gag formed in my gut, but I bit down. Her blood tasted bitter and sour. I swallowed to earn my freedom. Talia moaned as Alessia said she would, and I pulled away from her.

"Done," I said, my hunger satisfied. I shoved the woman back toward Alessia. She caught Talia with one arm.

"Very good," Alessia said. "I didn't even have to stop you. That never happens. Did Lilith give you her calling card?"

The medallion. I held out my hand with it. "Yes."

She ripped open the skin of her thumb and placed a bloody thumbprint on my medallion. "Prick your thumb and do the same. You can call her now. She doesn't give one of these to everyone. Just so you know."

I tore the skin on my thumb like she had and pressed it to the metal disk. *Lilith.*

A portal opened and sucked me through it. I landed on my back.

"That's quite an entrance and a quick pass from Alessia. You must have impressed her." Lilith showed a moment of surprise before the tension returned to her face. She held out her hand.

I took it, not wanting to refuse her in front of the blood-hounds. "Have you found anything?"

Lilith exuded calm in all situations no matter how dire, but she was all nerves. "No, but the hounds found her scent mixed with Amon's here. We're assuming he portaled her somewhere, but we don't know where that could be."

I'd gut him. Let him heal and do it again. How had he found her so fast?

"He's been removed from access to the safe houses?" I scanned the party here and recognized most. I'd been on missions with the lower-level demons in the last year. Their human forms tended to look like vagrants because it would allow them to slip through places unnoticed. They were Lucifer's best, but he wasn't here. With his daughter missing at Amon's hands, I thought he would be here.

"Yes, so he must have help." She wiped her hands down her pants.

The anger in me festered. I'd inflict punishment on the

conspirators. My sire bond with Lilith faded to almost nothing as I thought of Rena. She was all that mattered to me. I'd uncover Amon and return Rena to … well, I didn't know where but somewhere she would be safe. "I'll find her, Lilith. I promise this as my oath to her."

"Jax, if he…" she swallowed hard, glancing at the group and back to me. "We have to bring her home safe and sound. There is no other choice."

Sun beamed in from the windows. I'd never paid much attention to the time of day as a demon. *Damn being a vampire.* "As soon as the sun goes down, I'll go."

Her eyes met mine. "You are of me now. You share original blood." Her voice was so quiet I could barely hear her. "Jax, you can walk in the daylight."

I must have misunderstood her when I strained to hear the words. She was the only one, as the Mother of Night Children, who could step foot in daylight.

"Leave us," Lilith said to the others. "Wait for us outside."

She stepped closer. "Your eyes will be sensitive, so you'll want coverings."

It sunk in. I wasn't confined to night like the others. I had choices. Maybe there was a very slim chance for Rena and me. "I'll bring her home, Lilith."

Another portal formed, and Alessia joined us. She handed me a hoodie and a hat. There weren't any sunglasses. *Screw it.*

She brought casual clothes for Lilith too. Lilith excused herself to change. Alessia looked me up and down like she wasn't convinced I was up for the task. It made the air awkward in the room. I understood why Rena wasn't so fond of her.

Lilith returned and glanced between us like she considered separating us as if we were fighting siblings. *I guess we are.* "Alessia is the only other one of me still in existence in this hemisphere," Lilith said. "She'll be returning to Gothica."

Alessia sneered at me. "Don't break these and don't lose them." She handed me a pair of solid black sunglasses. "They are my favorite pair."

"I'm going with you," Lilith said.

I'd expected her to go. "And Lucifer?"

"He'll stay in Hell," she said, her voice shaking. "It took some convincing, but it is for the best. He's sending more forces."

Lilith was afraid of what Lucifer would do to the Overworld to save Morena, but I was afraid I would burn down Heaven, Hell, and Earth to save Rena from whatever Amon and Gabriel planned.

CHAPTER 13
JAX

Rena's soft scent of warmth mixed with the fiery smell of spirit floated around me. I hadn't noticed it before in the stench of so many mixed scents, but without the bloodhounds in the room, I honed in on it. Her aroma lingered around me. On me. Like it was connected to me. I let out a breath. She was alive. "I smell her," I said to Lilith. "It wasn't long ago."

"They had to have portaled." She kept her voice low.

"Yes." I studied the space. "Amon wasn't here at the same time. His scent isn't as strong."

I shuddered at the thought he was near her. I wanted to attempt a portal to find Amon and sever his head for daring to touch Rena. But Night Children couldn't portal and Lilith either had to have a demon call one for her or take the fall and deal with the strain of discomfort every time. Any attempt I made would be as useless as I felt being a vampire.

"Then who was with her?" Her forehead creased with worry.

I focused on the other scent mixed with Rena's. I knew it, but I didn't. It wasn't demonic.

"It's familiar," I said, frustrated I couldn't name the owner. "Like I've smelled something similar but not the same aroma exactly."

"Describe it to me," Lilith said.

"You are scenting it?"

"No," she said, her voice so quiet I could barely hear her even with my vampire hearing.

"It's like a…" I tried to pinpoint it, but there was only one thing that made sense. "An apple orchard. The soft sweetness in the air of one."

Lilith's throat bobbed up and down. "It couldn't have been Amon. She's gone somewhere he can't travel. Somewhere we can't travel."

Alarm twisted from the base of my spine up to my aching chest. *Where could Rena go we couldn't?* I stared at the Mother of Night Children. Her eyes were distant. "Where, Lilith?"

"To the angelic dimension. We live most of ours in the demonic realm. The angels have a similar place. It's not Heaven, but it's their home. Neither human nor demon can enter there." She stood immobile like she was paralyzed by the thought.

"How can she gain entrance there if we can't?"

"Because her father is an angel." Her focus returned to me, and I saw a mother frightened for her child. "He might be a Fallen, but he is still of angelic creation. Therefore, she is too."

Given the recent angelic visit Rena had, there was only one name on my lips.

"Gabriel."

"It would make sense." She hesitated as if she hadn't made the same connection. "Since your run-in with him."

"He tried to convince her she had a soul." I paused. The memory of the day my world changed was far too fresh. An ache of hunger burned my tongue and singed a path down my throat. I swallowed hard and shifted my thoughts to my sworn oath. Protect the heir of Hell with my life no matter how long or how short that may be. I'd bound myself to her when I took the oath. Lilith had supplied Rena's blood, and I never asked how she got it. It didn't matter. Rena was my duty. My heart. And I'd find her. "There has to be a way to get there."

"Not for us, Jax," she said. "We are damned, and we are not of angelic descent."

Gabriel said Lilith believed she didn't have a soul, but he was adamant both she and Rena did. *Would she go to this angelic dimension if she could? I would. Was she concerned what it would mean for the Night Children?*

A pattern appeared on the floor. I squatted down and ran my hands over where the portal had been. The lines intersected and told a story only someone with training could decipher. "This has been a frequent meeting place. Portals have opened here many times." I studied the orientation of the markings. "If it's Gabriel, he's too smart to come back here after taking her."

"You can still see the paths?" Lilith knelt next to me.

"Yes."

"Interesting. You should have lost that ability with the transition." She examined me, confusion on her face.

Her scrutinization made me uncomfortable. *So, I don't fit into the Night Children mold either. I'm good with that. Don't want to.*

"Can Re…" I cleared my throat. "Can Morena leave the angelic realm on her own or does she need Gabriel?" Rena had been curious about what Gabriel told her. She was stubborn enough to go with him to get answers, but I'd jumped between them, not believing the archangel.

"I don't know," Lilith said, shaking her head. "I'd think it would be like how it works for us. Requiring training and skill."

"So, we could summon her." I hoped for an option that didn't require us traveling there.

"We could try," she said. "She can't be summoned like a demon, Jax. Lucifer has tried and failed. It's one of the reasons we've been so protective of her."

I nodded. I'd sensed how different she was from a regular demon since I'd known her. "She has Lucifer's blade. What if we summoned the blade?"

"We might leave her stranded there." Lilith had tears in her eyes. She stood up and turned away from me. I'd never seen her cry. My hope drained with each option she deterred.

Light glinted from under a table beside her. I crawled under and grabbed it. *Lucifer's blade.* Dread dug deep in my chest. If Rena couldn't portal and she didn't have the blade, she was stuck. "Lilith?"

I stood up and handed it to her. "Morena wanted us to know she was here."

She flipped it over in her hand. "Jax, there are few who know this, but Gabriel was in love with me when I was human. I loved Morena's father from the day we met, but I valued my friendship with Gabriel. He was kind then. Much kinder than he is now. The years of loneliness hardened him I think."

I didn't tell her that I knew more than she thought I did. She didn't need to hear the gossip that still surrounded them after thousands of years. "Can you call him here?"

She pressed her lips together. When she spoke, her voice was the same whisper it had been at Gothica. "Yes. Or at least I could at one time. Not since I've become who I am now."

"Then do it. We have to try." I gritted my teeth, because I knew there was no guarantee he would bring Rena with him. "He took her to get your attention, didn't he? That's why you didn't want Lucifer to come to the Overworld."

"Yes," she said, her voice weak. "I feared that might be the reason, and I played down the seriousness to him."

I closed my eyes against the anger. When I opened them again, the room was painted in red. *I knew Lucifer would have been here himself. He doesn't know how dire this situation is.*

Lilith pulled a necklace out that was hidden under her shirt. She waved her hand over the small black medallion, and the metal changed colors to brilliant gold. It glittered and danced with the sunlight.

She'd had the ability to call him and hadn't. I ground my teeth together to keep my mouth closed. *If I wasn't sired to her...* I didn't finish the thought. No good would come of that thinking. Only more pain.

Lilith closed her eyes and pressed the charm between her hands. She muttered a summons for Gabriel in angelic song.

The melody was both beautiful and sad like how crystal makes a tinkling noise before it breaks.

Time passed, and my anxiety grew. *Had I been wrong that Gabriel would answer her call?*

The sweet scent of an apple orchard after a summer rain permeated the air around me. A bright light swirled in front of us. The heavenly light was like looking in the sun, and I shielded my eyes. When the brightness dimmed, Gabriel stood in front of us. No heavenly fire dripped from his wings this time.

I narrowed my eyes at him through a haze of red-hot anger. Morena wasn't with him. *Fuck. I was sure he wouldn't let her out of his sight.*

Gabriel glanced between Lilith and me. "You survived," he said to me. "But not without Lilith's touch."

My arm ached with phantom pain where his sword had pierced.

"Where's Rena?" I ground out.

Lilith held her hand out in front of me.

"Where is my daughter, Gabriel, and why have you taken her?" Lilith's voice was even and strong. She showed no weakness to the angel.

"I did not take her, Lilith. She came with me freely. You can ask her yourself." Gabriel held out a hand.

Rena stepped from behind him and took his hand. Relief came in waves that she was here, but it slipped away as I took in her appearance. Her face wasn't readable. No emotions. No expression. She looked like a statue. She looked drugged.

"What have you done to her?" I growled and took a step forward.

Lilith caught my arm and held me back. Her sharp nails pierced my skin. A tug snagged me. *The sire bond. Fuck that damn sire bond. My only bond is with Rena.*

"What do you want, Gabriel?" Lilith asked, her tone cold and lethal like she was ready to strike. Yet, she wouldn't let me attack.

"I want the family I was denied when you left me for Lucifer," he said, his voice as cold as Lilith's.

My fangs dropped, and a growl vibrated through me. Rena wasn't a pawn for his game. *I'll rip the archangel into pieces.*

"I was never more than your friend, Gabriel," she said. "But I will go with you if you release my daughter."

I tore my eyes away from Rena to look at her unable to speak. Shock shifted into full fear. There would be nowhere to hide. Lucifer would bring hell to the Overworld and anywhere else he could if she went with Gabriel. He wouldn't stand by and allow Gabriel to have either one of them. Lilith had to know that.

"Our daughter," Gabriel said. "She is our daughter, Lilith, and Lucifer will let her go if you tell him so."

This fucking angel is having a psychotic fucking breakdown.

Rena's expression never changed. No reaction. I took in the scene. I'm a new vampire who should be crazed, but I might be the only one in my right mind here. Gabriel was the catalyst. If I took him out of the equation, then problem solved. I reached for my swords only to remember they weren't there. I'd been in such a hurry to get to Rena, I'd failed to check for them. I couldn't take an archangel in hand-to-hand combat, but maybe I could distract him long enough to give Lilith time to escape with Rena.

"She's not your daughter." Lilith remained calm like she was talking a jumper away from the edge. She kept her eyes on Gabriel, but her grip loosened on my arm. She had a plan. "You are confused."

"No," he said, his angel voice rustling the air around me. "She is mine."

I'd never killed an archangel. I wasn't even sure how it was done or if it was possible by someone like me. The pure rage in my chest spiraled out. I wanted to kill Gabriel, but Lilith's slow stalking movements told me I might have to get in line.

"Morena has accepted it, and you must come with us to complete our family," Gabriel continued with his delusion.

"You know I cannot travel to the Realm of Angels with you," Lilith said. "I am soulless and will not be allowed entry."

"But Lilith, you do have a soul, and I can show you."

"All right," Lilith said, her voice soft. She held out her hand to him.

"Lilith..." I struggled to find words and understand her tactics. *Why would she give in so easily? Why didn't she fight?*

"He's right, Jax." She bordered on robotic.

Gabriel smiled and took her hand. She jerked him to her in one swift motion. Gabriel let out a high-pitched scream that rattled the building. Lilith stabbed him with Lucifer's blade. She stabbed an angel. *Fuck.*

"Get Morena and go. Take her to Hell where he can't touch her."

I nodded and grabbed Rena's hand. "Rena?"

She blinked but didn't move.

"Get her out of here now, Jax," Lilith said.

Maybe the portal would respond since I could still read the lines. There wasn't another option that would put more distance between us and psycho-angel. I was surprised when the portal opened for me. I shoved Morena toward it and grabbed her hand.

I flipped us around just in time for my back to hit the floor and shield Rena from the impact. She landed on top of me. She was out cold. I rolled her over onto her back and held her head in my lap. Her face was soft like it was when she slept. She stirred under my touch. I slumped over her and pressed a kiss to her forehead. My chest expanded that she was home, safe, and in my arms even if it was temporary. *Rena is in there. She has to be.*

Her eyes blinked several times. "Jax?"

"Yes," I said, thankful she seemed herself. "It's me."

"How did I get here?" Our trip through the portal or the boundary of Hell must have broken the hold Gabriel held on her.

"You don't remember where you've been?"

"No, not after I left Gothica," she said. "I was running down the street and then..." she paused and her forehead wrinkled. "Nothing."

"You were with Gabriel," I said. There was a hard conversation ahead of us, but I didn't regret being the one to tell her. She hadn't been a coward when she'd owned her decision to save me, and I would give her the truth today.

"The last time I saw him was when he stabbed you." She winced and grabbed her head.

"Your mother summoned him, and you were with him." I wasn't sure how she was going to take the next part, but I expected her to react the same way Lilith did for her.

Rena surveyed the room. "Where is Mother then?"

"She stabbed Gabriel so we could get away."

She pushed up from my lap. "We need to go back. What if Gabriel kills her? He's one of the few beings who can."

"He's in love with her, Rena," I said, not able to say Lilith was safe with Gabriel. "He's not going to kill her. Let me tell you everything I know."

She crisscrossed her legs and faced me. "We have to save her, Jax."

The unspoken words her stare held required me to acknowledge who I was now. "My oath is to you, Rena, and I will support you."

To not tell Lucifer was treason, but I was no longer his subject. I was a Night Child of Lilith's original blood and my oath to Rena was intact. Lucifer was no longer my king. I'd risk burning in Lucifer's flame for anything Rena wanted... as long as she was safe.

CHAPTER 14
RENA

I expected Jax to argue with me and was surprised he brought up the oath. "I'm going. I'd appreciate your help in figuring out how to get there. You can stay here if you want, but don't tell Father—"

"Don't tell Father what, my dear daughter?" My father's voice surrounded me from behind.

My eyes widened as far as they could to will Jax to keep his mouth shut. Father's love for Mother was what legends were written about, and he would make the skies rain fire if that's what it took to get her back. I needed to find her before he figured out Gabriel was involved. Jax looked up at Father.

"Lucifer," he said, his tone even.

I turned and smiled at him. "Hi, Dad." My voice came out in a squeak. *Not suspicious at all since I rarely called him dad.*

"I'm pleased to see your mother found you safe." He kissed my forehead. When he stepped back, he looked around. "Where is Lilith?"

"Go..." I cleared my throat and tried the lie again. "Gothica."

"She stayed?"

"Yes," I said. "We're actually going back."

"That's not a good idea. Your mother was panicked earlier. You two will stay here until your mother comes home."

"But I'm supposed to be there for a year," I said, knowing it sounded pouty, but there was no other argument I could use without telling him about Gabriel.

"I think we can see that experiment was a bad idea, Morena," Father said, his voice softened. "Maybe after some more training and a couple of years."

Mother might not have years, but I can't say that without risking him starting a war.

"But Jax is a vampire now. He needs to go back to Gothica."

He glanced and Jax, but smiled when his eyes landed on me. "He'll be fine here for a while, Morena." He looked back at Jax. "Won't you?"

"Yes, Lucifer," Jax said.

I wanted to kick him in the shin. He could have at least asked Father to send him back.

"See, Morena," Father said. "He'll be fine until your mother returns."

Fuck. I'd call a portal myself if I had to. I had no training, but I saw it done plenty of times. I'd figure it out.

I smiled at Father. "You're right, of course."

"We had a sighting of Amon," he said. "I need to go consult with the generals. I'm just glad he didn't have you."

I gritted my teeth against a jolt of pain in my head. Amon had found me and handed me over to Gabriel, but I couldn't answer that without telling him about Gabriel. "Yes. Good thing he didn't."

Father glanced between us and met my gaze. "You two stay here in the study until we confirm Amon's whereabouts."

"Okay, Father." I'd never lied to him, at least not for something so big, but I'd never been kidnapped by an angel before either.

Father left us alone, and I made sure he was out of earshot before I whirled around to face Jax.

"What the actual fuck, Jax?"

"Rena, he was never going to let us leave," he said. "And my duty is to keep you safe."

"Portal us back," I said, scratching an itch at my back. I rolled my shoulders, not quite able to reach it.

"No," Jax said.

"Then I'll portal myself." I performed a sequence. Nothing happened. I tried again and failed. "Just do it, Jax."

"You are safer here," he said, crossing his arms and assuming a power pose. I could foot sweep his legs out from under him, but that wasn't going to help the situation. "I can go without you if you wish."

"My mother might be dying or dead. Does that not mean anything to you?"

"It does," he said. "But you matter more."

If it was a different moment when I wasn't worried about my mother, that would have affected me. My back itched. It was intense and couldn't be ignored. I unfurled my wings and scratched. A single white feather drifted to the ground. I picked it up. *Gabriel's.*

I could go wherever he was... even the Angel's realm. I met Jax's gaze.

"No, Morena." He shook his head. His face was full of surprise and maybe a touch of anger. "Don't do it."

I whispered the first line of Gabriel's call. Jax lunged for me. I jumped back.

"Don't try to stop me."

He tackled me to the floor, his face inches from me. "Rena, she's not dead. I'd know. You'd know."

"Because you think her line would die," I whispered. "We have no way of knowing if that's true."

"When one of her Night Children dies, don't all those the Night Child created cease to exist?"

"Yes," I whispered.

"Then, put the feather away. She is fine." He let go of my wrists. I tucked the feather under my cuff.

He stood up and held out his hand. I placed mine in his, and he pulled me up from the floor. I crashed into him.

My breath quickened, and the rise and fall of my chest pressed against his. I looked up into his eyes and met a heated gaze. My cheeks burned in response.

Jax's hand slipped into my hair and the other around my waist. He lowered his head. His lips brushed against mine.

I wanted more and twisted my hand in the hair at the nape of his neck.

His mouth opened.

I'd wanted this, but it was never the right moment and

this wasn't the right time. Mother was my focus. I pushed Jax away.

"So—"

I pressed a finger to his lips like I had the other day. "No apologies. Once we find my mother, we'll talk."

He nodded, taking a step back from me.

"The safe house where you found me with Gabriel…" I said. "Is there a windowless room we can go to until the sun sets?"

"We don't have to wait for the sun," he said matter-of-factly as if I should understand.

It clicked. There were so few I'd forgotten. "Right. Like Alessia, you are of Mother. I'm assuming you know to keep it quiet?"

"Yes, I know you think I'm an idiot, but I do know to keep it to myself."

I smirked. "Good. Now portal us back to where Mother stabbed Gabriel," I whispered as if Father would hear me.

"I don't agree with this, but I will do it for you," he said. My heart sped up as Jax formed the symbols, and all my worry for her settled in my chest as we crossed the threshold.

CHAPTER 15

RENA

Neither Mother nor Gabriel was anywhere to be found in the old warehouse office. I hadn't actually expected them to be there, but it still disappointed me.

"I can't believe I disobeyed Lucifer." Jax sounded lost. "We're lucky the hounds aren't still here." Father must have recalled them with news of my safety.

"Well, you're technically Mother's subject now, so you obey her not him," I said.

"I don't think your father will see it that way," he said. "And Rena, always remember my oath is to you."

My chest warmed from his declaration, but if I looked at him I'd lose my resolve, so I averted my eyes. "It doesn't even look like they were here. I don't see any angel blood."

"They were using this location for a while. Amon or Gabriel or both. Someone could have cleaned it before they vacated." Jax inhaled around us and studied the area. "I don't see any other portals used after ours, but their scent is faint, almost non-existent."

"I don't think they could have cleared out in the hour or so we were gone. But the faded scent is interesting. Think they deliberately masked it?"

"Possibly," Jax said. "Or maybe the apple smell is covering it up."

"The what?" A splitting pain shot through my head.

"The Angelic Realm carries the scent of an orchard after the rain when everything is refreshed and alive." He narrowed his eyes on me like he was skeptical I didn't know that.

Recognition triggered. I inhaled deeply to catch some of the scent. The brightness of the realm came back to me. "Jax, he gave me some angel blood. It was like getting a lobotomy. I knew things were happening around me, but I couldn't react."

An archangel drugged me. *Wasn't that against their code? Oh, he will pay for that.*

Jax grimaced. A low rumble came from his chest. "Yeah, I noticed."

"I wonder if my blood would do the same to him?"

"He's an archangel. I doubt it would have the same effect. Besides you have angel blood from Lucifer."

"But mine is different from his." I was allowed passage into the angel realm. Into their most private sanctuary. Gabriel had kept me sequestered, and I hadn't seen much in the short time I was there. "I'm also half Lilith's daughter. If I could gain entry there, then she might too. I think he's going to try to take her there."

"He had said that was his intent, but why after all this time? Could he make it injured?"

Jax alluded to how it was hard but not impossible for a demon to portal injured, but I had no idea if that applied to angels. "I don't know, but I suspect it has something to do with Amon. Hopefully, Father collects him soon."

"He hasn't," a voice came from the shadows.

My gut twisted. I spun in the direction of the sound and conjured my demon voice. "Show yourself, demon."

Amon walked from the shadows, looking uninjured and fine to my disappointment.

Jax growled.

I reached for Father's blade, but it wasn't in its usual place. I remembered Mother had used it to stab Gabriel. *Damn.* Amon was too powerful even if Jax and I worked together.

"Gabriel has betrayed us all, Morena," Amon said, his voice neutral.

"You can tell it to Father," I said with zero plan on how to make that happen without the dagger.

"No, not today at least," he bemused.

"What do you mean he betrayed us all?" Jax took a step toward him.

"He can't take Lilith to his home, so he plans to make one here with her," Amon said.

"How does he think he can do that? He can't stay here unless he permanently falls to Earth," Jax said.

"No, just like Lilith can't stay in Hell unless she chooses to make the ultimate fall there like Lucifer did for her," Amon said.

Mother refused to abandon the Night Children, among other things, and Father knew this. She was a different being than Father or Gabriel. Her origins were from an alternate path. There was no guarantee what would happen to the Night Children if she committed to Hell.

Amon's words sank in. I understood what he suggested, but I rejected the implication. "But Gabriel can't make a life here with her without drawing my Father's wrath to the Overworld. There would be no peace. No world left to live in. He has to know that."

"He knows," Amon said. "And it's only a matter of time before your father realizes what is happening."

Yet, Gabriel moves forward with his plan. That doesn't sound like an archangel at all. A dull ache formed in the back of my throat. I swallowed to clear it, but it was no use. I wanted to go to Hell and hide under the covers of my bed, but that wasn't the most rational response either. My elders had lost all sense. Amon stood in front of me, and I asked what I thought would be an obvious question to test his honesty. "And what is your role in it besides kidnapping me?"

Jax growled again beside me. He was almost feral.

"I was to bring you here. He said he wanted to convince you that you and your mother had souls."

"He tried that on me too. I actually believed him." Disappointment gouged into my stomach.

"So did I," Amon said, his tone solemn. "That's the only reason I agreed with his plan."

A high-ranking demon who cared if the Queen of Hell and her daughter had a soul seemed a bit of a stretch to me, but he seemed genuine in his response.

I narrowed my eyes at him. "Where did he take Mother?"

Amon's shoulders sagged. "If I knew, I would tell you, Morena."

"Would you?" I moved closer to him, ready to strike if it came to it. "I'm not convinced."

Jax mirrored my movements.

"You've known me your whole life. You should know if I'm telling the truth." The dejection on his face was almost believable had he not kidnapped me a short time ago.

I sweetened my tone. "You've been a spy my whole life, so trust in your words isn't likely."

"Do you know of other safe houses he might use?" Jax asked.

Amon shook his head. "No safe houses, but I know where he wanted to live with Lilith. Somewhere they wouldn't be disturbed."

I exchanged a look with Jax. "Picher," I said. "He took her to Picher."

"Since the humans believe the land to be toxic, he thought they would be undisturbed there."

"He is so delusional. Why would you help him? What did he promise you?"

"The angel realm."

I blinked, mulling that idea. It couldn't be done. Amon must be as deranged as Gabriel. "Why? You can't even travel there."

"If your Uncle Gabriel renounces his claim there, he can pass his right to someone else."

"And you think that's you? You will never be granted entrance. I'm not sure why I was," I blurted out.

"You've been?" His eyebrows shot up.

Damn. He didn't need to know that. "Where did you think he took me?"

"To Picher," he said. "I thought he wanted to lure Lilith there."

"No, he took me to the angel realm." I stepped away from Amon. "Jax, take us to Picher."

"What about me?" Amon asked.

"You've navigated this far on your own. I'm sure you'll be fine." I turned to Jax. "Same place we were last time."

Jax moved closer to me. "I'll do my best."

"A vampire that can portal?" Amon laughed.

I wanted to punch him, but we'd wasted enough time with Amon. "That's not the strangest thing I've heard today."

Jax spun the portal into existence. Blue light spread in front of us. He took my hand, and we stepped through into the dark room we were in a few days ago. Jax slammed his hands together, and the portal closed. Amon would not follow us today.

I scanned the room, and it looked the same as when we were here the first time. The sterile smell remained. No scent of apples or of Mother. This room sealed tight when closed, so that didn't mean they weren't here.

"Shall we?" Jax gestured toward the door.

"That's what we're here for." I inhaled a deep breath and let it out. We would find Mother and get her back home to Hell before Father noticed. We would stop what Gabriel set in motion and prevent war. "Do you smell anything to point us where to look?"

"This way," Jax said.

CHAPTER 16

RENA

We wandered through the empty streets of Picher. The sun began its descent, and it wouldn't be long before Mother's children wandered out. Jax's ability to walk in daylight would be questioned. Not many knew. Father was afraid they'd drain Mother if more were aware of the unique gift she could give. Mother said she'd tried with others, and it wouldn't work unless it was part of their initial transition. I did see Father's point. Some would still want to try to feel the sunlight again. *Father. I wonder if he knows we're gone yet. Maybe he's still focused on Amon.* I didn't want to be on the receiving end of his anger, but I'd rather face it after we had Mother home.

"We're going to have to tell Lucifer," Jax whispered. "If it gets back to him that you knew and didn't tell him..." Jax's voice trailed off.

"I know." Guilt snaked around my stomach and squeezed. "If we don't find Mother soon, I'll have to. I need to figure out how to tell him without him bringing all of the demons from Hell here to battle."

"Since when do you care so much about the Overworld?" Jax glanced at me with a small smile.

When had I started to care? Didn't I always? This was Mother's world and, therefore, part of mine. And it was Stassi's home. Maybe it meant a little more since someone I care about can't live without this world.

"I've never not cared about it, Jax."

His smile widened like he could sense that I wasn't telling the whole truth.

"Back to Father," I said. "Any ideas on how to tell him?"

"Nope." Jax walked faster.

"Jax, I'm serious."

"Me too." He looked over his shoulder. "The way I see it, this is a family issue for your family, and I'm not part of it."

"Except you're here with me... and you might as well be family."

"Fuck, Rena," Jax whispered and waited for me to catch up. "I don't know how this ends well."

"I'm scared for what might happen," I said, unable to keep the tremble out of my voice. Father's banishment from Heaven was a terrible time in ancient history, and humans almost didn't survive. If he brought Hell to Earth this time... "And I can't remember the last time I was scared before you got stabbed by Gabriel. It seems like I've been nothing but afraid since then." Tears pooled in my eyes and I swiped at them, ashamed of the weakness.

Jax grabbed my upper arms. He stared into my eyes. His forehead wrinkled, and he crushed his mouth against mine. I allowed him in and wrapped my arms around him. His arms brought safety. His kiss washed away the fear. His touch gave me strength.

He pulled back. His hand slipped into mine. "We need to move. Eyes are on us."

I felt them too. Mother's children watched our every move. "Where are they?"

"All around us." Jax rolled his shoulders.

I snuck a peek at our hands. His was warm in mine. So natural. I scanned around the dilapidated city. "Not the vampires. Mother and Gabriel."

"Right." He studied our surroundings. "The mine?"

"Eww," I said, amused he would even suggest Mother would go there anytime other than to cull. "Besides, I can't see Gabriel hiding in a mine. I don't think they are here anymore."

"I think you're right. Their scent is faint."

"Let's go check Gothica." I doubted she would take him to a place so personal to her, but the other option was going to Hell to tell Father. At least we could find out from Alessia if she'd heard from her. "Maybe she took him to her apartment there because he was injured."

Jax gulped.

"He's an angel, Jax. An archangel. He can't be made into a vampire. The only thing he can do is..."

"What? Rena?" Jax stopped in the middle of the street.

"Fall," I said. "But when an angel Falls to Earth, it isn't like when we fall from Hell. They can never enter their home again. They are bound to Earth forever. Still immortal beings." And stuck in a world they don't belong to for eternity. A few had sought Father out over time to join him in Hell. Gabriel could be so consumed by his obsession with Mother he didn't realize his actual fate. Not to mention Father would not show mercy even if Gabriel was his favorite sibling.

"So, like a vampire but without the blood-drinking?"

"Yes, exactly," I said. "And he might think that will allow him to be with Mother. Call the portal."

He made the symbols, and we traveled to Gothica. We landed on the rug.

"I'm starting to hate this place." I surveyed the room, unable to block the images from coming of Jax lying on the couch or sending me away.

"They've been here." Jax inhaled a deep breath. "Recently."

I didn't see any signs of them. The bedroom door was closed. *Father will lose his shit if they are in there together.* For the first time in my life, I considered my mother might betray my father, and he wouldn't care if it was to save me.

My eyes were locked on the door and my throat tightened. "What if —"

"I've got it, Rena." Jax barged toward the door. He opened it in a swift motion and peered around the room. "They're not here."

I released a breath. Relief rained over me.

The front door opened, and Jax jumped in front of me. I shoved him to the side.

Alessia stood there. She looked Jax up and down and smiled. "You don't look like a new vampire. Are you hungry?"

I wanted to punch her in the jaw until she couldn't open

her mouth, even if I had to do it over and over again because she healed.

"If you are looking for our mother, she is downstairs." Alessia paused, a strange look passed over her face. "With many children."

I didn't like the way she said it. I'd never understood why Mother favored her, but she was nothing if not loyal to Mother. The way Alessia's forehead wrinkled wasn't the normal way she referred to the coven.

Jax slipped his hand in mine, and sparks licked at my palm. I noted to ask him later.

I resisted the urge to smile when Alessia's eyes took it in.

"My hunger is in check." Jax tugged on my hand. "We should find your mother." He emphasized that Lilith was my mother, but here she was all the Night Children's mother. I'd accepted it even when it hurt.

I led Jax through the halls of Gothica. It looked the same as it had the first time I'd come here with Mother. Dark and mysterious. It had once been a church, with a school above it. But that had been over two hundred years ago. When Mother claimed it for her children, she had the windows blacked out on the first few floors to keep the Night Children safe from the sun. Everyone thought it was an exclusive club. There were even rumors of a sex club. I guess all those were true in some form or fashion. The membership price was high here though.

Hushed conversations billowed out from what I called the throne room, but it was an old chapel. The seats were once for the priests. Mother had them refurbished with plush cushions and velvet, but she hated it when I called them the vampire thrones.

Mother sat in the center chair dressed in one of the long black dresses she'd made her signature, and as Alessia said, many Night Children had gathered on the steps below her. She looked like a queen with her subjects whether she wanted to believe it or not.

I walked toward her with Jax at my side. She looked up.

"Morena, what are you and Jax doing here?" She asked, her voice tense but even. I'm not sure anyone else would have picked up on it but me.

"Looking for you, Mother," I said, keeping my tone calm as well. I cut my eyes to scan around the room as much as I could without moving my head, but I didn't see Gabriel anywhere.

The Night Children's lack of motion weirded me out. They were still enough they could substitute for the gargoyles on the outside of the roof.

Jax's fingers tightened around mine. I glanced at him, but his gaze was fixed above us. I followed it.

Gabriel hovered high at the top of the room. *Fuck.* I didn't want him to die, but healed was dangerous, especially if Father showed up. Gabriel floated down and took one of the seats next to Mother. *Had he fallen? How would I tell without asking him?* His features were harder, but he looked the same.

"Mother, I was worried about you, but I see you are in good health."

"I am." She kept her gaze trained on me.

"And will you not ask about my well-being, Morena?" Gabriel rested his hand on his stomach.

"I can see you are fine, Gabriel. Archangels heal in a most immortal way I hear."

"Yes, it's true. We do. Even from my brother's blade," he said. "I do want to ask you something."

Dread washed over me, and sweat formed between my and Jax's clenched hands. "What is it?"

"I want you to take my place. Will you accept this honor?"

Fuck no probably wasn't the appropriate response or the one he wanted.

"I am a child of Hell," I said. "My place is there, so unfortunately, I must decline."

"You are a child of an angel. The only one who is not Nephilim. That makes you uniquely qualified to take my place."

I'd never compared myself to a Nephilim because I wasn't half-human and half-angel. I was born of two immortal beings, but I didn't see how that made me better to serve in his place than a Nephilim unless their human half prevented it.

There were plenty of Nephilim. *Why not choose one of them if he wanted to fall?* They seemed to be more qualified than me. "Gabriel, I'm pretty sure the part where I was born in Hell disqualifies me."

He shook his head. "Nephilim are half-angel and human. You are half-angel and half Lilith." He stared lovingly at my mother, and vomit rose to the top of my throat. He continued, "Nephilim will eventually age and die. You are an immortal like us."

"But I'm not an angel. I don't have angel blood like

them." His arguments were well constructed but then again, most psychopaths' streams of logic were.

"You are as much angel as your father, but it's not about what pumps through your veins. For lack of a better description, it's the power and energy inside you."

"I'm sure my demon face would be well accepted in the angel realm and Heaven." I scoffed. I was not Heaven or angel material. I'd known this my whole life. *What happened that made Gabriel so delusional?*

He floated lower, and I saw the subtle changes that differed from when we were in the field. His eyes were sunken with shadows around them, and he didn't have the shimmer to his skin.

"Are you sure your wound is healed?" I asked, genuine concern in my voice. A dead angel without a replacement offered challenges. They each had a purpose, and his was to deliver messages. Without a messenger in place, communications would cease between angels and Hell and the human world.

"I appreciate your concern, but I am fine." He took Mother's hand.

She stiffened. I stepped forward.

"No, Morena," Mother said, her eyes locked on mine. "As you can see, he's fine." She didn't want me to come closer. Or was she telling me Gabriel wasn't healing?

I ran through the history and lore around my father's blade. I'd used it multiple times and never had any issues. I looked at my hand, and it had healed with no scars like any other wound I'd had.

Gabriel looked sick, though, like a human. His skin was

sallow, and his feathers were dulled. The dagger was Father's before he gave it to me. There was significance there I tried to recall.

"We all have our roles, Gabriel. Yours is not here." I gestured to the room full of vampires whose sluggish movements were abnormal.

"But it will be when I fall," he said. "I just need someone to be the messenger that is worthy of it, and that is you."

"I can barely land standing up when I go through a portal. Why would you think I'll make a good messenger?" And I lied to the Devil, my father. That didn't seem becoming of a messenger or an angel.

"I told you why, Morena. You need to accept it," he said. "I'm not a human who cannot determine the difference between reality and fantasy. I am very aware of my decision and what I am passing on to you."

He made it seem like he was of sound mind, and I didn't want to say it, but there was a giant elephant in the room. I feared it would set him off, but I straightened my spine to do it.

"What about my father?"

"You know we must keep the balance. He would tip the scale too far. Who would rule the demon realm?" Gabriel shook his head.

"I'd rule it," I said. The decision had always been there. I was a fool to think there was another one. My place was Hell. No one else could take Father's place but me. It had to be me.

Mother gasped. Jax tightened his fingers on mine until they were painful. I accepted my fate to save my family.

Father's second chance might save Mother from a life here with Gabriel.

"I'm the only heir. It's what I was born to do. What I've been groomed for. I am Morena, daughter of Lucifer and Lilith, and the future Queen of Hell."

CHAPTER 17
RENA

"What the fuck are you doing?" Jax leaned in and whispered to me. He must have come to the same conclusion I had. If I took Father's place, I would be bound there for eternity and separated from Jax. It would repeat my parent's existence.

"It's been over two thousand years since your father has been banished," Gabriel said.

"For choosing to fall and live with my mother. Are you choosing the same fate?" I baited him.

A flash of white light sent the vampires scrambling, except for Mother and Jax. The building shook with a loud clap.

An angel appeared near us. He wore battle gear like he prepared for war, and scars marked his otherwise perfect skin. An archangel healed, but he chose to wear these as reminders. A warrior stood in front of us, and I recognized this uncle although I'd only seen him twice in my life. *Michael.*

"Brother, you know this is not the divine path. What has your mind so twisted?" Michael's voice boomed loud like he spoke through a megaphone.

He turned. Jax moved in front of me. Michael looked Jax over, sadness in his eyes. "Step aside young vampire. I am truly sorry."

Sorry? For what? Jax remained planted in place. He had no intention of stepping aside.

I stepped around Jax. "Uncle Michael." I tasted the bitterness of his name on my lips.

"My niece, you are so young yet so willing to sacrifice yourself for a war that is not yours. This is not your fate." His voice deepened with sadness.

"Since when do you care about my fate, Uncle? You stood against Father and supported his fall. My fate is my own to choose," I blasted back.

Mother sat in silence. She didn't move or speak. It was like she couldn't or was afraid to. Her Night Children remained in the corners where they'd been ever since Michael appeared.

Gabriel stood and strode up to Michael. They were inches apart. "Brother." Gabriel drew the word out. "My brothers stand against me. Lucifer took my love. You seek to deny me what is mine."

"You are sick, Gabriel. Let me help you," Michael said.

Gabriel swayed and leaned against Michael like he was intoxicated.

"He was stabbed with Lucifer's blade," Jax offered.

I dropped his hand and gaped at him. When I turned

back toward my uncles, Michael and Mother both stared at Jax.

"Is this true?" Michael faced his brother. "Lucifer stabbed you?"

"No, not Lucifer." Gabriel's words slurred.

Michael's eyes searched mine first, then Jax, but settled on Mother. "Where is the blade, Mother of Night Children?"

"Where it belongs," she answered.

I slipped a hand to her waist where the blade should be, but nothing was there. I met Mother's gaze. Her face hardened. She'd made a decision. A fate-changing decision and we were all in line to pay for it.

"Mother?" I whispered.

Mother was old and had knowledge of ancient ways... of angelic ways.

"It will kill him." Michael's hands roamed over Gabriel. "You must remove it."

"No," Mother answered, and I expected to see ice form around her mouth from how cold she was. "He has threatened my family, and only one solution will save them. He has made that clear."

"What are they talking about?" Jax asked me.

"I don't know," I said. "Father and I never got sick from it."

"You cannot kill the messenger of Heaven, Lilith," Michael said, his tone harsh. "There is no one to replace him. It will upset the balance and damn this world."

"Mother, if you are doing this to Gabriel, stop," I pleaded.

Mother's face was like stone. "He wants to punish your father and break up our family."

Gabriel leaned on Michael. "I love Lilith, Brother. I always have."

"I know." Michael led Gabriel to the chair he'd occupied next to Lilith. He sat next to his brother.

"Our fates are not worth damning the Overworld," I said. "Is the blade still inside him?"

"Yes," Mother inclined her head. "It's eating away his power and will remove the threat."

"He's an archangel, Mother. This is wrong," I took a step toward her.

"Your daughter is wise, Lilith. Listen to her," Michael said. "Do not start a war. Lucifer already lost once at great cost."

Mother raised an eyebrow. "Did he?"

Michael did not soften his words. "You are aware of what he lost, Mother of Night Children."

She bowed her head. When she looked up, she found me. Her eyes were full of tears. "I want to protect you, Rena."

"Mother, you have, but this is not the way." I turned to Michael. "I'll remove it."

"Only the one who dares to spear the angel can remove it," Michael said.

"That's not entirely true." Father's demon voice reverberated around us.

I spun around, shocked to hear his voice. Father found us. This was going to become ugly fast.

He stepped from the shadows, flanked by the other Fallen angels who supported him. "No one told me we had a family reunion planned."

Michael stood. Father was the taller of the two, but they

both carried a strong presence. Father's white wings unfurled, making him look larger. Michael's were still tucked away.

"Brother." Michael stood next to where Grabriel was seated.

"You haven't referred to me as your brother since my fall, and Gabriel visited me, yet he has betrayed me," Father said.

"You were the one who betrayed us and our ways," Michael said. His words were harsh, but his tone softened as if he cared for my father.

Jax inched closer to me like he could shield me from the chaos that would erupt with four ancient beings in the room. There wasn't anything either of us could do against their power.

"Our ways were flawed, and I paid for that decision." Father stepped toward Gabriel. Gabriel's eyes were thin slits like he was barely there. "But I will save him this time because he was my bother."

Father held out his palm and uttered words I didn't understand. The blade materialized in his hand. Gabriel didn't respond, and I assumed it would take time. "He will survive, but get him out of my sight before I change my mind."

"You have done a good deed, Brother." Michael put his hand on Father's shoulder.

"Have I?" Father plucked Michael's hand away and dropped it.

Michael picked Gabriel up. His wings expanded, and he flew up, disappearing at the ceiling.

I moved to stand in front of Mother, but I felt alone and vulnerable without Jax by my side.

"Clear the room," Lilith said. "Jax, you stay."

His gaze found mine, and I shrugged.

Father nodded to his subjects. They bowed and left the room. Mother waved to the Night Children, and they filed out still dazed but more alert.

Father leveled his gaze on Mother and me. His voice was quiet. "Why do I hear of this from my brother Dagon instead of you?"

I fidgeted like I did when I was twelve and accidentally banished one of the bloodhounds. Why did his angry face turn me into this kid version of myself? I tried to formulate an answer, but Mother spoke first.

"Because I didn't want to distract you for something so minor."

"You tried to kill my brother, Lilith. Did you not think of the consequences?" He sounded pained.

"He wanted Morena to take his place in the other realm, Lucifer. I couldn't let him do that to her. Take away her free will forever." Tears streamed down her face.

My eyes burned for the sacrifice she almost made.

"And you couldn't tell me so I could help?" Father's voice shook the building.

I stepped back, ready to run if he started to lose it, but there wasn't an escape from his anger if he wanted to reach someone. I wouldn't leave Mother alone to deal with him either. Anger boiled the blood in my veins. *Did he not see how we walked on eggshells around him? Did he not care?*

Father composed himself.

"It's my fault, Father. I'm the one who took off from here without thinking." I refused to cry like Mother. If it weren't for his anger issues, we would have told him. "If you are mad at someone, it should be me."

Not many would speak to the Devil with such vehemence, but I didn't fear him.

"No, it was my fault," Jax said. The surprised look on his face told me the words came out before he considered the consequences, but he continued. "I jumped in front of Gabriel's sword. If I hadn't done that, Rena wouldn't have asked Lilith to change me, and I wouldn't have told Rena to leave because I wasn't sure who I was anymore."

Their eyes all focused on Jax, and he wasn't to blame. It was me and my fucking trip.

"Jax, you are the least guilty here," I said and faced Father. "We didn't tell you because we were afraid of what you would do to get Mother back."

"What I would do to get you and your mother back, Rena. I don't agree with that, but I do not think this was Jax's fault," Father said. "Gabriel was going to take the risk no matter what."

My eyes flicked to Jax in time to see his shoulders relax.

"I'm sorry, Lucifer," Mother said.

Father pointed to Jax and me. "You two go to the apartment and wait for us. My wife and I need to have a private discussion."

CHAPTER 18
RENA

I paced the floor like I had our first night here, worried a battle royale was taking place below. "How much longer do you think they will be?"

"I have no idea, Rena. Why don't you sit down?" Jax moved into my path.

"They never fight, Jax." I sidestepped him. "Never."

"Everyone argues. They are no exception." He stood in front of me.

"Well, they are. Even when they disagree on something, they don't argue." Panic gripped me. *Would this set Father off? Would he start a war just to prove a point?*

The door opened, and Mother walked in. *Alone.* She wrapped her arms around herself. *This can't be good. Fuck.*

"Where's Father?"

Mother swallowed hard and stared out the window. When she met my gaze, her eyes were cold. "He needs some time on his own to think. I'm going to stay here for a while."

Mother staying in the Overworld periodically wasn't unusual. Father needing solo time was.

"Where did he go?" Hell wasn't somewhere you could go for solitude.

"I don't know," she said.

"When will he be back?"

"I don't know, Morena." She fought the frustration in her voice. "He just said he needed time and left."

Something created pressure on my side. I reached for it to find Father's blade materialized back in its sheath. Guilt riddled the relief I felt for its return. He wanted me to be able to reach him, but he wanted space from Mother.

"It's going to be fine, dear. I'm going to lie down for a while." Mother walked toward the primary bedroom.

I chewed on my fingernail and waited for her to shut the door.

"Jax," I whispered and pulled the blade out. "It's back. Father wanted me to have it."

"He gave it to you for a reason. Did you think he wouldn't give it back?" Jax ran his fingers across my cheek and along my jawline.

Had I? I'd thought he was mad at me, but I wanted to believe there was a reason he returned the dagger. "It just felt like he was sending me a message."

"He was. He was telling you he's still here for you despite whatever is going on between him and Lilith."

"Yes, I need to find him, so I can figure out how to fix this. I caused this. This is my fault, and I need to make it right." I looked in Jax's eyes, but I didn't find the judgment I expected. I found love looking back at me.

"No, you didn't. Gabriel did this. Let your Father have his time." He cradled my cheeks in his hands.

"That never ends well." My stomach dropped remembering the way Mother described the years when Father's anger had been unstoppable. One of his siblings had been killed, and he wanted vengeance. "The last time he was upset there was a world war. We can't let that happen."

"I think you should trust he won't do that and go take care of your mom for now." Jax pulled me to him. I let him envelop me with the comfort his arms provided.

"She has all of her Night Children and Alessia. Father is out there by himself on some solo trek." *And hopefully not thinking up ways to make others pay for the issue with him and Mother.*

"As he wanted to be, and you are your mother's only born child. The others are bound to her. You have a choice to love her. They don't."

His words were meant to show me how important I was to my mother, but they made me realize I'd been acting like a spoiled brat. Not just today but since I'd come to the Overworld.

"I need to go talk to her." I pulled away from Jax. I owed her an apology that she had every right to refuse, but I'd learned things are better said sooner rather than later in our family.

I knocked on the door and entered. "Mother?"

"I'm here, Rena." She was on the armed chaise lounge chair in the corner with her knees drawn up to her chest. The room was dim with no lights on. I should have waited. She wouldn't say it, but I'd intruded on her.

"You never call me Rena," I sat on the end of the chair.

"It's what you prefer, isn't it?" she asked, her voice unsure, but then she smiled. "Or is that only from Jax?"

My cheeks burned with what I was sure was a blush as red as demon eyes. "No, not just Jax."

"You are young." She curled her legs over the side and leaned forward to take my hand. "You have plenty of time to sort out your feelings for Jax. Don't look at this disagreement between your father and me as a reason to push Jax and his love away."

Tears formed in my eyes. I hadn't planned to talk about Jax or my feelings for him, but she thought of me first. Guilt ground its way into my chest.

Mother wiped my tears away. "Don't cry. He's not going anywhere I assure you. He loves you. You do love him too, right?"

"I…" I paused to think. "I don't know. I want him around, and I don't like it when he's not."

"Does he give you butterflies in your stomach?"

"I wouldn't call it butterflies. I get weird like I've lost my ability to form sentences."

Mother laughed. "I think you are in love, Rena."

I cleared my throat not sure if I was ready to admit that out loud yet, but she was right. I'd known it for a while, but I wouldn't say it first. Whether or not I was in love with Jax wasn't why I was here.

"Mother," I said, but it felt too formal with her calling me Rena. "Mom, I owe you an apology."

"Whatever for? You've done nothing but try to protect your family. I would have and did do the same," she said.

"No excuses. I've been a big fucking brat." I covered my mouth. I hadn't cursed in front of her. Not that she hadn't heard those words in her long life. "A big brat, and for that, I am truly sorry."

"Oh, all children go through that," Mother said. "But you are an adult now and are growing out of it. It's part of life. You'll see one day when you and Jax have children."

That wasn't even an option.

"But he's a vampire now," I blurted out. Not that I'd been thinking about children, but the Night Children couldn't have kids.

"You never know," she said. "I didn't think your father and I would be able to have children, but we had you."

I needed to change the subject. Children weren't something I was comfortable talking about yet if ever. "Are you worried about Father?"

Her smile dropped to a heavy frown. "I am." She smoothed out her dress. "I've never seen him so angry at me."

My fears were justified. I had to find him and direct the blame on myself, where it should be.

"I've seen him angrier for sure but never at me," she continued.

"What do you think he will do?"

"He'll come back. He has a realm to run, and he misses us when we are not with him." She patted my hand. Mother knew him better than anyone else, but there would be a cost in Hell for his absence. Without a strong leader, those who wished to cause chaos would have an open door.

"Who is running Hell if we are all here?" I asked, curious who he put in place with us here.

"Your Uncle Azazel," she said.

Azazel? He was a warrior like Michael and loved to show the humans how to make new weapons. "Mom, Azazel will have the world in a war like Father did."

"No, your father gave him instructions. He wouldn't disobey him."

"Maybe not disobey, but he likes to bend the rules because he knows Father is lenient with him. Father feels guilty for the sacrifice Azazel made, leaving his beloved in the angelic realm, and Azazel knows it." Panic scattered my thoughts. I forced myself to focus. There were two very good reasons to prevent a war, and they were both here in this apartment. "I have to go back and sit the throne."

Mother's eyes widened. "Morena, that choice cannot be undone. Once you sit in your father's place, you are conceding to life as his heir."

"I understand." The decision meant my year on Earth was forfeit. "I accept the consequences of my choice."

"That is thousands of years of commitment," she said. "You need at least a century behind you of living before you decide that."

"I only had a year, Mother. That was the deal we struck."

"We thought you would ask for more time after that year." She took my hands in hers.

"My decision is made," I said. The consequences would be mine, and I would bear them like the Queen of Hell.

CHAPTER 19

RENA

"Neither of you should return to Hell right now." Mother paced almost the same path in the living room I had the first night Jax and I were here. That day seemed years ago versus just over a week. "I can't go with you, per Lucifer's request, and power is the ultimate game in Hell."

"Mom, for the first time since I knew I'd have to make this decision, I understand what the choice really means. It's bigger than me, and someone needs to sit the throne who doesn't want to destroy the world. That's not Azazel even in a temporary placement." I wouldn't put it past him to have started ten wars already.

She sighed. "You are so strong, Morena, but this isn't your fight or your time."

"I just hope I am as strong as everyone thinks. I'm going to need it." I hugged her. "Trust me, Mom. Believe in me. That's what I need from you now."

"I can't decide for you, but I do not want this for you."

The sorrow in her voice poured into me, and I almost relented. She held on, and I squeezed back.

This decree could not be undone by anyone other than my father once I did it, but my position in Hell was the right one for her world and mine. When she released me, I turned to Jax. "Let's do this."

His features hardened in displeasure but he nodded. "My oath is yours and yours alone."

He called the portal, a portal so smooth it was like sliding on silk. I landed on my feet with Jax beside me in Mother's private study. It was undisturbed. I caught sight of myself in the mirror. My disheveled appearance didn't give the air of power.

"I need to change into something that looks a little more queenly," I said.

The halls were quiet as we made our way to my room. None of the usual noise. Dread hit me like a gut punch.

I changed into a black outfit that had leather panels designed to hide weapons. A stash I owned but never carried was hidden in my room. I secured my hair in a high ponytail. Jax ran his eyes up and down over me when I walked out of the bathroom.

"That's a look." His gaze heated.

My nerves skittered into a burning blush on my cheeks. *Damn.* I inhaled a shaky breath.

"Yep, it's a look." I tucked my father's blade in its sheath at my waist and pulled the top down over it. "Let's go see what in the hell is going on in Hell."

"I'm concerned about what we are going to find," Jax said, his voice a little unsteady.

"Me too." I held my confidence in the commitment to Hell and sitting the throne. "But I'm not avoiding it."

Jax took my hand, causing sparks to flare between us.

"Do you feel that?" I looked into his eyes.

"I do, and if you keep looking at me like that, we're going to find out all the body parts where it happens." He squeezed my hand.

Oh... Arousal coiled in my belly. Our timing sucked.

Jax guided me down the hall to the main gathering area.

It was empty except for a tapping noise. Azazel's shit-stirring started early it appeared. "Do you hear that?"

"Yes," he said, his voice lowered. "The torture level."

"Father closed most of it down," I said. Father's wrath would end Azazel if he tortured the demons of Hell.

"Someone has reopened it," he said. His eyes mirrored the apprehension building in me.

"En masse," I added.

I hurried down to the level with Jax right behind me. Few knew of the shadowed paths, and I used them to my advantage. Jax and I stood around the corner of the entrance. Vocalizations saturated the space, but no cries of pain stood out. Their cries demanded freedom and questioned where their king was. Most of the demons of Hell were imprisoned here from what I could tell. "Who would do this?"

One utterance grew clearer to me. My name was called over and over again. "Morena."

I listened for a voice I recognized. "Azazel is here. I hear him."

Jax listened like he honed in on Azazel specifically. "He's close."

The narrow corridor was long like in the nightmares of humans. I looked in each of the cells as we passed. The small spaces were crowded with too many demons. I recognized some but others I didn't. "Azazel?"

"Here, Princess," he said.

I followed his voice a dozen cells away. He'd been a victim like the others. *Who could have done this?* "What happened?"

"Amon. He surprised us with a legion of minions." Azazel's voice came out in weak puffs as if his strength had been stolen by speaking of Amon and his followers.

I yanked on the gate, but it wouldn't open. "How do I open the door?"

"Only Lucifer's blood can open these," he said.

"I am Lucifer's blood." It hit me what he meant. Literal blood. If I cut myself with the dagger, I'd be sent to my Father, and I hadn't grabbed anything from my private cache of weapons. *Stupid.* I held my thumb out to Jax. "Fangs, please."

"I can't Morena," he said, staring at my upturned hand. "I'm not sure I'll be able to stop."

"You can. Just prick the skin. I trust you."

He sighed and lifted my hand like it was porcelain. He turned the pad of my thumb toward him and positioned it under one tooth. His fang pierced the skin, and I fought back a moan. *Why does that feel good? Was it like that for him too?* He dropped my hand and turned away from me.

Desire pooled in parts of my body new to me. I inhaled to tamp it down.

I pressed my thumb against the lock, and the door

popped open. Azazel and the other occupants of this room filed out. Azazel's pale skin was dotted with purplish bruises, but the others appeared to be untouched. Strange the contusions remained visible. Amon wasn't known for compassion, but angels healed fast. And Azazel was a fallen angel after all. "Do you know what Amon's plan is?"

"He said he would rule somewhere. If not here, then Heaven," Azazel said. I slid my shoulder under his arm to support him. He was a warrior, but he was battered like he'd spent the last century at war.

"He can't even get into Heaven." I shook my head. "We need to find him, and I can't open all these doors a thumbprint at a time."

"Princess, I think he was going after Lucifer to use his blood for entry."

"It doesn't work like that. I heard directly from an archangel it takes more than blood." I propped Azazel up against the wall near the door to the level. "We need to find Father and find him now." I pulled the blade from my waist. "Will you come with me?"

Azazel bowed his head. "But the other demons need to be freed, Princess."

My wound had healed, and there must be hundreds if not thousands of doors. I glimpsed a sight of Jax, and he cringed away. That one prick of my finger was too much. Sweet angel's ass it was almost too much for me too. I couldn't ask him again.

"Is there some way I can do a mass release of the doors?" I asked Azazel.

He nodded. "The throne."

I lifted Azazel from the wall and shifted his weight to Jax. "The throne it is then." I glanced at the small crowd around us. Their faces bore the signs of weariness, and it would no doubt only get worse until we captured Amon. "Follow me."

The hallways were still empty. Amon hadn't left any guards, which meant he didn't plan to return. Maybe he thought it would distract me while he found my father. The throne room was vacant much to my relief. When I was little, the onyx-hued monstrosity of a throne scared me. The royal seat stood on a raised platform like a brutal giant with the edges deliberately left rough for anyone who got too close. I'd vanquished my fear a decade ago when Father sat me on the coveted spot and told me one day his kingdom would be mine if I desired it. That was the day I saw the jewels embedded from top to bottom in the throne. Rubies were embedded so tightly with the metal they became one in a mix of rich black and the darkest red. I regretted not asking Father if the combination represented him and Mother, but I thought the unification of them might.

"I can stand on my own, Jax. Thank you." Azazel walked toward the throne. "Here, Princess."

A spike protruded from the unassuming spot. My thumb hovered for a moment before I pushed down against the spike. The pinch from the puncture was excruciating, but I held my gasp in so as not to alarm the others. I placed my free hand over the impelled one and pressed. My blood spilled down the throne over the leg and into the floor. Jax moved to my side like he understood the cost of this act. His hand rubbed my back and allowed my focus to drift from the pain.

"They're free. Doors are open. I can hear only cheers and no more cries. You can release your hand now, Rena," Jax whispered in my ear.

I retracted my thumb and watched the wound close. The drain was immense on me. The fatigue ran deep in my muscles and bone, but I couldn't wait any longer to find my father.

"Everyone put their hand on someone's shoulder," I said. Jax wrapped his hand around my wrist. Azazel rested his hand on Jax's shoulder, and the next demon put his on Azazel's and so forth until the group from one cell was linked like a chain. I sliced my palm with the blade. Blood pooled as expected. Our group of six dove into our ride to the Overworld.

There were trees and a stream that smelled like fresh water, but I didn't recognize this place. The scents of spring filled the air even though we were long past summer.

"Where are we?" I turned around, gasping at the unmatched beauty. I'd never seen anything like it.

"The Garden of Eden," Azazel said, not nearly as dazzled by it as me. "It's been hidden from all for so long. How did you find it?"

"I didn't. This is where Father is," I said. The blade wasn't meant to take me to Hell. It was always meant to bring me to Father but not directly. It settled me at a safe distance. He put my protection first, and guilt tinged in my chest not for what I said to him earlier but the way I'd said some of it in anger. "It's bigger than I imagined."

"It's a maze," Azazel said. "Not many know that besides your Father. He knows these gardens better than anyone."

I understood Azazel's apprehensiveness. The thrill of the beauty diminished when I learned our path would be a game.

"If it's a maze, how are we going to find him?" Jax asked.

"We split up," Azazel said.

Dread formed a knot in my stomach. "That doesn't sound like a good idea."

"He could be anywhere in the vastness of this maze," he said.

"Azazel's right," Jax said, taking my hand. "We should split up. You and I can go together. Everyone can split into pairs."

"But how will we know if someone finds him?" I looked up at Jax.

"We'll meet back here in an hour." Azazel motioned to one of the demons. "Sophia, you can come with me."

An hour seemed like a long time with Amon on the loose doing hell knew what. I nodded, not wanting to waste any more time. I pulled my cell out. No reception as expected, but I set the timer. "An hour."

Azazel did the same and slipped his phone into his pocket. The other two demons paired off.

"I trust you two can tell time," Azazel said to them.

I cut my eyes to Azazel. *Joke or not, that's rude.*

When I turned back to the pair, I recognized one. She was not much older than me and had sparred with me on occasion since Jax. "Britt, I believe what Azazel meant to ask is if you have a cell or watch to know when an hour has passed."

Her eyes widened but returned to neutral right away. "Yes, Morena. I have a mobile."

I smiled at her, but she lowered her eyes. I turned back to Azazel. "I think we're set."

"Yes, Princess." He motioned for Sophia to follow him down a path, and I watched as Britt and the other one I didn't know took the direction straight ahead.

Jax had blocked the only path left, claiming it. He took my arm as we walked.

"I smell your father's scent," Jax whispered when we were out of earshot. "But I smell Amon's too."

"You think it's a trap?" I craned my head back to look at him. His eyes confirmed the dread I felt.

"I do," he said. "I think it's better we are alone."

After the weird display at our arrival in Eden, I agreed with him. Jax was the only person I trusted here.

The maze seemed never-ending. I retrieved the phone from my pocket to check the time. We'd only been walking for ten minutes, but it seemed an eternity since we landed in the garden. "Are you sure you smell Father?"

"Yes, his scent is getting stronger. We should be getting close to him," he said, picking up the pace.

"I don't know how you can smell it over all the floral scents. They are overpowering my senses."

Jax turned another corner. "That's probably why he chose the location."

We ran into a dead end. *Seriously.* "Wrong turn."

"No." He skimmed his hands over the greenery.

I pointed to the green, vine-covered wall. "Jax, there's a wall in front of us."

He turned around and studied the narrow space like he was assessing something. *Something I didn't see.*

The vines appeared like a solid wall on the three sides around us. I took a few steps back the way we came to examine it like he was, but I saw nothing. "Jax?"

I turned around, but he was gone. I walked to the corner and looked in all directions as if he could have slipped by me in the narrow space. Fear spiked at his missing presence. Chills ran up my arms. I took several steps back.

Pressure gripped my shoulder. There were fingers there. My heart pounded. I let out a high-pitched screech only a demon could. *Run, Rena.* My feet didn't listen to my command. They rooted me in the garden like a tree.

"Rena, it's me. Look at me." Jax's words floated to me in a soft soothing melody.

I took a couple of deep breaths and faced him. My cheeks burned with my embarrassment. "Jax, you scared me."

He chuckled. "I can tell."

I flashed my demon face at him. "Not funny."

"I'm sorry. Don't devil out on me. I didn't mean to sneak up on you." He held his hands up. "I promise."

"Never mind that. Where did you go?" I looked around him and still saw the green walls on three sides.

"Let me show you." He took my hand and led me to the corner. His hand passed through.

My muscles tightened. This was more than a maze. It reminded me of video games with hidden cheats in them.

Jax marveled, impressed more than me. "It's a hidden door, similar to a portal I think. I believe that's where your father is. Although, his scent ends here."

A knot formed in my stomach. *Why would his scent end here?* "What about Amon's?"

"His, too, ends here," Jax said, his tone grave.

"And what did you see when you went through?" It could be a trap of some sort. This whole place was a trap.

"I'm not sure how to describe it," Jax said. "I walked through a soundless space into a garden similar to this one."

"Another garden?"

"Yes, it's like they were connected by the space between."

"And my father knew where to find it."

If Amon set a trap for Father and now us, death waited on the other side. The risk weighed heavy on my heart. I was condemning both of us and leaving Hell without a ruler. But Jax had gone through and was fine, so maybe the risk wasn't as great as I suspected. I met Jax's patient gaze. "Show me."

He pulled me through. The area that followed was like a waiting place or passthrough. I tried to speak to Jax but nothing came out. I rubbed my hand at the base of my throat. I opened my mouth in a scream but silence persisted. It was soundless, as Jax had said, by design.

Jax laced our fingers together and guided me forward. There was no charge in our touch, and it made me despise this place more. Jax and I stepped onto the deep, green grass together. The rustle of our feet against it let me know sound was present here.

The release from the smothering suppression dazed me as noise surrounded me. It wasn't just sound. The scents of the flowers warmed the air, but there was no smell in the area between not even a sterile clinical smell like in Picher. It was nothing and then everything again.

My disorientation cleared, and I wandered forward unable to believe what was in front of me. I studied the vines and maze of the other garden and walked toward the opening. The view in each direction wasn't just similar to what we had left behind. It was identical only flipped. The garden became more mysterious to me, but dread rose up in equal portions. As the daughter of the Devil, I could sense evil in its most basic form, and the vibrations here were nefarious.

"I think it's a mirror of the one we just came through," I said, touching the vines of the wall. The beauty served to mislead the occupants. Make them feel safe when they should feel anything but.

"Two Gardens of Eden?" Jax asked, one brow lifted.

"It appears so." I stared down the path that would have been the opposite of the way we came. "And you still don't smell Father's or even Amon's scent?"

"No, nothing."

"All I smell is the same floral scent we smelled on the other side. We're here, and there aren't any other options. If their smells lead us here, we should see if we can find them." My hope dwindled. This maze was built like it wasn't meant to be solved.

CHAPTER 20

RENA

Jax and I wandered up and down the various aisles. I replayed the events that lead us here. My trip. The Nephilim. Gabriel's sword. Jax's sacrifice. My choices. It had all been my choices, and I had to fix my mistakes for those I loved.

"Nothing?" I asked for probably the tenth time.

"No." Jax scratched at the back of his neck.

I was drawn to the space. To the garden. Even though I sensed the deadliness of it, I couldn't ignore the enchantment. There was something or someone here we were meant to find, and it had to be my father.

"Maybe we should go back," Jax said. "We haven't seen anyone, and there is nothing in the air indicating they are here."

"I have a feeling, though, like we're supposed to be here. You don't have that feeling?"

"No." He shook his head. "I don't have any feeling about this place except dread."

"It's not like you to be so dramatic." I eyed him.

"I'm not being dramatic. I'm …" He paused. "I'm uncomfortable here."

I stopped and looked at him. He paced in front of me and scratched the back of his neck. He'd done that earlier. Being here irritated him. Demon senses provided us with a warning, and I knew from my time with Mother's Night Children that they did the same. "Tell me about it."

"I'm not sure how to describe it. It feels heavy here," he said, rolling his shoulders as if that would relieve the pressure.

"Like a weight or dense?"

"It's like a weight coming from all sides." He rubbed his chest.

"And it's not panic?" I asked.

Jax narrowed his eyes at me. "No, I know the difference, Rena. If it was panic, I'd tell you." His agitation increased.

"Okay." He clearly sensed a force I didn't, but I did have an awareness of an unfamiliar power I was unable to name. It, whatever it was, affected us in different ways.

"The deeper we go, the heavier the weight becomes," he said. His hand massaged the same place on his chest … where his heart was but it no longer beat.

"Interesting," I said, keeping my voice calm despite my growing anxiety. "Do you want to go back? I can move forward on my own." I didn't want him to keep going if it could hurt him, but I was fine and wouldn't stop until I found my father.

"I'm not leaving you here alone," he said. "We don't know who or what is in this garden."

Footsteps ambled our way. My heart sped up, and I reached for the dagger at my back.

Father emerged in front of us. His head tilted to the side. "Morena, what are you doing here?"

My heart swelled at the sight of him. He was fine. Healthy and uninjured. My eyes fell to his feet. *And barefoot.* Lucifer walking barefoot in a garden was not what I expected to find.

"Looking for you." I hurried to him and wrapped my arms around his neck. "Are you okay?"

He hugged me back. "Yes, my sweet, selfless daughter. I am fine."

"Jax smelled Amon's scent, and we were worried he had brought his legion here to kill you."

"His legion? Morena, what are you talking about?" He held me out at arm's length.

Jax tensed beside me.

"Amon locked up everyone in the dungeon of Hell, including Azazel." I rushed out. "Azazel said Amon was bringing the legion he raised to kill you and take over Hell."

"Morena, no one was locked up in the dungeon except for Azazel and his followers," Father said.

"What? I thought Mother said you chose him to lead while you were away," I said, confused. A shaky breath passed over my lips, and I squeezed my eyes shut. *I let him go. I led him here.*

"I did. He immediately tried to stage a coup as soon as I left Hell. I got word not long after and enlisted Amon's help to stop them."

Oh, shit. I fucked up. "But Amon betrayed you too."

"And he paid his penance. I stripped him of his rank and most of his power."

I'm such an idiot. The emptiness of Hell. Azazel calling my name. I'd done exactly what he needed me to do.

Jax's hand rested against the small of my back and gave me the strength I needed for what I'd have to tell Father.

"So you trust Amon over Azazel."

"I don't trust either of them, but Amon wants my favor. He escorted me here and should have been guarding the entrance. He was not there?"

"No, he wasn't," I said.

"As long as Azazel is locked in the dungeon, there should be no concerns. Amon was to return periodically to check on Hell."

I really fucked up. "I need to tell you something."

"Do you want me to explain?" Jax's fingers made small circles on my back.

"No, it's my story to tell."

Father crossed his arms over his chest. "Morena, what?"

The words left my mouth in a rush. "I let Azazel out of the dungeon because I didn't know about the coup." *And your daughter is an idiot but that part is obvious.*

"How? You need my—"

"Blood. Yep, have that," I said, wiggling my thumb.

"Why were you even in Hell? You should have been with your mother," he said.

It stung that he didn't think I was the right choice to sit his throne in his absence, but look at what I'd done in—the alarm on my phone went off. What I'd done in just over an hour. I silenced the alarm. "I went to stand in for you. Azazel has always been a warmonger, and I thought it was my duty."

Father let out a long sigh. "Morena." He swiped his hand over his face. "You are young and there is plenty of time to learn to be a leader. I'm not mad at you, because your intentions were righteous." He walked toward the path Jax and I had just come from.

"Well, they seem stupid now." *Fuck.* "I believed Azazel because I knew Amon had betrayed our family, and it gets worse. I brought Azazel and the ones in the cell with him here."

Father's Devil face flashed for a split second. *He's going to lock me up in the dungeon for this massive fuck up.* He let out a breath so hard it stirred up a warm breeze.

"You didn't know," he said. "We are going to have to fix this, and if Amon went without his full power, he will be in danger too."

Jax slipped his hand in mine. I squeezed it, thankful for his support.

A flash of light blinded me. *Now? An archangel appears now?* Michael took shape and blocked the way. His wings unfurled in their full glory, but he tucked them in as he walked toward us.

"Michael," Father said. "We have other things to attend to versus a conversation about Gabriel right now."

"This was your meeting, Lucifer. You asked me to meet you here," he said. "We can talk about our brother or not, but I have seen what Azazel is doing." Michael glanced at me. It looked like pity in his eyes, and I didn't want that.

"Yes, I screwed up." I narrowed my eyes at him.

"No one is blaming you, Morena," Father said and leveled a stare at Michael.

They postured but never intimidated each other.

"Gabriel has recovered," Michael said. "If you were wondering, Brother."

"Then he can explain himself after I deal with Azazel. Are you here to help or interfere, Michael?" Father held Michael's gaze.

"I cannot defend you or Hell's minions. You know this," he said, his tone devoid of emotion.

He won't help, but he loves to judge.

"Then be gone, so I can deal with this foolishness." Father waved a hand at Michael.

"But I can tell you where I would go if I wanted to stop Azazel from dragging minions to Hell." Michael stepped closer.

Michael was helping in the only way he could.

Father straightened. "And where is that?"

"Gothica," he said.

Panic rippled through me. I looked at Jax, and he clutched his chest. *The heavy feeling. It wasn't the garden. It was Gothica.* Vampires were easy targets to turn into demons since they are already undead. "Mother... Jax, call a portal now," I said, my hands shaking.

"On it." He was already performing the motions.

Michael's wings spread out, and he shot into the air.

"Come children. Behind me but be ready. We have work to do." Father stepped through the portal first.

The scent of death slammed into me as soon as I touched the floor inside Gothica. The throne room was empty, but piles of ash littered the ground. *Dozens of piles.* These were Night Children. *Were.*

My stomach roiled, and my head was light. "We need to find Mom. She'll be defending her children." I refused to believe she could be one of these piles.

"I think you and Jax should stay here," Father said, his tone solemn.

I looked at Jax for reassurance.

"She's still alive Morena. I would know," he said.

"We can't separate, Father. We need to stay together. We are stronger as a group than if we split up."

"I am the Devil, daughter. There is none stronger than me. I can seal the door where no one can get to you."

"You can't protect me forever, and if Mother is in danger, I'm the one who left her alone. I need to do this. And someone needs to have your back." He was immortal, but there were heavenly artifacts that could kill an archangel.

His mouth pinched together but he conceded. "Stay behind me," he said. "And Jax, you stand behind her. She stays between us at all times."

"Yes, sir," Jax said.

Father peered out the door and motioned for us to follow him. Dread grew like a mountain in my gut as if every pile of ash added a layer to it. He navigated us down the hall through more piles of ash. *Mother's children. She will be distraught.* She mourned each loss no matter how long they had been her children. So many dead vampires would have her frantic.

"It doesn't look like he's recruiting. It looks like he is

culling," I whispered, my heart breaking for the loss my mother experienced.

"Shhh," Father whispered.

Jax's hand rested on my lower back. Warmth spread from the contact, and it calmed my nerves a little only for them to return as we passed by more powdery residue.

I crept up the stairs behind Father as we stepped over even more ash. *A lot more.* They must have been defending Mother. Several feet in front of the door to her suite was solid black soot. I was confused about why they would come here versus taking her Night Children. Her children could be made demons, but she couldn't.

There was no noise in Gothica. None. It was completely silent except for our movements. The only way to get to the door required stepping on vampire remains. My stomach roiled as the ash crunched under our feet. "I feel sick. It's like we are walking on death."

"They were already dead, Rena," Jax whispered.

"Still," I said.

Father turned around and gave us a look that rivaled his Devil face. I cringed and leaned back. Jax's chest pressed against my back as if he were a wall that held me up. Father opened the door. The room, like everything else in Gothica, seemed empty.

"Lilith?" Father called out. There was no answer. She wasn't in her apartment.

CHAPTER 21

RENA

"Lilith?" Father called out to her again from the center of the living room.

"Lucifer," a weak, barely audible voice answered, but it wasn't Mother.

"It's coming from the pantry," Jax said. The pantry was the size of a walk-in closet. He went to the door and opened it. "Alessia…"

Mother's second-in-command lay on the floor with two other vampires. Alessia's injuries were numerous, but the most concerning one was the puncture near her heart. She wasn't healing. The other two appeared to be in as grave condition. Their skin dulled.

Jax knelt beside her. "How can we help you?"

Father crowded the door, but I pushed through and dropped down next to them. "Where's Mother?"

Alessia reached for my hand and squeezed. It was weak for a vampire. "Eden. She knew Azazel couldn't follow her there."

Except he can. Renewed panic skated over me. I looked up at Father.

Father squatted down and pressed a hand to Alessia's shoulder. "Alessia, you have been a faithful follower of Lilith for centuries, but you are of her, and I cannot turn you into a demon to save you. She is the only one who can."

My gut twisted.

"I know." She struggled to speak. "Save Tashara and Forest."

Father stepped over her to the two behind her. "You created them?"

"Yes," she said. "They are mine."

Father ripped open his thumb and dripped blood into Tashara's mouth. He repeated the action over Forest. "Jax, create a portal and make it strong. We're all going to Eden."

"I can't," Alessia said, her eyes closing.

"You can. Open your eyes." I tightened my grip on her hand. "We have a passage."

"The silent room?" Jax asked Father.

"Yes." Father lifted Tashara over one shoulder and Forest over the other. Their grey complexions appeared more translucent now. They looked better already. "Can you two carry Alessia?"

Jax formed the portal.

"I've got her." Jax scooped her up in his arms. He lifted her with ease. She groaned a gut-wrenching sound. I held onto her hand. We had to get her to Mother right away, or she'd be gone.

The silent room on the other side was empty. I sighed,

but there was no audible sound. Father led us out into the secret side of Eden where we'd found him earlier.

"Lilith is here," he said.

"Mother..." I whispered in relief.

"I smell her," Jax said.

Tashara and Forest came around, and Father sat them on their feet. "Breathe through it. You are no longer a vampire."

They both looked at Alessia in Jax's arms.

I'd observed Night Children's deaths in many ways over the years. Never one so slow. Alessia faded, but the fact she fought every second gave me hope we'd find Mother in time.

Father spoke to Tashara and Forest in a commander's tone, like the King of Hell. "We need to find Lilith to heal Alessia. Right now, you need to focus on finding Lilith."

They nodded like robots. I'd never seen his control take over someone so fully. That is why Azazel wanted vampires, and why Michael knew that was where Azazel would go. Azazel intended to create an army he could control without question, but he must have wanted to weaken Mother to make it easier.

The two former vampires led us forward like the bloodhounds from Hell, and I wondered if the current bloodhounds had once been Night Children.

"Is it always like this Father?"

"The vampires?" He raised an eyebrow at me.

"Yes, when you turn them into demons."

"When I turn them to demons, yes. When others do, no," he said.

"And if I did?" I asked, wondering if I could turn Jax back

into a demon to give him his life back. But I wouldn't want him to be a dog following my orders like the two ahead of us.

"I don't know, Morena," he said. "You are both the daughter of Hell and the daughter of Night. There is no other like you."

There was no way to test if it would work on Jax. I'd never risk him like that. He meant too much to me. And like me, his situation was a little unique. Not many demons were made vampires.

Mother turned the corner and met Father's gaze. My legs weakened, and I stumbled forward. *She's alive.*

Relief relaxed her expression, but the tension returned. Father took deliberate steps toward her. His arms enveloped her in an embrace of pure love. She melted into him. I glanced at Jax.

He cut his gaze in my direction but didn't meet my eyes.

"Take Alessia to Mother." I rubbed his arm.

He looked between Father and me and nodded. His steps were slow as he approached my parents.

"How are they here?" She looked at Alessia. Alessia struggled to stay lucid, but she raised her head when Mother spoke.

"It's always been possible," Father said. "Fear was the tool that kept them away."

And knowing it even existed … I didn't know Eden was a real place until today.

"Lay her flat on the ground, Jax," Mother said.

He did as she instructed. Alessia cried out.

Mother pulled her sleeve back and sliced open her arm with her fingernail. She pressed it to Alessia's lips. Alessia latched on like a leech and sucked. Mother stroked her hair. "Drink what you need, child."

Jax stepped back. I entwined my fingers with his. He gripped mine in a vice.

Alessia had her fill and wiped her mouth. "Thank you, Mother."

A twinge of jealousy stabbed at my gut, but it shouldn't. This was what Mother did. She wasn't just my mother. She had many children.

Mother looked at the two former vampires. She stood up, and Alessia stood beside her. She faced Father, her voice soft. "Was it necessary?"

"It was either that or let them die." He matched her softness.

"I understand," she said like she was familiar with what their life would be like now. They would be servants of Hell obedient to Lucifer. Mother faced Alessia, who functioned but not at her normal pace. "The others?"

The piles of thick soot on the floor at Gothica flooded my mind.

Alessia shook her head. "Most are gone. We did evacuate about twenty-five through the passage."

Mother wiped tears from her face. "I knew the loss was great, but not so great."

"I know you need to grieve, my love, but this place is not safe. Azazel has traveled to the garden." Father slid his arm around her waist.

Mother leaned into him. Their love was enduring and everlasting, but this wasn't the first time it caused death or even a war. I met Jax's eyes. His face was lined with worry, and I wondered if his thoughts were similar to mine. No matter how much we wanted to be together, the result might be the same. I could walk in both the demonic and the heavenly realms. A target would be on me as long as I lived, and I could not pull him into that. A life without me offered more peace for him.

My hand slipped from his, and he let me go. The anguish dug inside me and twisted far worse than the pain of making the fall from Hell.

"Where are we going then, Father?" I asked.

"Home, of course," he said. "To Hell."

I looked around the group and stopped on Alessia. She was the only one with fear on her face. She'd never been to Hell, at least not to my knowledge.

Mother noticed her frightened expression. "You'll be fine, Alessia. Just stay with me."

Alessia nodded.

"Jax, take us home," Father said, but I didn't miss his grim tone.

CHAPTER 22

RENA

Azazel's devotees had vacated Hell. Father summoned his own followers as soon as we arrived. The room was full of generals and all ranks of demons. I'd never seen so many all in Hell at the same time.

"If you are loyal to your king, show me now," Father said in his booming Devil voice. It shook the walls like an earthquake.

Every single demon took a knee in front of him, even the two former vampires. He left them there for some time like he wanted them to remember the moment. *Is it a test? He's known for testing his subjects.*

He looked at me. His eyes weren't the warm honey color I was accustomed to. They were a deep red like the rubies in his throne. "This is loyalty, Morena."

I stared out over the crowd. Not one of them flinched. *No, not loyalty. This is fear. Fear they will be punished by their king.* A bitter tang formed on my tongue and swept down my throat.

The forced loyalty he used disgusted me. *I didn't want to and I wouldn't rule like this.*

"Rise, my subjects," Father said. He continued his monologue, but my thoughts drifted.

I'd heard him say the power phrase on many occasions in my life, but this time I consumed the words differently. He wanted to destroy Azazel, and I didn't disagree with his intentions. The power over these demons was what bothered me, and I never saw it like that until the two vampires joined the ranks.

Mother came to my side and placed a hand around my waist. "I see the confusion on your face, and I was there once," she said. "Remember, there is a balance to be maintained, and your father is the largest weight on one side of the scale."

"But—"

She shook her head. "Not now. We'll talk about it later."

"Mother, we're literally taking Hell to the Overworld. That can't be right for the balance either."

"Not here, dear," she said without anger.

I turned to Jax, and fear dotted his eyes. "Do you agree with this?"

"I agree with your mother that this is not the place," he said, his voice firm.

Was that him or the sire bond talking?

"We'll leave in three waves." Father was wrapping up his speech. "Go to your designated portal as assigned." The lieutenants stationed themselves at various points in the vast area. "We will defeat Azazel and his army."

The minions, low-ranking demons, cheered like a

sporting event. Maybe they didn't mind the fear if it meant they got to fight. Either way, this was wrong. Father was about to rain Hell down in the Overworld, and the humans, like Stassi, would be unsuspecting victims.

"Father, I need to talk to you," I said. "In private."

"Now, Morena?"

"Yes, now. It's important."

"My office then." He led the way.

I didn't look back to see if Mother and Jax followed, so I wasn't sure if the footsteps behind us were theirs. My palms dampened as we marched the short distance to his private office. I wiped them on my pants. He might take my objections as betrayal, and I didn't know what he would do to me if he did. *Probably not kill me ... Banish me.*

Father ushered me in and closed the door before I could peek back in the hall to see if anyone was there. One eyebrow raised, his face portrayed annoyance. "What is so important that it couldn't wait until after we capture Azazel?"

"At what cost, Father?"

I trembled and braced myself for the anger I anticipated from him.

"Pardon me?" He narrowed his eyes at me as he leaned back against his grand black desk.

"You're not taking this war to a celestial realm. It is going to the Overworld. Demons will perish. Angels, your brothers and sisters, will perish. Humans, many who don't know or don't believe in our existence, will perish. Taking this war to the Overworld with this kind of force is bringing Hell to Earth."

"So, you would let my enemy go? My brother, who

murdered your mother's children he could not or simply would not turn?" His face was strained, and the anger grew in his voice. "That cannot be allowed."

"Father, this will tip the balance that you, Gabriel, and Michael have talked about many times. Can he not be lured to a celestial realm instead?"

His face relaxed and his anger softened. "A temporary incursion will not tip the balance, my daughter. Is that what you are worried about?"

"What is temporary for you is not temporary for humans. Temporary to you could be a hundred years with little impact, but that impact could be felt for generations of humans."

"You are being too sensitive. Their lives are a blip. Inconsequential."

I stared at him. My father was not the person I thought he was. His ego was damaged, and he wanted revenge. Revenge I understood, but I recognized the ramifications of it too. Father didn't care about the consequences. He wasn't my father or Lucifer. He was the Devil as the humans named him.

"What would you have me do, Morena?" he asked.

"Fight this battle anywhere but in the Overworld," I said, my voice soft, fully aware I wouldn't change his mind, but with hope, I'd reach him.

He sighed. "I love you and would do anything to keep you safe, but I cannot change course on the inexperienced view of one so young. You are welcome to stay behind. I'll make sure you have protection."

If I stayed behind, it would be the same as ignoring it.

But if I did stay, I could try to enlist some help to keep the balance. My mind ticked through slim choices and people I didn't want to contact but would.

"Yes, I'd prefer to stay here."

Disappointment crossed his face. "Very well. I'll ask your mother to stay, too, but I cannot guarantee she will not want her revenge."

"I understand," I said. "Can Jax stay too?"

"If he so wishes, he can stay without any repercussions."

"Thank you, Father." I wrapped my arms around him and hugged him. "Regardless of our disagreement, I love you."

He wrapped me up in a warm father's embrace. "You are my daughter, Morena. Stubborn, smart, and steadfast in your ideas. Don't forget who you are."

I knew what he meant. *I am the daughter of Lucifer and Lilith. The future Queen of Hell.*

Father walked the distance to Mother's study with me. "I'll let your mother and Jax know to meet you there." He kissed the top of my head.

"Thank you," I said. "Be safe."

"I'll be fine. Keep your mother from worrying too much."

"Will do," I said.

I paced the floor of the study and debated whether or not I'd be able to follow through with my plan. *Would Mother and Jax agree with me? Would Father banish me or worse?* I'd take banishment to keep the balance and save humanity.

The door flew open. Mother and Jax entered with a group of guards on their heels.

"Wait outside," Mother commanded them.

The guards backed out, and she shut the door.

Jax looked pissed. He and Mother were owed the most revenge. Father carried the sword for Mother's vengeance, and there was no one to carry his. I hoped he would trust me when the treasonous words left my mouth.

"Your father said you weren't going," Mother said.

"No, and we need to figure out a way to stop Father before he sends all these demons to the Overworld."

"The first wave is leaving right now, Morena," Jax groused.

Damn. "This is going to tip the delicate balance you and Father and his siblings are always talking about."

Mother wrapped her arm around my shoulders. "I don't disagree, Morena, but I will not stand against your father."

I'd expected some version of that, but I'd hoped she'd lean more on my side.

"So you will let demons, angels, and humans die for this?"

"And what of my Night Children who died at Azazel's hands? Who avenges them? They are earthbound creatures too."

The validity of her argument wasn't in error. She wanted revenge just as Father had said. Jax stared at me but didn't say a word. I'd face consequences for what I was about to do, and I'd accept them. "If neither of you will stand with me on this, then I will call Michael to help."

Jax lifted his head, and his eyes widened. He understood the risk I was taking calling the fucking warrior of Heaven to Hell.

Mother stepped back to face me. "You cannot do this. Your father might not forgive you."

"I understand that. But do you understand what taking this army to Earth will do? Your children need humans. What if they destroy that world and your children with it?"

"Your father would never let that happen," she said, her tone convinced.

"He is consumed with making Azazel pay at all costs. He does not care about the consequences," I said.

"He is your father and the ruler of Hell. Show some respect." Her words cut through the air like a knife.

"I'm just stating facts," I said.

"As you see them, Morena. I'm not denying your father's obsessive personality, but you are looking at it with young eyes."

"Urrggh." I inhaled a deep breath. "Then I will go somewhere else to call Michael if you do not wish to be part of my plan."

Mother shook her head. "No, Morena. Your Father will see this as a betrayal, and he might never forgive you."

I should care, but I'd made up my mind just like when I wanted to fix my own mistakes. This war would be stopped one way or another. "Jax, can you call a portal for us?"

He didn't move.

"Jax?"

"My oath is to protect you, and I'm not sure I can do that if we leave here."

I scrubbed my hands over my face. My heart pounded in my chest. I didn't want to incriminate them if they didn't want to be a part of it, but they weren't leaving me much choice.

"Let me be clear. I am calling Michael whether you want

me to or not. If you do not wish to be a part of it, then you either need to leave or let me leave." I kept my voice quiet but firm.

Mother nodded at Jax. "Take her to Gothica. She should be safe there. No one will think to look in my house right now."

My stomach churned. All the blackened ash from the vampires who sacrificed themselves for my mother was still there. Mother was right though. *Who would think to look among the soot for us?*

"I can't stand against your father, but Jax will travel with you," she said. "I hope you do comprehend what this will do to your father and our family."

"Mother, this is bigger than us," I said, thinking of how Stassi was never afraid to call me on my bullshit even after she found out I was the Devil's daughter. She wasn't afraid, and if a human could have that kind of bravery, what I was doing hardly counted as such. "One day, you may see that and be proud of my choice."

"I'm always proud of you." She hugged me.

I held on tightly to her for a minute. "I need to go."

"Keep her safe," she said to Jax. "She is the future for you and all of us."

I blinked back tears.

Jax nodded. His unusual quietness disturbed me on some level.

He spun up the portal and held out his hand. I slipped mine in his, and he entwined our fingers. The charge between us was so strong I gasped. Jax didn't flinch. "As your mother stands by your father, I stand by you."

"Thank you," I said, my voice lost in the tunnel of the portal. The gravity of his words ground into me. His declaration was treason to my father, and it was obvious Father still considered him a subject. They may have asked for his oath to me, but my parents were still the king and queen of Hell. Mother wouldn't be able to protect him against Father's wrath. I had to get this right.

He brought us to a smooth landing in the all too familiar apartment on the top level of Gothica.

"Thank you, Jax," I said.

"No need to thank me for what is my duty," he said, his tone steady.

Duty. Ouch. Is that what I am now because I'm committing treason?

I shook my head.

"Michael, archangel and great captain, I summon thee here." I used my demon voice to add power to the summons.

White light flashed in front of me and blotted out the room. When it dimmed, Michael stood in front of us. His annoyance was written all over his face.

"Morena, you are my niece, but you cannot summon me like one of your father's minions."

"I'm not requesting your presence like a follower of my father. The balance you hold so dear is at risk, Uncle." The words came out full of more venom than I meant. I wasn't a fan of my uncle, but I needed his help today.

He narrowed his eyes at me. "What do you mean the balance is at risk?"

"My father is bringing his entire army from Hell here to resolve the Azazel matter."

He rubbed his thumb and pointer finger back and forth along his chin. "Here? To the human's domain?"

"That's what I said."

"When?"

"They have already started to arrive," I said.

"Does your father know you are here?" he asked.

"No, he doesn't yet." I paused. "I tried to reach him, but his vengeance is ruling his decision-making." *A traitor. Telling Michael makes me nothing less than a traitor. It didn't make my choice wrong, but it made me feel like shit.*

"I cannot interfere, Morena," Michael said.

"Even if the balance is in jeopardy?" *He has to help.* My teeth ground together. I drew in a slow breath to steady myself.

"If the scales were to tip in your father's favor by some act, then I could intervene to restore balance," he said. "But I cannot restrict decision-making, especially that of another archangel, and I cannot impede a path someone has chosen."

My hands clenched and released at my sides. *Slugging an archangel probably wasn't helpful.* "So, we just let him bring this massive army here and fight Azazel regardless of the devastation it will cause to the people here and the Overworld?"

"I cannot," he said. "No matter how much I want to."

"That is bullshit, Michael," I said. He enjoyed the fight as much as Father or Amon did.

"I do not expect you to understand," he said. "Even giving your father the hint I did threatens the line I'm not allowed to cross."

"You are a hypocrite. You say you are a protector of men

and must keep the balance, but when you have a chance to help, you turn your back."

"It's not like that, Morena."

"Oh, it is exactly that. Go, Michael. I don't want to look at you anymore," I said.

The blinding light of Heaven flashed, and Michael was gone.

"I've never seen anyone talk to an archangel like that other than your father," Jax said.

He meant it as a compliment, but it felt like anything but that. We had to stop my father, and Michael was my plan. Without him, I'd have to come up with something only the daughter of Lucifer could do.

CHAPTER 23
JAX

Rena paced the floor, and it wasn't the first time in this apartment at Gothica she'd done it. I worried about what desperation would drive her to do. She had a point about her father, and my oath was to her. I'd follow her to the death if needed. The one thing I couldn't do was let her take over the angel's realm because I couldn't go there.

She paused in her steps. "Jax?"

"Hmm."

"What if I claimed the throne?"

I swallowed hard to control my fear. She hadn't made it that far when we learned Lucifer was in danger and abandoned the plan. Lucifer loved her, but he was prideful. Claiming her right as heir was one thing, but if she were to try to take his throne, he'd take it as a betrayal and likely not spare her life. That wasn't an option, and if it came to it, I'd offer mine in trade.

I shuddered. She could not die. I would not live this

damned life without her. "I don't think that's the answer, Rena."

"I know." She returned to her pacing. "But if I did, what do you think would happen to him?"

"He's ruled Hell for thousands of years. How would any of us know? It could be catastrophic or apocalyptic." From what we were told, Hell was created as a prison, and it wasn't until Lucifer chose to fall from his state of grace that the Underworld had a ruler. It was his home, and I imagined the fight. She had a valid point in that it might bring him back to Hell. *But was she ready to imprison him if that was what it took? Or actually fight him?* I wasn't convinced.

"I'd have to keep the balance in check," she said.

"And more, calm the constant conflict that erupts among the demon generals. They are not as forgiving as your father."

"Hmph." She looked out the window. "He doesn't seem very forgiving from where I stand."

"He has lived so long, Rena. He's seen the world nearly collapse multiple times. Do you not trust his ability to see what needs to be done?" I asked.

"Not this time," Rena said. "He's blinded."

She was blinded too. She couldn't see it, and I struggled to find a way to show her. "And what about Michael?"

"He's a coward," she said.

Michael could never be called a coward. He'd stood with many peoples in his lifetime. He was a self-righteous smug bastard, but he did want to do the right thing. "Rena, you know that's not true."

She sighed. "No, it's not. He is an ass though."

I bit back a smile. "That is true."

She smiled at me. "My family is the biggest bunch of dysfunctional assholes."

I chuckled. "No comment."

My father was absent most of my life, and I didn't know my mother at all. I wasn't qualified to judge.

"That means it's true," she said. "There is one other person I trust who I can call. She might be able to persuade others to help us." She paused. "Help me."

She had my heart and my oath. "I'm at your side as long as I can stand, Rena."

"Then stand back, because she's known for her entrances."

I scooted back, and Rena's head tilted upward like the humans did when they talked to the Heavens. She was more like them than she wanted to admit.

"Jophiel, I need you. Hear my call," Rena whispered.

The lights of Heaven flashed around us. The sweet apple smell permeated the room and mixed with the scent of burnt, dead vampire.

"Morena." Jophiel sheathed her sword, flaming with Heaven's light, behind her back. Jophiel stood as tall as me, and her strawberry-blonde hair waved down over her shoulders. She smiled and held her arms out.

Rena closed the distance and held tight to the angel. "Aunt Jophiel. I've missed you."

She never mentioned to me she knew Jophiel, the angel of beauty and creativity, and I failed to grasp how she would help return Lucifer's sanity.

"I've missed you too. You have grown, my beautiful niece," she said.

"It's been a few years," Rena said, pulling back.

"Have you been keeping up with your studies?" Jophiel asked.

"I'm a little old for studies," Rena said.

"One is never too old to learn and expand their mind," Jophiel said with a brilliant smile. She extended her hand in my direction. "And this must be Jax."

I gulped, her beauty almost blinding like Heaven's light head-on, and took her hand. "Yes, it's nice to meet you." I recalled seeing her in Hell from time to time but never knew she was an angel.

"It's nice to meet you too," she said. Warmth spread from her hand to mine. I felt like a half-human half-demon again. She withdrew her hand, and the retreat left mine cool. I ran my fingers over my palm missing the sensation.

She looked around at the dark soot on the floor and concern creased her otherwise perfect, tan face. "Where is your mother? Is she well?"

"She's in Hell," Rena said. "And is safe there."

"What has happened here then? Are you safe in Gothica?"

"Azazel is what happened. He's trying to take over Hell, and his first attempt was using Mother," Rena said.

"Our little brother can be quite aggressive," Jophiel said. "I assume Lucifer has it under control."

Were the other archangels this oblivious to what happens here and what their siblings are doing? Rena appeared to trust

Jophiel and believe her, but I didn't share the trust for any angel.

"Do you not see all from where you sit?" I asked.

Jophiel inclined her head in my direction, but Rena moved on before she could respond.

"Control, he has, but not the right kind," Rena said. "He's bringing the war here to the Overworld. It's going to shift the balance and tear this world apart."

Jophiel ran her fingertips over Rena's cheek. "My dearest niece, Lucifer has been to this world many times for war. He will not cross the line. He's well aware of the boundaries that must be maintained."

"But he's bringing the entire army of Hell, Jophiel."

Jopheil's fingertips glowed as they rested against Rena's skin. She cared for her niece.

"Do not fear, Morena. You are the bridge between all. Let the wisdom be yours to make decisions that are thoughtful and righteous. Be strong but pliable. Listen with your heart and mind. Love with your soul."

She wasn't hurting Morena, but she wasn't helping the cause either. "Rena?"

"But I don't have a soul," Rena whispered to Jophiel and ignored me.

I moved closer.

Jophiel smiled a sad smile. "Do you believe such a harsh untruth about yourself?"

"Yes." Rena lowered her head, her voice so small it didn't sound like her.

My shriveled heart broke at her confession. I wanted to wrap my arms around her until her pain faded away.

"While you must find many answers on your own, that is one I can give you in the purest form of truth. You have a soul. It's not a human soul. You are the child of an angel and carry the heavy burden of an angelic soul."

Gabriel told the truth. It wasn't all nonsense he'd spewed. Rena could travel anywhere she wanted.

"So, Gabriel was telling the truth?" I asked.

"He was," Jophiel said. "He's the messenger. Lies are forbidden in most cases."

Rena looked up at Jophiel, relief on her face. "How did I not know?"

"You did not wish to know. The knowledge was always there. You carry the weight with you just as you are today in your concern for your father's actions."

Tears ran down Rena's face, and I wanted to kiss her until she forgot them. To hold her tight and love her until the tears stopped. Instead, Rena's arms wrapped around Jophiel.

"Thank you," she said. "You have helped me more than I can say."

"You are welcome," Jophiel said. "I'm always here for you. You were a good student, Morena. Don't overlook the value one gets from studying a situation from all angles."

"I understand, Aunt Jophiel."

"Hug your parents for me," Jophiel said. "I must go."

Rena nodded, looking less than convinced she could fulfill that request. She certainly wouldn't if she went forward with her plans for the throne.

Heaven's bright white light flashed in front of us again, and Jophiel was gone.

My mind swam. *Rena has a soul.* I didn't deserve her, but I was hers however she needed me to be.

I closed the distance between us and pulled Rena to me. "You are always enough, Rena."

She hugged me back, but it wasn't the tight embrace I expected.

I leaned back and looked into her face. She looked sad. "Are you okay?"

"No, and I don't know if I ever will be."

The unsteadiness of her voice sent worry scurrying up my spine.

"Not even after what Jophiel said?" I studied her, but her face gave away no emotion.

"It doesn't change anything," she said. "You should go back to Hell, Jax. My mother needs protection."

"But my oath —"

"Damn your oath, Jax," she said. Fresh tears pooled in her eyes, and she stepped out of my arms. "I release you from your oath. You are no longer bound to me. You are free to choose your loyalty, but I wish you to return to Hell and protect my mother."

My chest tightened. I grabbed it and staggered, dizzy from the impact of her words. The agony of Gabriel's sword couldn't compare to the gaping hole of suffering that opened up inside me.

CHAPTER 24

RENA

Alone in the Gothica apartment surrounded by remnants of vampires, it was like I was already on a battlefield. It gutted me to send Jax away, but my actions would be mine and no one else would be held accountable. *It was the right thing to do.* "So why do I feel like shit?"

"Because you hurt someone you love."

I jumped, startled by Gabriel's voice. *How long has he been here?*

He looked more like an archangel than the psycho-angel he was last time I saw him. His features relaxed, and he appeared in control.

"What are you doing here?"

"Looking for your mother." He dropped his head as if in veneration. "To apologize."

"Well, she's not here," I said, disgusted he would show his face in the place he'd made a graveyard. Maybe not personally, but he set the cards in motion for Azazel to maneuver his way into a coup.

"I'm sorry, Morena," he said. "I need to apologize to you too."

"Gabriel, I neither have the time nor the demeanor right now to have this conversation."

My anger perforated me until I was sure he could see it spilling out, and I struggled to find it in me to calm it. I dismissed him with a wave and turned my back on him.

"You do not mean that. It is not the Morena I know. You sound like your father."

I lunged at him. Something in me snapped, and I had him by the throat pressed against the wall.

"Do not compare me to my father." My demon voice projected around us.

"You cannot kill me this way, Morena." Gabriel gasped out.

I loosened my grip and let him drop to the floor. He landed on his feet. I didn't want to kill him. *Did I?* I looked around at the black ash remains of the vampires he, and I too, wanted vengeance for them. They died protecting my mother from a domino effect my birthday trip caused. *I caused.*

"These deaths are on your hands even though you didn't strike the blow. You gave Azazel the opening he needed," I said, my words full of venom. "What penance will you pay, Gabriel? What repercussions are there for an archangel?" There was no penance to make amends for this kind of mass murder.

Gabriel clasped his hands. "The same as for you, Morena."

"I'm not an archangel. I'm not even an angel," I said. "Just because I have a soul doesn't make me either of those things."

"No, you are so much more, and one day, you will realize how much." He unfurled his wings.

I let my purplish-black wings loose and readied to call Hell's fire to them if he wanted a fight. There was a time I would have been afraid to take on an archangel, but that time was gone.

Instead, bright white light flashed and the whip of his wings beating against the air stirred up the vampire dust.

I spit ash from my mouth. "That is so gross."

Gabriel's last words stuck with me. *What did he mean that I was more than an angel or an archangel?* I'm the daughter of the King of Hell and the Mother of Night Children, and I couldn't be further from angelic, even with a soul.

I tucked it all back in my brain because the more time I spent on it meant the more time Father had to bring troops to the Overworld. *If only I could close the portals…*

"Holy Hell, could I do that?" I asked the empty room.

There was a time in our history, long before me, when the portals had been closed for angels and demons. Neither could travel outside of their realm and if they were somewhere other than their home realm, they were trapped. Documentation revealed nothing about if how the portals were reopened was the same as when they were closed, but the closure period was well documented.

Jophiel had departed some knowledge on me with her

touch, but I hadn't unlocked it. Her way was to gift a path to learn, so it was a bit of a scavenger hunt. Gabriel's appearance couldn't have been happenstance. He was a messenger delivering his message, and I believed they were related. I needed to put it together.

"Why is everything they do in riddles? Thousands of fucking years, and they can't just speak in a modern tongue," I said. "And I look crazy grumbling to a room full of ash."

Wings flapped above me, and I unfurled mine. "Not again. I don't have time for more cryptic conversations."

"Zadkiel," I said. Known for being the life guide, he stood in for Michael many times in his absence.

"Hello, my niece," Zadkiel drifted down in front of me. He reminded me of a monk. His head was shaved and his robes were even similar to them. His brown eyes danced like he was happy to see me.

"Am I going to get a visit from all of you today?" I asked. "It's like the ghosts of Christmas, and I'm the cranky old person."

His head tilted to the side. "I do not understand."

"Of course not," I said. "Never mind. Why are you here?"

"I'll be brief because I know the situation is urgent." He plucked a feather from his wing and held it in his hand. Warm white light glowed. He handed the light-infused feather to me. The brightness faded to a soft gold.

"A feather. Thanks. That will go a long way in stopping my father," I said, defeated by the arcane shit. I just wanted answers.

He smiled. "You know it's never that simple." He paused.

"This feather will allow you passage to where the answer you seek resides."

"How to control the portals?" My barely contained excitement to get something useful from my extended family bubbled out.

Zadkiel closed his eyes and gave one nod. He met my gaze. "The feather will guide you to the answers. Choose wisely, Morena."

"Thank you, Zadkiel. You've been the most helpful today."

"I think you will find it was a team effort," he said. "And I hope this meets your request for modern language."

I cringed inwardly. *They heard that.*

"It does," I said.

"Then ask the feather to help you answer your question. The time is short." He squeezed my shoulder and shot into the air. A bright flash of Heaven's light marked his leave.

I looked at Zadkiel's feather in my hand. "Feather, it's you and me. How can we close the portals and stop my father?" The air around me swirled and stirred up more vampire ash. "Not a dust storm with dead vampire ash." Light threaded through the space and encircled me. I was hurled through the expanse, and my fear spiked. *What the fuck, Zadkiel?*

A wood floor appeared ahead of me. I tried to turn so I'd land on my feet, but I couldn't. I landed hard on my side and rolled across the room. The feather slipped out of my hand and skidded away.

"Ouch." I sat up and rubbed my shoulder. "He could have warned me."

I stood up and was in awe of the vast library. It was bigger than any library I'd seen. I picked up the feather and twirled it in my fingers. "What do we do now?"

The books on the shelf had no titles on the spines. "This is insane. How do you know what they are?"

Realization settled on me. I gasped. This wasn't any library. It was *the* Library. The Library of Knowledge and only angels could step foot here. Zadkiel had given me a pass with his feather. *A key...*

I sat the feather in my hand and blew a light stream of air under it. "Show me the answer to my question."

The feather floated out from my hand and down the aisles of books. I looked around, but I didn't see any angels. *Guess they don't care about growing their knowledge.* I followed it until it hovered in front of one. Golden light warmed the space around the book. "Wow... that is some angelic power at work."

I pulled the book from the shelf. It was white with pages edged in gold. "Beautiful." I ran my fingers over the outside and flipped it open.

The book was written in a language I didn't know. *Seriously.* "How am I supposed to read this? I've never seen this much less know how to read it."

The words blurred on the page. I rubbed my eyes to try to adjust. Sentences reformed and unscrambled in front of me. It was a language I knew well. An old abandoned one I complained about in my lessons. *Jophiel. It's like she knew this day would come.* The archangels were crossing some lines today, and I liked it.

CHAPTER 25
JAX

"The first wave is almost through, Lilith," I said. The generals moved the demons into the portals with urgency, but it would still take time for that many demons to cross through. They would pause to regroup between waves and let the portal summoners eat to recharge their power.

"You should go find her, Jax," Lilith said. "I have Alessia here to protect me."

"No offense to you or Alessia, but she almost died," I said. *And Morena sent me here to protect you.* I shut off the pain when it ticked up my throat. *A perk of being vampire.*

"She is healed now, and she almost died protecting me," Lilith said. "It's not the first time, and it will not be the last. That is love, Jax."

I saw the sincerity on her face. *Was it love or blind loyalty or fear?* In the case of Alessia, I did believe she had love for Lilith.

"Rena doesn't want me with her," I said, my gut tightening. I searched in my senses for how to lock the new level of hurt down. "She released me from my oath and sent me to you."

"Morena doesn't know what she asked of you, Jax. Don't take it to heart. In her way, she was protecting you as much as me. It's not that different from what Lucifer would have done, and your body cannot be broken so easily." She smiled.

The door opened, and I unsheathed my swords.

Alessia stood in the doorway. Her gaze drifted from me to my swords to Lilith. She smirked.

I returned my swords to their holder. "Feeling better?"

Alessia rolled her eyes. "I'm a Night Child. I'm fine. You will understand one day." She faced Lilith. "He sent a runner to ask if you would join him in the final wave."

She only has one choice. She doesn't see it yet, but she will go with Lucifer. I fully expect it.

Lilith stared at the floor. "I don't know what to do. I agree with my daughter, but I cannot betray my husband."

"I've never seen him so..." Alessia's voice trailed off.

"Obsessed," Lilith said, her voice a whisper. "I haven't, either, and I thought I'd seen him at his worst."

"Gabriel's actions were also obsessive and out of character," I said, noting the similarity in their focus.

Lilith met my gaze. "He was very different than normal."

An archangel could become lost and need to be brought back to the present, there were stories over the years, but two in such a short time was odd. "Could a being, angelic or demonic, cause this?"

"I don't know of one, but I'm sure Lucifer would."

"We can't exactly ask him," I said.

Lilith glanced between me and Alessia, but then her gaze settled on Alessia. "Jax and I cannot walk among demons without being noticed, but you can. Go mingle with them. Listen for anything out of the ordinary and look for anyone who doesn't belong."

"Of course, Mother." Alessia ducked out the door.

"Aren't you afraid she'll get lost? Or caught spying?" Lucifer made examples of spies and enjoyed handing them over to other demons to do so.

"No, she has been there many times." Lilith smiled.

"You've had her spy on activities in Hell?" I asked.

"From time to time, but always for Lucifer," she said, her eyes turning distant. "Not ever on him."

THE DOOR OPENED after not even a half hour to Alessia slinking in with a smile on her face.

"You look proud of yourself," I said.

Alessia sneered at me. "I'm older and stronger than you, baby boy. Remember that."

"I carried you until we found Lilith. Remember that."

"Unlike you, I do not wish for death, but I'm not afraid of it."

She opened my box of pain back up. I was afraid of death, but only because I was afraid of being separated from Rena.

"Any who..." She moved on. "Azazel has a very interesting medallion in his possession."

"Uriel's Ascendant?" Lilith asked.

"No one has been close enough to see it, but I would wager my undead life on it." Alessia crossed her arms.

"What is Uriel's Ascendant?" I asked.

Alessia rolled her eyes.

Lilith answered. "Many years ago, Uriel infused a medallion with his angelic power. He almost died but healed with his power restored. The medallion retained the power he committed to it."

"So anyone who has it can use it?" I shook my head. "Why would he allow it to fall into someone else's hands?"

"Not only use the power but control others. The rumors were it was hidden where no one could find it," Alessia said, her tone flat like I'd asked the dumbest question in the history of dumb questions.

It made sense. Both Gabriel and Lucifer acted out of character and Azazel had access to Lucifer when he was temporarily in charge. "Well, those rumors were wrong," I said. "How do we break the spell it has on Gabriel and Lucifer?"

"We cannot," Lilith said. "Only Uriel or the one possessing the Ascendant can."

"Fuck." *Shit.* "My apologies, Lilith."

She smiled. "I'm married to Lucifer. I've heard far worse."

I nodded. "Capturing Azazel would be difficult with the size of his force. Can you summon Uriel here?"

"He's been in seclusion for two centuries," Lilith said. "And even if he wasn't, he would never cross the demonic boundary."

"We need to return to the Overworld and summon him," I said.

"Uriel has not left seclusion for any summons," Lilith said in an ambivalent tone.

"Then we find something that will make him want to," I said. "Don't you want to free Lucifer of Azazel's control?"

"Yes, but I don't want Uriel's wrath either. It's almost as bad as Lucifer's, and the last factor we need is a fight that will divide the siblings again. Besides, the only thing Uriel ever cared about was purging the Nephilim after his own mate and child died in childbirth." Lilith exhaled like the memory was painful for her.

"Easy then. We bring the Nephilim to the fight." Since they seem to know our moves before we do, all we need to do is step out in the open in the Overworld.

Lilith laughed. "You're so optimistic, Jax. There is no way the Nephilim will come fight with us."

"They don't have to. We just need a large number of them at the battle. Then we can summon Uriel." I kept the assertiveness in my voice.

"He will not discriminate between demon and Nephilim," Lilith warned.

Any other day, I might pause for that, but in the current situation, it was a price I would pay to restore order and ensure Rena's safety.

Alessia shifted her weight from one foot to another. *The plan made her nervous.*

"Alessia? Something to add?"

"Uriel is the worst of the angels in my opinion. He would strike down his own family. If he has an issue with Nephilim, what will he do if he sees Morena?"

I closed the gap between us. "He will do nothing to Rena.

If we must sacrifice the Nephilim and all the demons of Hell to protect her, we will."

"Jax?" Lilith called. I turned to find her scowling.

"Apologies, Alessia." I stepped back, reining in my anger. "Just understand I will sacrifice anything and everything including myself if Rena is in jeopardy."

Lilith stood. "Morena wants to make sure the balance required for all our survival is maintained, and we can help with that. We'll follow your plan, Jax, but if it fails, we will all lose."

"I understand. I'm open to other options, but we are out of time and Morena is not here."

Lilith took Alessia's hands in hers. "Sneak through the portal with this wave and go to the Overworld. Scatter the message far and wide for the Nephilim to meet the demons of Hell on the battlefield."

Alessia swallowed hard. "As you wish, Mother." She was gone at vampire speed.

"I hope you know what this price will be, Jax. A lot of blood will spill before this ends."

My only care was for Morena and her safety. I'd die a thousand deaths, vampire or demon, to save her.

CHAPTER 26

RENA

A map? Why would Jophiel and Zadkiel send me to a map, and what is it for?

"That's Uriel's symbol." I studied the placement. It was here in the library. He'd been a bit of a rebel from what I understood. *Could he have been responsible for closing the portals?*

I recalled what I'd learned of him from various texts. Uriel had been in seclusion since before my birth. He'd been on a mission to cleanse the Overworld of Nephilim, and many demons had sided with him. *Because, hello, Nephilim hate demons. Was his seclusion here, and were they telling me to find him? Did I need him to close the portals?*

I got my bearings in the library and made my way through. The map led me to a dead end. "There is supposed to be a door here according to the map."

In the Garden of Eden, there had been a hidden door to a secret side of Eden. Jax had found it, but he did it by feeling around the greenery. "Here goes nothing."

I touched various books and moved some. *Nothing. Sweet angel's ass I'd go nuts if I were an angel only capable of saying things that had to be decoded.* I studied the map again and backtracked my steps to my last turn. "Hmm..."

There were walls on either side, but this intersection of the library was like a crossroads. I could go straight, right, left, or back the way I came. The turn I made that was a dead end looked like the right place on the map. I took several steps forward and stood at the corner of it. There wasn't anything that looked remotely like it could be a door.

I pulled Zadkiel's feather out of my pocket. "Do you know where to go or what I'm supposed to find here?"

The feather glowed with the same warm, white light from earlier. I held it up in the palm of my hand and blew a burst of air under it. The feather floated up, but it didn't go down to the dead end. Instead, it hovered at the wall next to me.

"I don't see anything." I shook my head. "And I'm talking to a feather."

The feather remained in the same spot. I leaned in closer, looking for anything that could be related to Uriel. I couldn't grasp what this message was, and my frustration grew. The feather gave no more answers.

I ran my fingers over the books. The texture of one was different. It was rough and not smooth like the others. I went back to it and pulled it out. The invisible door opened.

The room was like a museum. I stepped through the door to find dozens of artifacts like Zadkiel's harp that entranced humans and Michael's broken shield from the war caused when Father fell. The feather floated next to me as I explored.

I'd heard of many of them, but only from stories that took place before my birth. The power in this room was thick and suffocating.

"Were they telling me I need one of them?" I asked the feather. It danced and moved deeper into the room. There was a symbol on the back wall, and I walked close enough I could read it.

"Uriel," I whispered as I touched the intricate medallion. "I've never met you, but maybe it's time." I placed my hand flat over the symbol and pushed. A marble slab in the floor slid away.

"Creepy." I peered inside the hole expecting to see Uriel in some form of stasis, but instead, there was a small wooden box with Uriel's symbol on it. *He's not dead, right? He can't be.* I retrieved it and sat on the floor beside the opening. The wood was painted black, and the box was heavy. The feather made a series of rapid movements over it. "I get it."

I placed the feather on top of the book. Uriel was a bit of an enigma among the angels, at least that was what Jophiel told me during our lessons.

Hopefully, there's not some kind of plague inside. Plagues weren't Uriel's style, so I wasn't too worried. I flipped open the box not sure what I expected to be in it. I didn't envision it would be empty, but it was.

"What the fuck, Zadkiel?" I asked, beyond frustrated. I stuck my hand down in the dark box, but there was nothing in there. "This was a waste of time."

I slammed the box shut. "Was this whole thing a ruse to get me off track?"

The feather lifted off the book and danced wildly over the box. "I don't understand."

I studied the symbol on the lid and ran my hand across it. The symbol was Uriel's, but there were other inscriptions. I squinted to read them. "That can't be right."

The feather zigzagged like it was trying to confirm what I saw.

"The Ascendant. Uriel's Ascendant."

I opened up the box and ran my hand all over the dark fabric to make sure I hadn't missed it in some way. "Where is it?"

Not good. Really, really bad. Someone had Uriel's Ascendant, a medallion I thought was folklore. If the rumors were true, the being who possessed it could control anyone they wanted. It was like they had the same power as Uriel.

"How would Azazel have ever found it or even gotten into the Library of Knowledge after he was banished?" I looked around and knew exactly what I needed to do.

I put the feather in my pocket and returned the box back to the hidden compartment, watching the floor hide its location. Next, I returned the book with the map to its proper place.

"Time to go back to Hell." I couldn't use Father's blade. It would alert him to my return. I pulled the feather out of my pocket. "Can you get me home without my father knowing?"

The feather's glow brightened to a white light, and I snapped through it. I landed on my feet, facing Mother in her study.

Her eyes widened with surprise. "Morena?"

I took in the room to find Jax there. Jax kept his word to

stay with Mother. Warmth spread across my chest. He avoided eye contact with me, and the warmth disappeared.

"We can hug it out later. I have news to share. Azazel has Uriel's Ascendant."

"We know," Jax said. "And we have a plan."

CHAPTER 27
RENA

"Do you have any idea how many demons, Nephilim, and probably humans will die like this?" I asked Jax. He explained the plan they'd come up with in my absence, and it was only moderately better than my father's.

"We're running out of time, Rena. The generals started sending the second wave through moments ago."

"We need Uriel," I said. "I don't disagree, but luring him with Nephilim is disastrous for all of us. His hatred is massive. I think it will cause him to become unhinged."

"Rena, how did you come by passage to the Library of Knowledge?" Mother asked.

"Zadkiel," I said. "He gave me a key of sorts."

Mother looked distant like she was trapped in a memory. "He doesn't usually offer assistance unless —"

"The balance is threatened or off course," I finished. An event must have veered off the path for them to help me.

Mother returned to the present. "So, it's already tipped."

"Possibly," I said. "Likely."

"Then we must act fast. Unless you have another idea, Rena, we must move forward with the original plan," Jax said.

"Alessia is already spreading the invitation to the Nephilim to meet us on the battlefield," Mother said.

"Invitation?" I snorted. "It's not a party. We're inviting them to their deaths."

"We'll do everything we can to stop it before then," she said.

I held her gaze for a moment in disbelief. "Like what? Unless you can summon Uriel right now, there are no guarantees."

"Of course, I just meant we will not let it go any longer than necessary," she said.

"And they are Nephilim, Rena. It's not like we haven't killed many of them," Jax said, his tone a little too nonchalant for what was laid out in front of us.

I'd shared his same thoughts many times, but this was different. "Random battles and self-defense is not the same as inviting them to a slaughter at the hands of the person who thinks they are abominations."

"He thinks we're abominations too," Jax said.

"But it wasn't his life's goal to eradicate us. He knew we were important to the balance. He does not feel the same way about the Nephilim, and if you read the history, you will know his biggest concern was their ability to yield Heaven's light as a weapon."

"He's a hypocrite," Jax said. "Like most of them."

"Jax." Mother's tone warned him not to go there.

"Yes, Lilith," he said. "What other option do you have, Morena?" His tone was formal with me, and I hated it. Hated I sent him away but knew it was necessary. Zadkiel would not have given Jax passage to the Library and might not have granted it to me if he was there.

The feather twitched in my pocket. I held it up. *Of course.* "What if we didn't need Uriel? What if Zadkiel's feather led us to the Ascendant?"

"Zadkiel could not intervene," Mother said.

"If the balance has tipped, he could," I said. "And I think he infused it with the ability to answer my questions. If I ask it, it might answer. Once we have the Ascendant, I'll return it to the library." I made it sound way easier to them than I expected it to be. Jax's plan was probably the quickest, but we could spare lives my way.

"But someone got to it there," Jax said.

"Then I'll find somewhere else to hide it," I said. I had to try to stop the madness.

"The power of the medallion is strong. Pure angelic power. There is a chance that it will control you, Rena. You could take on Uriel's desire for vengeance," Mother said.

I'd wanted vengeance, but I'd let it go when I realized the consequences. Would mine look like my father's if I took it on?

"It won't happen to me." I thought back on how Azazel seemed very much himself. "And it doesn't seem like Azazel is under its influence."

"He has his own dark vengeance he feels the need to yield," she said. "I don't think you are the same."

She was right. I didn't have a great vendetta, but I did

want to restore the balance between angel and demon. "We don't know that for sure, and my biggest desire is for harmony between the realms."

"We need to go through with the next wave," Jax said. "If we wait for the final wave, there will be no chance to end the battle before it starts.

I nodded, ready to do my part and more if it was required of me. "Then we should leave immediately."

Mother looked hesitant. "Your father might not forgive us even after the spell is broken. It will be ingrained in his being. Do not hold it against him."

"He will be begging for your forgiveness, Mother. He loves you and has for two thousand years."

"Things have been strained though," she said. "For a while. This might be it." Her face dropped.

"No, he's been under the control of that medallion, and we don't know for how long," I said. "Have faith in your love. It has lasted lifetimes, and it will last many more.

"I hope you are right, my wise daughter."

"I do too," I said under my breath. I cleared my throat. "We're going to need disguises. How do we hide our appearance in a place where everyone knows us?"

"My dear daughter, you are a powerful demon with a demon face," Mother said. "You can change your appearance whenever you want."

"My demon face has been seen by most of the Underworld," I said.

"But you're not limited to that. It is your opposite but not the only option. You can make yourself look however you want."

"Seriously? Why did no one tell me this when I was going through that awkward phase at thirteen?" I asked, shaking my head. "Never mind. How do I do it?"

"Just think of what you want to change."

"And how do I go back?"

"You think it as well," she said.

I walked to the mirror. "Give me dark hair and the face of a thirty-year-old." My features transformed into an older version of myself. *Is that what I will look like? Not bad.* My hair darkened from silver-blonde to a deep black like Mother's. I ran my fingers through it. "I like the dark hair."

"It looks good on you," Jax said. His gaze heated. It stirred something deep inside me.

I averted my eyes and focused on Mother, hoping she hadn't noticed. "What about you and Jax?"

She walked to a closet door and opened it. "Since our appearances are frozen in time, we'll go with robes."

Our disguises in place, Jax led us down to the portals. Mother went through one portal, and Jax and I through another one together. I landed on my feet in the Overworld. The number of times I'd gone back and forth was whiplash inducing.

Jax took my hand, but I dropped it. It wasn't that I didn't want to hold his hand, but I owed him an explanation before I did. He looked me up and down like he assessed my motive. I pushed forward, looking for my mother.

She found us first. "Come. I know where we are and where we can go to talk."

CHAPTER 28

RENA

My pentagram-shaped birthmark sizzled and burned. "Nephilim are near."

"We need to move fast then," Mother said, her tone urgent.

"If this fails..." My voice trailed off. I cleared my throat but couldn't bring myself to acknowledge failure.

"It won't," Jax said. "You will succeed. But don't you want to do it as yourself?"

"Oh, thanks." I'd forgotten my disguise. I wanted Azazel to know who came for him and stopped him. I wanted him to know who dealt vengeance today. No mirror in sight, I swiped my hand in front of my face. *Restore my face and my hair.*

The color and length of my hair returned to the silver-white blonde the locks had been my entire life. "Do I look like me?"

"Yes," Jax said. He shifted uncomfortably.

I swear these awkward moments for us had the worst timing. Sweet angel's ass.

Jax moved a little closer. "Rena, when you ask the feather the question, ask it to take us on a route that will lead us around the populace."

I nodded and retrieved the feather. "Zadkiel gave you to me for a reason, and I believe this was it." I held it up between my fingers. "Guide us down a private path that will lead us to Uriel's Ascendant without interference."

The feather glowed with a golden light. It was dimmer than it had been before. "I think the feather is going as incognito as it can."

It floated up and out in front of us. I followed it along the edge of the woods just out of sight from the demons. Mother and Jax were close behind me.

"We're headed to the base of the hill," Mother said.

"How do you know?" I asked.

"Because it protects Azazel and his army on two sides," Jax said.

"Lucifer did the same thing in a battle before he and the others fell from grace," Mother said, her voice not more than a whisper.

"Why would Azazel do that?"

"He wants to rewrite history," Mother said.

My birthmark burned like the molten fires in Hell. I pressed my hand against it. "There are Nephilim near," I whispered. "Very near."

Jax grabbed my wrist. "Hold up," he said, his voice low. "I smell them."

One appeared in front of me, a sandy-blond male, but

the searing pain from my birthmark said he was not alone. I cut my eyes to the left and caught sight of a female Nephilim with golden-blonde hair. "Mother, come toward us."

Our backs against each other, I readied to fight. The tension coiled in me. My anticipation for the blows built in my body. "Two in my line."

"Two in mine," Jax echoed.

"I see one," Mother said.

Five Nephilim would be easy, but taking them down without alerting the demons to our location would not be so easy.

"Jax, remember the time we snuck out and took out the guards along the way so no one would know?" Jax and I had hit those guards quick and hard.

"Yes," he said. "But we had the element of surprise and not all of them at once."

"I don't know what you two are talking about," Lilith whispered. "But I can handle five Nephilim. You two cause a distraction, and I'll deal with them."

"Mother," I said. "We're not leaving you."

"Go," she said. "I'll catch up."

"Lilith, these Nephilim are skilled fighters," Jax said.

"I've lived through many battles, Jax," she said, her voice confident.

The Nephilim in front of me moved closer. His eyes flickered to the glowing feather.

"What are you doing with an angel's feather?" The blond Nephilim male looked about my age.

"It was given to me," I said.

"Why would an angel gift a disgusting demon a feather? I think you stole it."

"I don't have to steal," I said, unfurling my wings to show power.

He assessed me with a disgust-filled sneer. "Silver hair and purple wings. You are the abomination who will inherit Hell."

"The same abomination archangels frequently visit. How about you? What do they say to you?"

He narrowed his eyes on me but refocused on the feather. His weight shifted, and I saw the move coming. He lunged for the feather, and I launched myself at him. My foot connected with his chest and knocked him into the female.

"Morena, you and Jax go," Mother said. "You can't risk being caught here, and I've got these young half-angels."

If all three of us were caught, the plan would be over. As much as my heart said not to, I knew Mother was right.

"Be safe and do what you need to do, Mother," I said. "I'll see you soon."

"I'll meet you there," she said.

I glanced back at Mother, and her kick landed square in the chest of the blonde female. Mother held her own with the Nephilim.

Jax and I hurried through the opening with the feather leading the pace like it knew our urgency. The faster we moved, the faster it moved. I didn't risk flying, afraid I would be spotted.

I stopped inside the forest edge. The feather hovered in front of me like it waited on me to reason through my options. There was a large clearing to pass through in order to get to the camp Azazel and his army had set up. I didn't see a way in that wouldn't expose us. It was clear why Azazel had chosen the spot and why my father had before him.

I pinched my lips together and let go. "Jax, how are we going to get to the battle from here?"

"We could belly crawl," he said.

"I'm not crawling to Azazel," I said.

"You can't fly in, Rena, if that's what you're thinking."

"It would give away our element of surprise, and it's getting dark. It's also the last thing Azazel would ever expect from me. He was there for some of my training, and he knows how much I like to stalk."

"It's too dangerous," he said. "Maybe we should wait for Lilith."

She should be here by now. Five Nephilim should be an easy takedown. Sweat dampened my palms. I was worried about what might have happened. If word got out that she was on the battlefield, my father or Azazel might decide to push their timelines up. *And I don't know those timelines except that all the demons aren't here yet.*

"If we were to fly in—"

"No, Rena," Jax said. "They could kill you before you reach the ground on the other side."

"But it's dark and my wings are dark," I said. "I can fly in near silence and blend into the dark sky."

"Except for the glowing feather you are following."

The feather dimmed like it understood.

"Someone agrees with my plan," I said with a smile. "I'll create a distraction on the opposite side and then you can rush in when you see where the feather leads me."

"I don't like it," Jax said, a deep scowl across his face.

"You don't have to like it," I said. "You only have to agree to it."

"I'll follow you anywhere, Rena," he said. "You should know that by now."

He melted me inside like the molten streams in Hell. "Thank you, Jax."

"Thank me if we are both alive after all this," he said.

"I'll do more than that," I said, forgetting the conversation we needed to have or the apology I owed him.

"Go before I pin you down," he said, his eyes glowing.

I soared into the air, stretching my wings and flapping in careful strokes with the air. The opportunities were rare in Hell where I could fly. If I wasn't about to steal an angelic artifact, it would be relaxing. I glided silently along behind the feather. "We need to create a diversion first." I didn't know if it understood, but it hung with me.

The perfect distraction came into view. "Why in Heaven and Hell do they have human weapons stockpiled?"

I couldn't pass up on this gift and swooped down to the ground. I plucked one of my own feathers and willed it to ignite with the fires of Hell. There was a canvas tarp covering part of the stash. It was even bigger than I'd realized. *This is going to make a big boom.* I tossed my feather on the pile and leaped in the air.

The face of the mountain offered good cover. I hovered there in the deepest shadows and waited. It didn't take long for the explosions to start. The first few were small and sounded like firecrackers, which made their way to Hell often because demons love a good a prank. *Well, some do.* A massive boom shook the ground like an earthquake and tossed a fireball as high as the mountain. *That's what I was hoping for.* The demons ran in that direction.

I glided down with the feather leading the way to a small tent. It didn't look like it would be the command center for Azazel, so maybe it was his quarters. There was no light coming from inside, and it was quiet.

The shouts of the demons and random sounds of ammunition exploding blasted behind me. *That should keep them occupied.* I reached for the opening of the tent, worried it would be occupied, and peeked inside. Satisfied there wasn't anyone in there, the feather and I entered.

"It's here. Isn't it?" I whispered. "Why wouldn't he have it with him..."

The feather went to a large crate on the floor. It looked like an old trunk. Azazel apparently liked to hide things in plain sight. I opened it. The feather ducked inside and lit up the contents. The warm glow of the feather danced off a particularly shiny gold object. I'd never seen it in person, but I knew. *The Ascendant.*

I reached and put my hands around it. Nothing happened. It didn't imbue me with power. The feather hovered around my hand and dove back into the box. There was a black velvet bag there too. It was heavy, and I realized it was reinforced with a metal mesh. I placed the Ascendant in it and tucked it in my pocket.

"Time for us to get out of here," I said to the feather.

I made sure the coast was still clear. The explosions had tapered off from my distraction, but there still wasn't a sign of Jax. Maybe he decided to wait.

I took a few steps from the tent when voices drifted from nearby. I slipped back into the shadows. The feather started glowing ultra-bright. I snatched it from the air and pressed my hands around it, but the light peeked out. *Fuck.*

It was like a beacon. I shoved it in my pocket, but it glowed through there. *It's going to give me away.* I wanted to scream at Zadkiel. The only thing I could think to do was tuck the damn feather into my wings or up my ass. I shoved it in between some of my feathers and pulled my wings into me. *Finally.* I was afraid it might make me glow too.

My birthmark burned, and there was only one thing it alerted to. The voices nearby were louder. *Nephilim. Here? In Azazel's camp?*

I ducked down and inched around the tent closer to where they were, careful to stay in the deep shadows. It was the assholes from the forest line. I was ready to take them down, but I noticed another figure. *Mother?* I covered my mouth to hold in my gasp. *How had they captured her?* A second figure kicked a leg out and tripped one of them. *Jax.*

"We'll trade them to Azazel for The Ascendant. Then we can take the fight to Uriel," said the one I drop-kicked in the woods." Little did he know that Uriel would end him faster than I would. *Dumbasses.*

I couldn't let them take my mother and Jax to Azazel. There would be no stopping my father if Azazel held Mother captive. Lucifer would serve Azazel to the hounds of Hell and watch them feast until there was nothing left. *Literally nothing.*

The one I had now named Idiot looked way too smug for

me. I stepped out into the open. "You are making a big mistake," I said. "Huge."

"There's the other one," Idiot said. "The one with the angel feather."

"Um yeah. I just got your attention, Idiot," I said. "You have my mother and my..." I stammered over what to call Jax. "Friend."

"Why don't you come get them then?" The female said.

"Or you could just hand them over to me," I said. "Save yourself from a beating."

The female laughed. "You are outnumbered."

"I've had worse odds." I shrugged. "I guess this doesn't scare you then."

I blinked into my demon face. The female looked disgusted, but none of them seemed phased by it. They must have seen demon faces, which meant they had seen high-ranking demons.

One of the Nephilim tried to sneak around me. "Uh uh. I wouldn't do that if I were you. I was nice in the woods, but now you've taken people I care about. I'm done playing nice."

"Who said we were playing?" Idiot shoved my mother.

My anger took over, and I made no effort to check it. I pulled my father's blade out of my waistband and lunged into the air. I planted both feet in his chest and stood on him. I slid down until I straddled him with the dagger in my right hand. I dropped my arm and pierced his shoulder with the blade to make Idiot suffer.

Worried his friends would try to sneak behind me, I

rolled off him and turned to face them. I cut the binding around Mom's wrists with the blade.

She yanked down the gag they had put on her. "They are with Azazel."

I figured that. "Which means we need to get out of here."

"Did you get the —"

I held my finger up to my lips. I grabbed Jax by the arm and hauled him to his feet. He broke his bindings without my help. He'd let them take him. I'd have to ask him about that once we were out here.

"I'm the only one with wings, so hold on tight," I said to Mom and Jax.

Idiot was rolling on the ground crying like he was mortally injured.

I spread my wings. Zadkiel's feather was still embedded in mine. I plucked it and released it into the sky. "Take us somewhere we will be safe."

The feather floated up, and I held my arms out for Mother and Jax. They each took an arm, and I jumped into the sky, flapping my wings at top speed.

I followed the feather for miles, and it became clear where it was taking us. "Why is it taking us to Gothica?"

CHAPTER 29
RENA

It became clear why the feather brought us here as soon as we climbed the stairs to Mother's apartment. Perched on the couch was the same archangel who refused to help. *Michael.*

He waited for us like a lion waited for dinner. "What now, Uncle?"

"You veered from the path," he said.

"What path? I thought you weren't supposed to interfere?" I asked, being sarcastic. "Isn't that what you said?"

"I'm not interfering," he said, his tone solemn.

"Looks like you're about to," I said. "Why else would you be here? And now? It's because you know what we just did. The risk we took."

"Stop, Rena," Mother said. "Michael, tell us what you came to say."

"The Nephilim are aligning with Azazel to bring Uriel out of seclusion," he said, his voice grave. Interesting that tipped the scales enough for him to interfere, but my father bringing an army greater than all the countries put together in the Overworld didn't.

"We've met some of them," I said. "But why are they working with Azazel to call Uriel here?"

"They want their freedom, and they believe the only way they can get it is by killing Uriel," Michael said but his words were barely audible.

I might joke about killing my uncles and aunts on occasion, but I would never actually do it unless it was life or death. If they hurt my family, I'd devote my existence to destroying them. What the Nephilim sought to do was not only nearly impossible but a one-way ticket to eternal purgatory when you died. And archangels were dicks when it came to punishment.

"What makes them think Uriel would even come out of his blissfully ignorant slumber for them?" I asked to see what Michael would say, but we were essentially doing the same thing. Not to kill him but to help kill them.

A figure stepped from the shadows. An angel I'd never seen before. I had to pick my chin up off the floor from how beautiful this uncle was. *Uriel. The other angels should be jealous of him.*

"Because their stupidity has already awakened me, my niece." He held out his hand for me. I looked at Michael who did nothing. *He knew. Asshole.* And Uriel had to know what our plan was too. I glanced at my mother. She nodded, giving me the permission I was looking for.

I grasped his hand. His hand swallowed mine in a warm shake. "Hello, Uncle."

"You are very impressive," he said. "So, you saw Nephilim with Azazel?"

"No, first I saw them outside of the camp in the forest. Then, I saw them again inside the camp where they held my Mother, and my ..." I cleared my throat. "And Jax."

Awestruck by Uriel's beauty, my thoughts scattered. He was taller than Father with the darkest black hair and a strong face. I felt like I basically said, *I made big boom. Saw Nephilim. Ran with feather.*

"I don't trust him," Jax said, clearly not caring if Uriel heard him.

And I was on the fence. *I'm not sure how to trust someone who just woke up from a two-centuries-long sleep.*

"You are smart to speak your mind, but let the angels have their discussion," Uriel shot back.

"Hold up, Rip Van Winkle. First, don't talk to Jax like that. Second, I have a soul, but I'm not an angel," I said. *Why do I have to keep reminding everyone of that?*

"I don't know this Rip Van Winkle, but I can assure you that you are angelic. We can have that discussion another time," he said. Michael came to stand beside him. Uriel towered over him. I'd bet the ascendent he was a full foot taller than him.

"What made you return?" I asked, curious if he would speak in hidden meanings like the others tended to do.

"The Ascendant," he answered. "But the number of Nephilim has grown. The numbers need to be culled, and this is an easy place to do it."

I gave Michael a hard look and then turned my attention back to Uriel. "Why do none of you understand the literal

Hell you are bringing here with this stupid gang fight of a war?"

"Morena," Lilith said.

"What, Mother? You don't think they really give two shits about us, do you? You might be afraid of them." I glanced back at my uncles. Michael's arms were crossed, and he watched Uriel who looked bored. "But I'm not. They want something from us. That is why they are here. They want us to do something they do not want to sully their hands with." I turned my gaze back to the archangels. "Isn't that right, Uncles?"

"It's not like that, Morena," Michael said. "We can't do it."

"We don't need your mother or your Jax," Uriel said. "We need you."

I scoffed at the audacity. "Well, we're a package deal."

"It's not that their help isn't welcome." Michael paused. "There are things you can do that no one else in this room can do."

I scoffed. "You sound as crazy as Gabriel did earlier."

"What happened with Gabriel?" Uriel asked, his forehead wrinkled.

"We can go see him when we leave here, and he can explain it to you," Michael said.

"Or I can tell you. He completely lost his shit and tried to kidnap my mother, whom he professes to still be in love with. And he tried to force me to take his position in the Angelic Realm so he could fall here and live with her."

"Gabriel?" Uriel asked. "And you are certain?"

"Yes, I know Gabriel, but I think we all know he was

influenced by your fucking Ascendant." I baited him for a reaction to the artifact and hoped I did it well enough he didn't figure out what I was doing.

"That Azazel has," he said.

I started to reach for the Ascendant from my pocket, but I stopped myself. He hadn't told me what they wanted me to do, and I wasn't going to risk my one bargaining chip until I got some answers from both Uriel and Michael. Besides, it seemed he should have been able to sense his own angelic power.

Uriel's face twisted in confusion but then it returned to the hard expression that was his angelic RBF. His resting bitch face was strong. "Gabriel shouldn't be affected by The Ascendant though," Uriel said. "He's a messenger. He should be able to handle the power without being influenced."

"Brother, are you sure?" Michael asked.

Jax moved to my side. "What does your gut say?" he whispered to me.

I flicked my gaze in Uriel's direction. His eyes danced in amusement. "They can hear you just like you can hear when humans whisper."

"You haven't been a vampire long," Uriel said. "How have you come to gain the trust of the Mother of Night Children and the Heir of Hell so quickly?"

I held my hand up to Jax. "Uriel, he doesn't owe you any explanation. You are the only one who has questions to answer."

"I'm here for The Ascendant. To return my power back to me," he said.

I suspected he had a good idea The Ascendant was in my

possession, and I wondered why he didn't just outright ask for it. "So why are you in Gothica and not where Azazel is?"

Michael crossed his arms and stared at Uriel as he waited for the answer too.

"Well, angel?" Jax hurled the word as an insult.

Uriel took a step toward Jax, and I moved between them. Mother came to my side.

"You cannot touch him without harming my daughter, and I will not allow that, especially in the house of my children. You've been gone centuries, Uriel. You cannot come in and demand things of this house," Mother said, her voice strong.

"I slept too long." Pain flashed across his face. "You have done well with Morena."

"You don't know anything about me." *What a jerk.* I fought the urge to punch him in the face.

"I know more than you think," he said, his voice low.

"You are an even bigger ass than—"

"Morena." Michael shook his head.

"And Azazel is in command of The Ascendant?" Uriel asked.

"I saw it in his camp." It was the truth even if it was in my pocket now. "Why do you seem confused by that?"

"He shouldn't be powerful enough to hold it. Gabriel, Michael, and even your father are all archangels. They can hold and command artifacts. Azazel shouldn't."

I hated to tell him that I touched it, and I'm fine. Maybe it wasn't as powerful as it was two hundred years ago. "But wasn't that the point of putting your power in it? To allow others to use your power who wouldn't otherwise?"

"Not the entire reason," he said. "They must have the fortitude only an archangel has to touch it."

"So maybe he tricked Gabriel into getting it for him somehow?" I murmured, wondering how I touched it. I definitely wasn't an archangel. My father had been, sure, but I wasn't.

"Gabriel is not so easily tricked." Uriel's forehead wrinkled.

"Then what's your explanation?" I asked.

His brows pulled together in a tight line. "Someone or something has tainted the medallion."

My stomach sank. *If that thing is tainted and in my pocket, will it affect me? It is in the reinforced pouch. Is that enough to protect me from it?*

Shit.

I debated on whether to pull it out and toss it at Uriel's head. "But not everyone that has touched it is affected by it..."

Everyone was quiet and stared at me. *Sweet angel's ass.*

"Did I say that out loud?"

"Yes," Jax said with a mixture of amusement and confusion.

"What do you mean, Morena?" Michael asked.

Fuck it. I pulled the pouch out of my pocket. "When I found it in Azazel's camp, I touched it before Zadkiel's feather told me to put it in the pouch."

"Zadkiel's feather?" Michael scrunched up his face.

I opened the pouch.

"No," Michael stepped forward and grabbed my wrist. "Don't touch it."

"Release her arm," Jax growled.

Michael moved away from me.

"I agree with my brother," Uriel said. "We need to examine the contaminant first."

I held the bag out to him. Uriel didn't budge, and I imagined what it would look like if I thunked the thing against his pretty face.

"So, what do you want me to do with it?"

He turned to my mother. "Lilith, do you have a lab here?"

"No, but one of the children does." Mother looked at the ash on the floor and cleared her throat. "Did. She was a scientist."

Mother's pain was visible on her face, and if I wasn't potentially contaminated by Uriel's artifact, I'd hug her.

"Take us there," he said.

"Please." I met his eyes. "Be polite and you'll get more help."

Uriel narrowed his eyes at me and faced Mother. "Please, Lilith, will you take us to the lab?"

"I will," she said.

"And I guess you want me to be the transport for this object you think is tainted?"

Uriel looked me up and down. Jax stepped between us.

"Please," Uriel said, his voice tight.

"Since I might be the only one it's not affecting, I'll agree," I said. "Let's go."

CHAPTER 30

RENA

I paced the sidewalk in front of the building where the laboratory was housed and ducked around the corner to catch my breath away from all the eyes. The brick was warm through my shirt. I leaned my head back against it.

"Rena?" Stassi called my name. I blinked several times sure I imagined her standing there, but it was her. She and Alec, the remaining vampire guard I sent with her, were standing a few feet away.

I walked to her and hugged her. "Stassi, why are you here and not at home?"

She glanced up at Alec, and her eyes were full of fear.

I rubbed her arms. "You're okay. How did you find me though?"

She held up her cell. "I tracked you on that app we put on our phones."

"We..." She looked at Alec again. "We were at Gothica and..." She shook.

I pulled her into my arms. "You were there when the attack happened. It's okay. You're okay now." I squeezed Alec's arm. Stassi must have come to Gothica looking for me, but Alec kept her safe. "Thank you."

"We didn't know where to go," Alec said, looking shell-shocked.

"You can come with us for now. We'll figure the rest out later." I led them back to the group.

"For those of you who don't know, this is Stassi, and this is Alec."

Jax scowled in the back of the group.

"You're not bringing them inside," Uriel said.

"Yes, I am."

"Shall we get inside first? Then we can figure out who goes where," Mother said.

She pressed her hand to the entrance of the building and led us through a hallway and a series of doors. We stopped at a large thick door similar to the safe in a bank. Mother leaned forward with her hand on a panel about waist high. It scanned her hand and eye at the same time. The heavy door creaked open to the inner sanctum that made up the lab.

I looked around at the massive space in awe.

The lab was modern. Way more so than the human labs I'd used on occasion. Vampire money had to be funding it.

"Which vampire's lab was this?"

"Liz's," Mother said, her voice thick with sadness. Elizabeth, Liz, was one of Mother's favorites like Alessia. She was a kind but fierce woman, and I, as well as the others, were in her favorite place to be.

"Can we clear the room of nonrequired observers?" Uriel directed the question to me.

"There's a breakroom through those doors." Mother pointed to the far corner. "Alec, I believe you're familiar. Can you show Stassi?"

"Put the Ascendant in there." Uriel pointed to the large glovebox in the back of the lab. It had a clear front and sides with gloves to slip your hands into for experiments.

I stared at him without moving.

"Please," Uriel said with a forced smile. It looked so painful for him that I almost laughed.

"Fine." I walked to the back of the lab and opened the door on the side of the glovebox. I dumped the pouch upside down and let the medallion drop to the bottom of the box.

"Leave the bag in there too." Michael pointed to the box.

"It might contaminate the tests." If it was infected with the same tainted power, I doubted this box would protect any of us from it.

"We're looking for a contaminant. We can test it too," he said.

I tossed the bag to the corner of the box. "And I guess you're not going to do the tests. That will be me too." I dropped onto the stool in front of the rectangular container. I'd run tests like this hundreds of times and welcomed the distraction.

The glovebox was completely sealed, but it was awkward using the glove pockets to handle things.

"I'm ready. What are we testing for? It's not like we have a gauge for angel power," I said.

Jax chuckled.

"Test for elements," Uriel said.

"All elements?" I asked. "There are a hundred and eighteen of them."

"On Earth." Michael cocked his head to the side. "There are a vast many more in the universe."

"I'll start with the ones here," I pivoted on the stool to face the box. This lab was equipped for testing with an extremely small sample. "How am I supposed to get a piece off of it to do the tests?"

"Scrape some off of it," Uriel said. "That should be sufficient."

I found a scalpel in the box and did as Uriel asked. A flake, the size of an eraser and much thinner, came off. It would be enough for the elements in our periodic table.

The automated tester beeped as I placed the sample in it and programmed the thing to run tests for all the elements on the periodic table.

"It will produce a report with all the matches," I said. "It could take a while. What do we want to do in the meantime? Perhaps Uriel can tell us what he plans to do with the information once we have it?"

I moved to a seat at the large table in the room's center. Jax took the seat beside me and rested his hand on my knee. The contact was warm. I smiled at him, but I didn't know what to do with Stassi here. I had important things to talk about with both of them.

Uriel took the seat across from me, and Mother and Gabriel each took a seat.

"I'm not going to eliminate the Nephilim if that's what you are thinking, Morena," Uriel looked me straight in the eyes. His gaze was intense, and I understood why he was so intimidating to others. I refused to let him overpower me or anyone since he hid from responsibility for so long.

"Oh, I know you won't, because that might be the one time I'd fight against you." I deadpanned. I only killed them in self-defense. That was the difference between Uriel and me. "What are you going to do?"

"I'm only interested in doing what needs to be done to keep the balance, Morena," he said. "I believe we have that in common.

I assessed him and didn't see anything that looked like he was being dishonest. But nothing in me could muster trust in him. He wasn't readable, and it convinced me we had nothing in common.

"What do you want, Morena? You can have whatever you want." Uriel studied me as if he couldn't figure me out either.

I shifted on my seat, but the unease I had was from him not the chair. "That's a weird comment coming from an archangel."

"When you figure out what questions you have," he said, "I will answer them."

"We will answer them," Michael corrected him.

Michael's correction convinced me I was right not to trust Uriel.

"Where were you, Uriel?" I asked.

"Adrift." He offered no elaboration.

Michael gave his brother side-eye like he wanted the answer too.

"Uriel, are you going to try to punish my husband?" Mother asked.

"No," he said. "Lucifer is my brother. It's not my place to punish my brother."

"But you think he deserves it?" Mother asked.

"He broke the rules and continues to break them, Lilith. Anyone who did that would be subject to punishment," he said in a matter-of-fact tone.

Arrogant. Self-righteous asshole. "You would punish me then? And my mother too?"

Jax shifted but remained seated.

"I would punish anyone who broke the rules, even you or the great Lilith or the mighty Lucifer," he said.

Uriel is a pig.

"And who will punish you for creating this artifact?" The glovebox beeped in a rapid cadence. "Excuse me while I check on the tests."

The computer linked to the box flashed up many results. I combed through them, but I hadn't found anything that would explain the Ascendant being tainted. If anything, it wasn't tainted at all. It had made it through everything. None of the elements the system checked came back as a match for the medallion. *Strange.* Some of these elements were very common and in almost everything. There should have been a match to at least one if not a few of them.

"What is the base metal for this, Uriel?" I called out over my shoulder.

"It's not from here," he said. "Doesn't your test show that?"

"The test requires an identification of the primary substance to set the baseline." I fought back rolling my eyes.

"How are we supposed to do that if the metal isn't from Earth?"

Uriel unfurled his wings. The expanse was massive like Father's. His wings had a silvery-white glow more like the color of my hair than the typical angel light. He reached over and plucked a feather from his wing and handed it to me. "Will this do?"

I was confused. I looked at Jax, and his head was tilted. I glanced at Mother and Michael. They seemed less than surprised.

Uriel stalked closer to me, and I met him halfway. I reached for the feather.

"Careful," he said.

I studied the feather and saw the glint off of it. The feather was made of metal. The edges sharpened to a point. "I've never seen an angel feather like this."

"And you never will," Uriel said. "Mine are the only ones hardened, similar to the steel on this planet."

Michael seemed the more obvious choice for feathers like this. *Why Uriel?*

I grasped the edge of the feather and placed it in the glovebox. The recalibration of the test didn't take long to set the feather as the base metal. "Now, we wait again. It should be able to identify trace substances against it with the detail."

Uriel stood over my shoulder.

I glanced up at him. "Why are your feathers like that?"

"I cannot answer that question," Uriel said. "They have always been as such."

"And you don't know why they are different from the others?" I asked.

He cocked his head to the side. "They are all different, Morena."

"But not like this."

"Aren't your own a different color?"

"Yes, mine are a purple so dark it's almost black," I said. "And they drip fire from Hell, not Heaven's light like Gabriel's. But I'm not an angel."

"We all have our purposes, and our angelic powers, which include our wings, support that."

"But I'm not an angel with angelic powers, Uriel. I'm a demon, and my powers are rooted in Hell. I just happen to have a soul," I said.

"You don't believe that do you, Morena? Your father is an angel. You have angelic power in you." Pain crossed his face again, and I wondered if that was his normal face.

"That sounds like you are calling me Nephilim," I said. "Should I be afraid of you?"

"You are nothing like the Nephilim, my niece." He rested a hand on my shoulder. "You are much, much more than a Nephilim could ever hope to be."

"People keep saying that, but I don't get it. I'm half demon. My father is the original fallen angel, yes, but he is a demon now. He's been that for two thousand years."

"He likes to portray that to separate him from his loss, but he is still an angel. He will always be an angel. His sacrifice does not change that" Uriel squeezed my shoulder. If his touch was meant to bring me comfort, it didn't.

"To marry my mother." I shrugged his hand off. "That's

what you mean. Because he fell in love with the original vampire and chose to be with her, so he was cast out. I know the story, Uriel. I've heard it my whole life."

"Hmmm," he said, his voice quiet. "You've heard a story."

The testing system on the glovebox beeped again, this time with real data to evaluate.

"Congratulations, the Ascendant is ninety-seven-point-five percent your feather material."

His eyes narrowed. "It should be all mine. What is the other?"

"Whatever this is," I pointed to the screen. "I've never seen it before. Mother? Can you come take a look at this? You might be more familiar."

She walked over and looked at the results. Mother let out the faintest gasp.

"This is Uriel's feather material, but this," I said. "This isn't a makeup I know or can pull up in the database."

Jax and Michael joined us to look at the results, as curious as I was.

"That's because we deliberately keep it from any database." She glanced over her shoulder at Jax. Jax hadn't spent as much time in the lab as I had. *Why would she turn to him?* There was only one reason I could think of ...

"What is it, Mother?"

"It's vampire blood," she said. "What it is doing here, I do not know, but I am more than familiar with the makeup of it."

Questions rolled through my head. "I don't know where to start. Why is it here? How?"

"My Night Children would not participate in this kind of

act. They fear the angelic relics." She glanced at Uriel and Michael. "I suspect that was the real reason behind the attack that ended so many of my children."

The attack was a diversion. Nausea gurgled in my stomach. "Whoever is behind this wanted to distract you and maybe all of us to get the blood," Jax said. "Then, they'd use the Ascendant to control whatever being they wanted."

"But wasn't Gabriel already under the control of it before then?" I asked.

"Maybe," Jax said. "Maybe it was an act."

"Can you just suck it back up in you, Uriel?" I asked. "To stop it all?"

A slow smile crossed his face. "I cannot 'suck it back up in me,' as you said, with the vampire blood in it."

Michael laughed. "Morena thinks we need to learn the modern language. You have a long way to go, brother."

Uriel looked less than amused despite the smile.

Michael cleared his throat. "I don't think Azazel is smart enough to pull something like this off or even think of it."

"Agreed. He's all brute force and no smarts," I said. He had help whether by choice or by force.

"Someone was helping him then," Jax said.

We looked at Mother. She stiffened.

"My children would not help him," she said. "Nor would I if that is why you are all staring at me."

"Mother, I think you are going to have to accept that a Night Child was involved in some way, whether by complicit means or by force. Maybe they threatened you to get their help."

"Have you noticed anyone missing or acting strange?" Jax asked.

"There are lots of my children missing," she said, her voice thick with grief. "They are nothing more than ash."

My heart hurt for her. She loved me differently, but she loved all of her Night Children too. She knew when one was lost, and the scale of the pain she felt was related to how close the child was to her.

"Of course, Lilith," Jax said. "That was callous of me."

She patted his arm. Not all the tension was gone, but her demeanor relaxed. "I know you didn't mean it that way."

"So, do we just destroy the medallion?" I asked. "There's an incinerator on the other side of the room."

"You can try," Uriel said. "But I assure you it will come out unscathed."

I decided to try it anyway. With the vampire blood tainting it, maybe there was a chance. I grabbed some forceps and picked up the Ascendant from the glovebox.

"Are you sure this is a good idea, Rena?" Jax asked. He looked nervous.

"I've had worse. I'm sure," I said.

The incinerator had a grate system. I placed the Ascendant on the metal and watched it slide forward. The window closed. I observed until it entered the ignition cubicle and the door dropped there. The flame ignition was loud even outside the incinerator.

"I guess it's cooking now," I said, laughing at my own joke. A burnt smell flooded the air.

"Um, Morena?" Jax's voice was full of nerves, shaky even. I turned around to see why.

He held Mother and guided her to the ground. Michael was doing the same for Uriel.

My mouth dried. *What the...*

I rushed over to Mother's side. "What happened?"

"She started swaying, and I caught her," Jax said. "She feels warm."

Mother's cheeks were rosy and sweat beaded on her forehead. I pressed my hand to her face. "She's burning up."

"Uriel is too," Michael said.

I met Jax's gaze and saw straight-up fear. I turned to the incinerator. "Fuck." I jumped up and ran to the incinerator's emergency shut-off. The timer said it only had seconds on it, but I slammed my hand against the button. The fires shut down and went to the low roar they were before I put the Ascendant in there.

"Did it help?" I hurried back to her side and panicked at how red her face was.

"She's still warm, but I think she's cooling off," Jax said.

"Uriel is cooler, but he hasn't opened his eyes," Michael said. The archangel sounded worried.

"Mom?" I called to her like I did when I was a child. Her eyes remained closed. "Jax, why isn't she waking up?"

He shook his head. "I don't know."

I held her hand in mine. It was noticeably cooler. *Why did I put that stupid thing in the incinerator? I'm an idiot.* Guilt ate at me.

"Uriel?" Michael's sounded less tense. "Can you hear me?"

I glanced over Jax's shoulder to see Uriel sitting up. Relief sank in. "He's awake?"

"Yes," Uriel answered. He rubbed his forehead and looked at his hand. "What is this?"

"Perspiration," Michael answered.

I looked back at Mother. She stirred. "Mom? Can you open your eyes?"

Her eyes opened in slits.

"Open them," I said. "You can do it."

She complied like she'd heard me. Relief washed over me. "Why are you fussing over me?"

"Mother, you collapsed."

"I see." She pushed up. Jax helped her to her feet.

"Are you okay?" I asked.

"Yes." She smoothed out her clothes. "Yes, I'm fine."

Her color returned to normal, and she looked like the episode had never happened.

"Do you want to sit?" Jax asked, gesturing at a chair.

"No, I am perfectly fine." She straightened her spine. "What happened?"

"When I put the Ascendant in the incinerator, both you and Uriel passed out and were burning up." Guilt nagged at me. I'd let my desperation for a resolution get the better of me.

"Oh, that's why I thought I was on fire," she said, her voice too calm for me. "I thought it was a dream I couldn't wake from."

"That's called a nightmare, Mother." I looked to the only other person affected. "What about you, Uriel?"

"I don't remember." He didn't meet my eyes and his voice was distant.

My intuition told me he was lying.

"It's going to take the Ascendant a while to cool down," I said.

"No, it's already cooled," Uriel said, his eyes averted.

"How can you know that?"

"I can," he said. "And I do."

CHAPTER 31

JAX

I had zero trust in Rena's uncle. Not that I had much love for angels, but he was shadier than the others. I sensed he was testing her. *For what was the question.*

"Did you know before she put it in the incinerator?" I asked.

He didn't make eye contact with me. "I suspected."

Bastard. "You endangered yourself and Lilith for that?"

"I didn't know it would affect Lilith, but I thought it might have some impact on me. I didn't know the scale," he said, his expression pained. "I thought it would be tolerable."

Was his emotion real or more of his entrapment talk? I wanted to take him down right here, but he was an archangel with another archangel by his side. It wouldn't be as easy as taking down a Nephilim or a low-ranking angel. Demons weren't allowed to touch archangels without Lucifer's permission. I'd face his wrath if I did. But I'm a vampire now, and my allegiance is to Lilith.

I glanced at Lilith. Her face formed a vicious, heavy look

as she gazed at Uriel. The expression was hard, much harder than I'd ever seen on her face.

"Why would you take such a risk?" I asked.

"Because I wanted to know if it could be destroyed now that it was weakened." His face returned to the neutral expression he'd mastered.

"You could have mentioned that," Rena said.

"I didn't make it for myself or to be used as it has been," he said, the corners of his mouth drawn down.

"Enlighten us, Uncle," Rena said. "Why did you make it?"

Michael's eyes widened, and he shook his head at Rena like she'd crossed a line with the question.

Uriel closed his eyes and tilted his head up. When he looked back at Rena his eyes were heavy and had a tinge of gold in the corner. *Angel tears? Did angels cry?*

"I made it for my wife and child so that they might come live with me eventually," he said, his voice thick. "They never got the chance, and I filled it with my sorrow instead."

Rena opened her mouth and closed it. I glanced around our group. Michael and Lilith didn't seem shocked by his story. Michael's pained expression was of a brother who empathized with his brother. Rena stepped forward and touched Uriel's arm.

"Why didn't you tell us that from the beginning?" she asked, her voice soft.

"Because that is ancient history, Morena," Uriel said, his voice and expression back to neutral. "I want the reminder gone."

"But you can't erase the memories of your loved ones,

Uriel," she said. I assumed she was trying to reach and console her uncle, but I didn't like her so close to him.

"We are not like humans," he said. "We are not so sentimental."

She crossed her arms. Her gaze bored into him. "If I were to tell you that you are in denial, what would you say?"

"I would say you are wrong and trying to apply human emotions to an archangel. We are not the same." His face hardened almost like stone. He'd shut down and shut her out.

Rena liked challenges. She wouldn't back down just because he hurled an insult. Her shoulders squared, and she stood taller. Uriel should be afraid if she unleashed her ferocity on him. That fiery look on her face haunted my dreams, and I longed to have it leveled on me. I thought of her on top of me, giving me that look, and wanted to possess her in a way she would scream my name. My cock stiffened. I adjusted to hide it.

"We are more alike than you are willing to see, Uriel," she said, the softness returning to her voice. "You just need to open your eyes and see. The humans were created in the image of us. Well, you and the archangels. Not so much me specifically."

She stammered through her own identity. I wanted to comfort her, but the change she created at this moment was more important than my desire.

"You are young in years and are part of our divine path. As the years pass and you grow wiser, you will understand the loss of those attachments you form," Uriel said, his voice gentler to her.

Lilith met my gaze and gave me a tight smile. She went over to Rena. "Maybe we need to let this conversation be for a while." She steered Rena off to a corner of the room.

Uriel's eyes followed them, his intense focus on Rena. He shook his head and met my gaze. Pain flashed across his face, and it was a constant with him as if being in pain was his normal state.

"Jax?" Rena called from the corner.

I wanted to hurry, but I forced myself to go at a normal pace to her.

"What's up?" I asked.

"We've spent a lot of time here without much in the way of results." The wariness in her face betrayed her exhaustion, and I suspected it was mental more than physical. I wanted to take her away somewhere she could rest, but that wasn't an option we had right now. She looked down at her hands. "Mother thinks we need to find Alessia and get a message to Father."

"But he's under the control of the Ascendant. What message would you send?" I asked.

"That someone has declared war on the archangels. All of them," Lilith said, worry and tension present in her shoulders and face.

"Will he even care?" I asked. "It seems the Ascendant makes those possessed by it single-minded."

"If anything can break him out of it, this is it. The love he holds for his family." Lilith bit down on her lip like she was holding back.

That was true. He was most protective of his family.

"We would like for you to be the one to find Alessia and

give her the message to pass on." Rena took my hand in hers and squeezed.

"I'm not leaving your side." I ground my teeth.

"Rena and I will stay here with Michael and Uriel," Lilith said. "We would draw too much attention if we all traveled together, especially behind the lines of Lucifer's army."

"You would be recognized." I agreed they were right, but I didn't want to leave Rena here. *Especially with Uriel. Fucking fuck.* It had to be me. I was the only one who wasn't well-known enough to be recognized. "I will find Alessia and give her the message. Then, I will return here as soon as I can."

Rena's brow lowered. "Be safe."

I brushed my hand against her cheek and into her hair. Her eyes fluttered closed. I tilted her head back and devoured Rena's mouth with mine. Desire burned in me. I had to stop, or I'd take her here. I leaned her upright, and she opened her eyes. Her cheeks flushed.

"Jax." Her voice came out in breathless whisps. "I'll walk you out. There's something I need to tell you."

Rena took my arm. I was too scared to say anything as we walked. She waited until we were a good distance from the lab before she spoke.

"This feels so awkward." She wrung her hands. "But I want to be honest. The year you were away and didn't speak to me…"

Rena stopped and fidgeted with the zipper on the side of her top. Each time she slid it up a small area of skin was exposed. I wanted to still her hand and touch the exposed skin myself, but I didn't. I had a hunch about where she was going.

"You were with Stassi. Rena, we weren't together. But are we now? Because if we are, I know it's your right to have who you want, but I don't want to share you."

She let out a long slow breath and stared out the window by the door. When she met my gaze, tears pooled in her eyes. The hurt etched in her beautiful features crushed me. I reached to cup her face, and she rested her cheek in my hand.

She inhaled softly. "I care about Stassi. She helped me get through my pain. I missed you, Jax. It was like my best friend disappeared. She made me feel good again."

Oh... I was both intrigued and filled with hate at the images that conjured.

"But she wasn't you, Jax. I've never felt the spark from a touch with anyone else. I've never been as connected with someone else as I am with you."

I closed my eyes and let the relief loosen the tension in my shoulders. "You have no idea what those words do to me." My cock pressed against the zipper of my jeans, so she might know what I wanted to do to her, but not how I felt. "There wasn't one day in that year that I didn't think about you. The few times I did see you, my longing for you was so great all I could do was stare. And no, I haven't experienced that spark with anyone other than you, Rena." I rested my forehead against hers, desperate to be close to her.

"Jax," Lilith called from the end farthest from us. "We can't delay."

Rena leaned back. Her voice was like velvet. "Hurry back."

The soft sensual sound smoothed over me like a gentle caress. "Stay here, and don't do anything—"

"You wouldn't do," A small smile emerged on her face as she completed a phrase we'd used many times, but that wasn't what I meant.

"No, don't do anything." I brushed my lips over hers. "Stay here, and stay out of sight."

She didn't argue and nodded. I held her gaze for a moment and left on the journey to where I suspected I'd find Alessia.

CHAPTER 32

RENA

I ran my fingers over my lips. Jax's kiss still burned there. I didn't want his touch to fade.

"He'll be back, Rena," Mother said. "He's strong and capable."

"I hope so. I feel guilty staying here while he is out there." I stared at the lab door like he would walk back through right away.

"We have our own job to do." She inclined her head toward Uriel.

"Michael, come help me find some tea in the break room," Mother said.

He glanced between me and Mother. "Of course, Lilith."

Mother took his arm and walked into the adjoining room where Stassi and Alec still were.

"Uriel, I'm not sure how grief works for an angel. Father hasn't lost anyone important to him in my lifetime. I think you are struggling, and I want you to know that I'm here if you want to talk."

"It's been centuries, Morena." He stood stonelike near the table.

"Call me Rena," I said.

"Rena," he repeated. A tiny smile lit his face.

"I've done some bad things too," I said, hating I had to make myself vulnerable like this.

His eyes found mine, searching.

I took a deep breath. "I accidentally killed some humans when they summoned me. At first, I didn't think I cared. I shut off the feelings, but then, my brain and my heart registered I'd ended a life. A life that was already incredibly short. It haunted me for a while until I realized I couldn't take it back. Regret followed me like a Hellhound for killing those four souls. I didn't understand how precious human lives were. They had trapped me, but they didn't know what they were doing. I didn't have to kill them." It had been two years, but the anguish they felt rippled over me like when I took their lives.

"Rena." His voice sounded like silk. "You had to have been very young. You wouldn't have known better."

"I was, but I was very aware I was Lucifer and Lilith's daughter. I thought I had a reputation to live up to, but I was wrong. Mother and Father don't kill on a whim as I did. What I did was worse than anything they'd ever done."

Uriel rested his hand on my cheek like my father would when we would have our talks. "You made a mistake. You need to forgive yourself."

He pulled me into a hug, and I found comfort there similar to Father's. "It's time to let it go."

Light shined down over us. We were in a room with no

windows to the outside, but bright white light encircled us. *Please tell me there isn't another archangel about to drop down here.*

"Free yourself of this burden, Rena," he whispered.

The light warmed my skin, and a weight lifted. The lightness it gave startled me. "What's happening?"

"Truth," he said. "Because your heart is pure and your intention to not repeat your mistake is true, it is releasing you."

Relief. It was relief. I didn't know what else to call it.

"Thank you, Uriel." I looked up into his eyes.

A golden tear ran down his cheek and dripped onto my face.

"I didn't realize how heavy the burden was." A little guilt pitted in my stomach that maybe I was meant to carry it.

"It doesn't make you forget," he said. "It gives you peace, so you'll no longer be weighted by it. But Rena, they intended to trap you. You should not have felt guilty about it."

"Demons and angels both get summoned," I said. "We don't kill everyone who summons us."

"If it is them or us we do, even angels," Uriel said, his voice so soft it was like a gentle caress. "And it was in this case."

Something in the finality of the way he said it told me it was the truth, and peace washed over me like a rainstorm.

His smile was warm and welcoming. "Acceptance of the truth in a situation will bring peace. It's not always the peace you are looking for but peace nonetheless."

I moved from his embrace. "Your smile is nice, Uriel. It's not crazed like Michael's or Gabriel's. You should do it more."

He laughed a belly laugh. "Do not tell my brothers that. It would break their wings to think they disappointed their niece."

I laughed with him. "Really? I didn't think they cared that much about what I thought."

"They aren't very good at showing it, but they do," he said. "They sat at your cradle when you were a babe."

That was harder to believe. I couldn't picture any of them except maybe Jophiel sitting still that long. "How do you know?" I asked. "You were in seclusion."

"Many of our thoughts are shared when it is family. When I came out of my sabbatical, they flooded back to me. It was too fast to decipher, but when things happen, like this discussion, the relevant ones surface."

"That's kind of weird. It's like you eavesdrop on each other." *Could Father be reached that way?* "Do my father's come through too?"

"No, not since he fell from grace." Uriel's tone was pure sadness.

I studied the way the light dimmed in his eyes and the deep grooves that formed on his forehead. I saw loss there. "You miss him."

"I am the Angel of Truth, Rena. Tread lightly on the questions you ask me. But yes, I do miss my brother's thoughts. I miss my brother. Period." There was a warning in his words, but the anger he carried earlier seemed gone. "You may one day be part of the collective thoughts."

"That doesn't sound like something I would enjoy." Imagining these archangels and the crazy thoughts they probably have made me cringe inwardly.

Uriel smirked. "It's not as bad as you are imagining right now."

"What makes you think I'm imagining anything right now?" I asked.

"The left corner of your mouth is drawn up in disgust."

"Oh." Sweet angel's ass, I'd die if any of them had been reading my thoughts.

He rubbed my arm. "Relax. It's going to be fine."

An awkward silence built between us, and I wanted to break it.

"I wonder where Mother and Michael are with the tea." I looked towards the door of the breakroom. "And I need to speak with Stassi."

"I'm sure they will be back momentarily." Uriel's voice hardened.

A rustling noise came from the direction they had gone, and they emerged.

"Who wants tea?" Mother asked.

Michael smiled by her side. He took a sip. It was a strange sight to see an archangel drinking tea from a paper cup. I almost broke out in laughter. He handed Uriel a cup like his, and Mother handed me one.

"Well, don't we look like a bunch of humans sipping tea while the world is about to burn?" I looked at the clock on the wall. Dread twisted in my stomach and made me nauseous. Bile threatened to rise up my throat. I didn't need to be hiding here. I should be out there trying to stop this. "The second wave should be almost done."

"Rena," Mother warned. "You need to let Jax reach Alessia as planned."

I nodded. "I need to speak with Stassi before he gets back."

"She and Alec stepped into the hall," Michael said.

Mother peered at him. "There is a safe house we should send them to, Rena. Remember the one at the tip of Manhattan? It's small but secure."

She knew. She always knew. I smiled in gratitude. "Thank you."

I wandered into the hall and prepared myself for the conversation. The noises I heard were not what I expected. I rounded the corner to see Stassi up against the wall. Her hands were up Alec's shirt, and his mouth was over hers.

Maybe this conversation wasn't needed as urgently as I thought. I turned to walk away.

"Rena..." Stassi's breathless voice stopped me. "It just..."

"No explanation needed," I said. "I just came to tell you that Mother has given the approval for you two to go to a safe house. Alec, it's the small one at the tip of Manhattan. Are you familiar with it?"

He gave one nod, but there was genuine fear in his eyes.

I walked down the hall, and Stassi caught up to me.

"I like him, Rena," she said. "It happened when he took me home, and we haven't been apart since then."

"I'm happy for you, Stassi. I really am." I hugged her, and I was genuinely happy for her.

"You two should go though. That safe house is virtually unknown. You'll be out of harm's way there until this is done."

"Thank you," she said. "Be wise and make good decisions."

After walking them to the door, I returned to the lab.

Uriel and Michael both had stoic expressions like whatever their thoughts were they chose to hide them. I looked at Mother, but she averted her gaze.

"Mother, what are you not telling me?" I asked. "I can tell you are hiding something. You all are."

Michael and Uriel both looked at her instead of me.

"Tell her, Lilith," Uriel said, his tone cautionary. "She should know. I will tell her if you don't, but it should come from you."

Michael held up his hands in a defensive position and stepped back.

What in Heaven and Hell is going on?

CHAPTER 33
JAX

"Alessia?" I whispered, her scent strong in this area of the woods. "I smell you. Come out."

A limb cracked behind a nearby tree. I snaked my way over to it, stepping with silence only a supernatural could do.

Alessia was crumpled in a ball. She hissed when I approached. Her hands pressed against her stomach.

I crouched down next to her. "It's Jax," I said. "How did this happen?"

"Nephilim," she said, her word a gurgle of blood.

Her injuries were far worse than when Gothica was attacked. I needed to get her to Lilith, but the message to Lucifer was important. *Fuck.*

I stood up and turned around like the answer would be written in the trees on this moonless night. Alessia groaned. At least I could use a portal to get there and come back to pick up the task that would have been Alessia's.

"Hang on," I said, lifting her into my arms.

"No," she gurgled. "Leave me here. Go before they come back."

"The Nephilim?" I asked. "I'm not scared of them."

"No, the ones who killed the Nephilim," she said.

"Demons? I used to be one of them, Alessia."

"No, angels." She strained to speak.

But Uriel was with Rena, Lilith, and Michael. None of the other angels had an issue with the Nephilim. They thought the half-angels and their descendants were doing the work they should.

A flash of light blasted not too far from us. I called a portal and took Alessia to the lab.

I landed on my feet with Alessia secure in my arms. The room was quiet, and I thought they might have left. Until I looked up. Michael had his hands up like he was being robbed. Lilith gave a start that would have killed her if she wasn't already technically dead. Uriel's jaw tensed, and his hands were clenched by his side. Rena had one eyebrow up.

What in all that is Hell is going on here?

Something had happened while I was gone, and I'd dropped right in the middle of whatever this was. Rena was about to dish some serious shit in here by her expression.

Alessia shifted and whimpered.

"Lilith," I called. "She needs you."

Lilith turned to me. "What happened?"

"She was attacked, and it's bad." I laid Alessia on one of the tables. If these were regular Overworld wounds, she'd have healed by now.

"These don't look like demon wounds," Michael said.

"No, they were Nephilim," I said. "But she said something about the ones who killed the Nephilim. I think she's delirious. It had to be Nephilim, right?"

"Are you going back to end them?" Uriel asked.

"Alessia said that was taken care of by angels," I said, venom in my voice. I stared down the two angels in the room. "You two wouldn't know anything about that. Would you?"

They exchanged looks.

"I've never seen wounds like this," Lilith said, her tone engulfed with anguish. "They aren't even attempting to heal."

"You told me you have a collective brain thing," Rena said to Uriel.

Uriel met her gaze like they held a secret between them. "With archangels, Rena. Not with lower angels."

He called her Rena. I saw red. He did not get to use my name for her. *Fuck the consequences.* I lunged at him ready to pluck every feather from his fucking wings and dismember his body to feed to the hounds.

Strong arms wrapped around my waist and held me back. I jerked and reached for Uriel, but I couldn't move. The hands wrapped around me were too large for Rena or Lilith. *Michael.* I fought harder to get loose.

Rena appeared in front of me. "Focus on my voice," she said, her own full of concern. "Breathe with me. In for four. Out for four. One... two... three... four. Again."

I locked eyes with her and breathed through the anger. It

took far too many repetitions to bring me back to the present considering I didn't need air.

"I know you're upset." She stroked my face. I leaned into her touch. Her hands were smooth and felt like velvet against my skin.

"Rena, come help me," Lilith called, her voice panicked.

"I'm fine," I said. "Go."

She bit down on her lip but went over to assist Lilith.

"I meant it, Michael. I'm good. You can let me go."

He released me. I eyed Uriel, but I moved to see if I could aid Lilith and Rena.

"What can I do to help?" My anger simmered below my calm exterior.

Lilith ripped her wrist open with her teeth and let her blood pour into Alessia's mouth.

"Not in the wound?" I asked.

"She already tried that," Rena said, her voice grim. "It didn't do anything."

The wounds looked the same as when I found Alessia in the woods. Her skin was so translucent that she looked ghostlike.

Her skin shimmered.

"It's happening," Lilith said, her voice shaky. "I'm sorry, Alessia. I'm so sorry I couldn't save you this time."

Alessia's skin flaked off into ashy pieces, the edges red like burning coal. Ashes floated into the air. Alessia's body sparked and turned to black soot on the table.

Lilith sank to the floor and Rena went to her side, wrapping her arms around her Mother. Rena wasn't a fan of Alessia, but she never wanted to see her mother suffer, and right now, Lilith was feeling the loss of the Night Child closest to her. The one she chose as her second-in-command. Her love for Alessia would leave a hole in her. She'd lost so many today, and now she lost her most loyal and trusted child.

"I'm here, Mother," Rena said, her voice grim. "Tell me what you need."

"My blood should have been able to bring her back from almost anything," Lilith leaned into Rena's arms.

"Except angel fire," Rena whispered. She glanced at Uriel and Michael with an accusatory expression.

Like lower-level demons couldn't wield hell fire, most angels couldn't wield angel fire. It was Heaven's light in a flame, and typically higher-ranking angels and the archangels were the only ones strong enough to contain it in an artifact to use it.

"Did she say who it was, Jax?"

"Only Nephilim and that angels came for the Nephilim," I said. "And there is only one angel, an archangel, that I know of who wants to eradicate Nephilim."

Rena's gaze met Uriel's, and my vampire blood boiled. I didn't want to cause another scene, so I kept myself in check this time.

She continued, "But he was here with me the whole time."

"I had nothing to do with this, Rena," Uriel said. "I promise you."

His intimate address of her made me snarl. An angel's promise was a lie detector. They didn't make them on a whim like humans. Their promises were binding and sealed with the source of their power.

Rena visibly relaxed at his declaration, and it sickened me. I was losing her, not that she was mine to lose. He could lead her on a path that neither myself nor anyone from Hell could, and I hated him for it.

CHAPTER 34

RENA

The look on Jax's face was like he wanted to kill me or Uriel or both. *Why was he so angry?*

I rubbed Mother's back and pulled her close. Alessia was her closest Night Child. She loved her, and the loss to her would be great. She was in no position to battle or advise Father. The more I thought about it, the answer I came to was someone targeted Alessia to get to Mother. They knew she would want revenge, and she would deliver it in a swift fashion and likely with my father's help.

Michael and Uriel chatted among themselves, serious expressions on their faces. Jax stood with a snarl on his face aimed at Uriel.

"This wasn't an accident," I said. Everyone, including Mother, froze and looked at me. "Whoever did this wanted to hurt Mother. This was a decision, not a random act."

Jax's posture went rigid like he understood.

"I don't disagree," Uriel said.

"She's fucking right," Jax said. "Why can't you just say it?"

Uriel appraised him. "I just did."

Michael stepped between them. "Why would someone do that?"

"The better question is who." Jax's face was like stone.

"I want them to pay for all the vampire deaths and twice for Alessia's," Mother said, her voice filled with anger.

"We will, Mother," I assured her. "We'll deal out the end they deserve."

"I'll start the hunt now," Jax said.

"No," I said, my voice firm. "We will come up with a plan, and we will do it together. The four of us."

Jax narrowed his eyes on Uriel. *What was it with him?* His focus was important if we wanted to do this right. I needed to talk to him about what had him riled up.

"Michael?" I called him to me and gestured to Mother. "Will you?"

"Of course." He slipped into my place as I stood up.

Mother leaned against him, her gaze as distant as it could be.

"Jax, can you walk with me?"

He nodded, and I led him to the room where Mother and Michael had gone for tea. I glanced over my shoulder to see Uriel watching us.

I closed the door to the break room.

"What's going on, Jax? You seem off."

He stood silent in front of me and crossed his arms in front of his chest.

"Are you not talking? You've never not talked to me." I

placed my hands on his shoulders. "Well, except for this past year."

He pulled me to him with a force so strong I collided with his chest. He growled.

I looked up into his eyes and saw heat. "Jax," I whispered and wrapped my arms around his neck.

He lowered his mouth to mine. His lips met my own with an urgency like he had to claim me. He coaxed my lips apart. I welcomed him into my mouth. My body stirred to life.

I broke our kiss and met his gaze, a gaze full of desire. As much as I wanted this, and I did want it, this wasn't the right time or place.

His behavior wasn't normal for Jax. I suspected it had to do with being a new vampire. He was still learning to control the urges vampires have. Even as I reasoned through it, my heart fell. I've wanted him since I could remember but not due to some misguided vampire urge.

"What's going on with you?" I whispered, my voice rough with desire. I ran my fingers through his hair.

"You're mine," he said. "Not his."

Jax had never been the possessive type, and I wasn't his. I wasn't anybody's. "Who? I don't understand." I searched his eyes and watched the desire turn to rage.

"Uriel," he said, his tone acerbic. "The way he looks at you. I can't stand it. I don't want anyone else looking at you like that but me."

I narrowed my eyes at him and pushed him away. "You are acting like this because of my uncle? Gross, Jax." I stepped back out of his reach. "All the times I wanted you to touch me, kiss me, hold me... and it takes a weird uncle showing up for you to make a move like this? You didn't act like this when I told you about Stassi."

I paced back and forth and headed for the door. "Fuck you, Jax."

"Rena," he said, and gently touched my arm.

My name so soft on his lips that it made me turn to meet his eyes.

There was remorse and hurt in them. If I put it there, I needed to fix that.

"Tell me what is going through your head to make you think there is anything between my uncle and me. That's just sick," I said, my voice disgusted even though I tried to hide it.

"Demons and angels don't have the same boundaries or barriers that humans do. The way he looks at you is hard for me to watch."

"Jax, do you really think that is me? That I would do something like that?" I was insulted he would think I wanted anyone but him. I'd loved Jax most of my life. First as a friend and then as more, even before I realized it. I loved him even if I hadn't said it to him yet.

"No, but I don't trust him," he said.

"Then trust me," I said. "And when we get through this current crisis, we can figure out what we have here." I gestured between us. "Deal?"

"Deal," he said, and pulled me back to him. "A deal sealed with a kiss."

I leaned into him and gave into the moment. Gave in to his kiss. It deepened and all the worry and strife around us disappeared. The touch of his lips to mine washed away the rest of our world.

When he broke the kiss, he looked into my eyes and tucked a stray strand of hair behind my ear. His hand rested against my cheek. "I promise I'll try to do better, but if I kill your uncle, will you ever forgive me?"

I laughed. "I might kill my uncle." I focused on the seriousness of the situation. "We need to get along right now, Jax. All five of us, because we might be the only chance this world has for a future. We don't know what is going on, and we need to figure it out and fast."

"You're right. My loyalty, as always, is yours."

"Thank you," I said. "I'm glad you're here. There isn't anyone else I would want by my side to face whatever shitshow is waiting for us."

"I've got you." He took my hand and walked out the door.

Mother was upright and looking more herself. Michael was close to her like he was ready to catch her if she passed out. Uriel looked uncomfortable and averted his eyes from Jax and me.

Mother turned her weakened gaze at me. Strength looked back at me. "We think we know what is happening, and we have a plan."

CHAPTER 35
JAX

Lilith tried to reason with Rena, but her feelings for me got in the way.

"Absolutely not." Rena's voice was so enraged it trembled.

"I'm fine with it," I said. "I'm a soldier of Hell. I've faced worse."

"You are not going to be the bait to try to trap the angels who killed Alessia. She was a badass bitch, and they killed her. Not happening with you," she said, her tone obstinate.

I raised an eyebrow at her. "I'm a badass too, Rena."

"I didn't mean it like that, Jax," she said, her voice softening. "I just meant we don't know how many of them there are or what they used to wield angel fire. It could be a no-win situation to send someone into that scenario."

Of course, I knew what she meant, but I liked seeing her fuss over me, especially with Uriel here.

"And you are a vampire now. Not a demon. You don't have a demon's strength."

"I'm still very strong and capable. You are really taking all the jabs at my ego." I bantered with her not only to argue my point but with the hope it would help ease some of her stress.

"No," she said. "I know what you are capable of, but I don't want you to die either."

She whirled to her mother.

"It's the only way this plan will work," Lilith said. "Like serial killers, they have been targeting my children when they are isolated. That would suggest that they are few and not numerous."

"We need to think of something else," Rena said.

Uriel took a step forward, and I met his gaze. He stopped his advance toward her.

"Rena." Lilith's voice was gentle. "We are out of time and out of options. It has to be this, and it has to be now before they realize we know they're responsible."

Light flashed and Michael appeared from his mission to see what he could find on the angel gossip network.

"As we suspected, none of the archangels know about this group or what is going on," he said.

I deflated. The hope was that something would be out there.

"But," Michael said. I looked up. "I called in a favor with a friend, and there have been rumblings of an extremist group among the lower-level angels."

"Isn't it your job to keep them in line?" I asked.

"No, they have their tasks just as we do," Uriel answered.

I inched closer to Rena.

"What have they heard, Michael?" Lilith asked.

"The angels are taking up Uriel's fight from centuries ago. They want to rid the world of Nephilim but also of half demons and vampires. The group believes all are abominations who shouldn't be in existence."

"I am their dream come true then," I said. "I'm a former half demon who is now a vampire. I fulfill a sick fantasy for them."

Rena leveled me with her gaze. Her eyes narrowed on me. My cock twitched. Even when she was angry or annoyed by me, she was sexy as sin.

"I don't like this," she said. "We don't know much more than we did before Michael left."

"We do know where they are hunting at the moment," he said, his voice solemn and almost apologetic.

Uriel picked up the black velvet bag and headed to the incinerator. I watched him as Michael continued to talk.

"They hunt in smaller groups and focus on those separated," he said. "And there are several of these packs near the campsites of both Azazel's side and your Father's side."

Uriel slid the Ascendant into the velvet back and tied it to his waist. He didn't hide his actions, but I wondered why he retrieved it.

"I presume you know an optimal location where I can be staged?" I asked.

Michael watched his brother. Concern etched his face when he turned back to me. "Yes, I have the area where the group who we presume killed Alessia is stationed."

"What about Father? The final wave will be starting anytime," Rena said.

"Then we need to hurry. If we stop these angels," Uriel

said, his voice laden with disgust, "we can probably stop the war."

"For now," Michael whispered.

What did he mean for now? Was there something else that would draw the King of Hell to a war in the Overworld?

No one else seemed to have heard him, but Uriel shifted his weight. Nervous activity from an angel wasn't normal. He met my gaze, and I saw sadness there. For someone responsible for countless deaths in his long existence, he seemed concerned about what was to come. There would be death.

Michael went to the map on the wall. He pointed to a spot almost an equal distance from the camps but north into a portion of the forest. "Jax, can you portal us here?"

I zeroed in on the location and visualized it. "Yes, ready when you are."

"Everybody clear on their role today?" Michael asked the question to all of us, but his gaze settled on Rena.

Rena stared at me. I saw fear in her eyes. She wasn't afraid of anything, and I hated that I might be the reason it was there. I wanted to ask her to stay and not go, but she'd refuse and be angry with me for even asking. Demons were raised to fight. We lived for this shit.

"Don't die," she said to me and faced Michael. "Yes, totally clear on the plan."

I called the portal and we stepped through. The group dispersed to their designated locations. My adrenaline spiked, anticipating the coming attack. I sniffed the air for Nephilim, but I only smelled our group.

I wandered around in the path we determined, but nothing happened. I moved toward the opening from the forest into the clearing where Azazel and Lucifer would likely battle with their armies.

I inhaled the air. The field was damp, and the wet-grass scent filled my nostrils. A familiar rustling noise drew my eyes up. Two angels with grey wings, not black like Rena's but a dirty grey, landed on each side of me.

"What are you?" one of them asked and cocked his head. "You smell strange."

I'd never seen this kind of angel before. Their teeth were sharp like the fingernail shape Lilith favored, and their eyes were solid black orbs. But the odor in the air was angel. Nothing else.

"I could ask you the same thing," I said. "What the fuck are you?"

"Your nightmares," the other one said. He had a metal mace covered in sharp spikes in his hand. Angel fire dripped from it. That had to be the weapon that delivered the damage to Alessia and ended her existence. They picked the wrong ex-half-demon vampire to mess with today. But Alessia would have been able to handle these two weirdos.

Something rustled above me, and many more of these odd angels dropped around me. I was surrounded, and I had the answer as to how they defeated a proven warrior like Alessia.

"Are you alone, vampire?" the one with the mace asked.

"I'm the only vampire here," I answered.

The grey-winged angels moved in toward me. Rena and Lilith emerged from the woods, drawing catlike hisses from the crowd around me.

Michael and Uriel dropped with their white wings spread wide.

"I am Michael, and this is my brother, Uriel," he said. "Perhaps you have heard of us."

The odd angels exchanged looks. "What kind of angel are you?"

"We are the originals. The archangels," Uriel said. "Where are you from?"

One pointed toward Azazel's camp, and another one slapped her hand down.

"Judgement on you has been made by your seniors, and no mercy shall be shown. Your sentence is death," Michael said.

Zadkiel, Michael's favor he called in, dropped in position. He was easy to spot because he was the only bald angel. The help welcomed.

The archangels displayed their swords and other artifacts reserved for war. Angel fire poured from them. Each step was a precise movement that resulted in one of the grey wings losing its head. One rolled near my feet, and I punted the bastard away like a football.

A smaller, grey-winged angel took off running and leaped into the air. Rena had her wings unfurled and was flying after him.

I didn't have fucking wings, so I ran along the ground as fast as I could to follow them.

The pace to keep them in sight was brutal even for a vampire. I pushed forward. I wasn't letting them out of my sight. My eyes trained on Rena's movements. She was on his heels and close to catching him.

A blur exploded from the forest and collided with my side. I slammed into a tree. Pain radiated through my body. The agony was like nothing I'd experienced save when Gabriel's sword impaled me.

"What are you?" The words were a hiss in my ear.

I pushed against the beast on top of me. "People keep asking me that, and I keep returning the favor. What the fuck are you?"

My back was broken, and it wasn't going to be an instant heal. I wasn't sure if I could fight this thing off of me in this condition while my insides stitched back together. But I'd go as long as I could. I shoved hard against the thing. *Fuck. Lucifer in Hell, that hurt.* The beast landed a few feet away, and I got a good look at it. It was another one of those dingy, grey-winged fuckers, but this one was twice the size of the biggest one over there, easily taller than Uriel.

I gritted through pain and forced myself to stand. I wasn't going down without a fight. My back wouldn't straighten, and I was acutely aware that my torso leaned to the left. My legs would be useless for hand-to-hand combat, and I wasn't sure my arms were going to be helpful either. I tightened the muscles in my core and let out a groan. *Fuck this motherfucker.*

The ugly bastard ran toward me at full speed. I prepared myself against the pain and dove at his leg. The bone snapped with a loud crack, and I rolled away. The creature howled like he was being gutted.

"Shut the fuck up," I said, my voice shaking from pain.

His moaning stopped, and he stood, his recovery faster than mine.

I tried to stand, but I couldn't get to my feet, my back further damaged from the dive I'd performed. I reached for my demon dagger, but it wasn't on my hip. I'd left it in Hell, thinking a vampire shouldn't carry it.

The grotesque angel stalked closer to me.

"It's a shame to kill you," he said. "You are a formidable adversary."

"I'm sure there's a compliment in there, but I'll pass on what you are serving." I resigned myself to death, but not without regrets. I wanted one more moment with Rena. One more kiss from her lips. One chance to show her how much I loved her.

He withdrew a sword. Angel fire dripped from the metal, and I knew from my experience Gabriel's blade, it was going to feel like I would explode. *Maybe I would.*

Rena, I hope you are safe. I love you.

I opened my eyes, and the hideous bastard was right in front of me.

He drew the sword back, and I steeled myself, ready for death.

A zing passed my ear, and I caught sight of a blade. I followed it to its destination. Right into the angel's chest. He jerked and waited. I recognized the blade. It was Lucifer's. The one he gifted to Rena.

I glanced over my shoulder and saw her leap into the air with one flap of her wings. She planted her foot against the hilt of the blade and drove it in deep. I let out a breath even though I didn't need air. She'd saved me again. Rena grasped the handle and retrieved the blade. She wiped the blood from the angel on his clothes. It was black like his eyes.

"He was a big one." Rena held out her hand to me.

I shook my head. "My back is broken."

She sat down next to me. Her hand rested on my cheek. Warmth spread in me from her touch. "Thanks for not dying, but we can't stay here. There are more of them out there."

CHAPTER 36

RENA

"Are you doing okay?" I asked Jax again and didn't care if it annoyed him as long as it distracted him. Seeing him in pain reminded me of how close to death he was before when I asked Mother to turn him. The fear gripped me in the same way and sweat was beading on my forehead from the nerves.

He shifted in my arms. "I think I can stand now. Set me down."

I set him on his feet. He grimaced and rocked a little, obviously still in pain. I reached out to him, and he pushed my hand away.

"It's almost healed," he said with a forced smile. "I can walk from here."

"We should be getting close to the others," I said.

Jax inhaled the air deep in his lungs. "I smell all four of them." He paused. Disgust twisted his face. "There is another scent. It's like angel but mixed with rotted garbage in a back alley."

"That's the blood from the new angels," I said.

"New angels?"

"That's what I'm calling them in my head. Someone created them. They are not part of the normal rank and file."

"Why would someone create those?" Jax wondered aloud, looking around.

"For war," I said, unable to keep the disdain out of my voice. "They were preparing for a battle we didn't know was coming."

"You have always hated surprises." Jax's labored steps were painful to watch, but he moved faster with each one.

"Yes, it's never been my thing, and we've been caught off guard every step of the way since this all started," I said. "I don't know how to get ahead of them when we don't know what their end game is."

"It's unusual for you to get flustered." Jax's steps smoothed out and his back straightened.

"I'm always flustered around you." *Fucking A. Did I just say that out loud?* My cheeks burned, and I was sure they were the bright crimson of Hell's fires. "Like when you would best me on the mat."

A broad smile was plastered across Jax's face, and I glanced into the woods.

"Rena?" Jax's voice turned serious.

My senses went on alert. I studied our surroundings. "What do you see? Smell one?"

"No, nothing like that. I thought I was going to die back there or turn to ash as vampires do." He cleared his throat and stopped.

I turned to look at him.

"There was only one thought on my mind when I understood the outcome of that fight." He locked eyes with me. There was something powerful there, and it caused me to be lightheaded. My heart fluttered. "It was you, Rena. You were the only thought for me."

"Jax." I rested my hand against his face and rubbed my thumb across his cheek. His eyes closed, and I pulled him to my chest.

He wrapped his arm around my back and squeezed me. It was too tight, but I didn't dare tell him. He pulled back and cupped my face in his hands.

His eyes were full of love. He dipped his head and brushed his lips across mine. The touch was a gentle kiss, but the meaning felt significant. The act wasn't a kiss of need but a promise of what the future could be.

Jax had been my love even before I realized, but our futures were uncertain. I didn't know what awaited us or what surprise was next. As much as I loved him, I had to focus on my father, Azazel, and whatever the fuck these new angels were. I was suddenly nervous and pulled back. "We better find to the others."

Mother ran over to us. She never ran. Her arms wrapped around both of us. "I was worried about you."

Carnage was strewn around us from the punishment Michael, Uriel, and Zadkiel unleashed, but one of them was missing.

"Where's Zadkiel?"

"He left as soon as it was done," Michael said. "He doesn't like the cleanup."

"I don't blame him." My nose wrinkled at the sight. "What do we do with them?"

"We should burn them," Uriel said.

"If we make a bonfire out of these corpses, we're going to draw attention."

"I think we've already done that." Michael smirked. "They know we know."

I punched his arm. "Do you know that for sure? Like from your angel hive-mind thing?"

Michael laughed. "Something like that. The archangels are all aware, and we weren't removing a threat inside a cone of silence."

"Truth," I said. "But it will be like a lighthouse shining the way to us."

"There are two archangels and the Mother of Night Children, who have all lived thousands of years here. We'll be fine," Michael said.

I nodded, but a sick feeling formed in my gut. "We better get to work then."

CHAPTER 37

RENA

"Last one." Jax slung the headless corpse on top of the pile. Uriel tossed a head into the mix.

Michael extended his wings and plucked a feather. Angel fire erupted from it, and Michael tossed it onto the mound. Uriel repeated the action. As the only other one here with wings, it seemed natural I should do the same. I unfurled my wings and yanked one out. *Damn. That one hurt.*

Hell's fire dripped like small streams of lava off my feather, and I concentrated on it. The fire grew, and it was too hot for me to hold. I tossed the flaming quill onto the heap. The angel and demon fires merged together and enveloped the stack of bodies.

"We should go," Michael said, turning to Jax. "Are you able to call a portal to take us back to the lab?"

"What?" He couldn't be serious. There was way more to do. "We can't leave a fire burning in the middle of the woods."

"Our fires will not burn the woods down, because we do not wish it so," Uriel said.

"But we haven't stopped anything and only got minimal answers. We need to push forward," I said.

"What do you want to do, Rena?" Uriel asked. His gaze burned so intensely it was like a pressure hold on me.

Jax moved to my side. I relaxed having him near and let out a breath.

"Why do you want to save the humans?" Uriel asked. "Save this world?"

Everyone waited for my response, and my chest felt like it caved in on me. *Why did I want to save the people and this world? Because it was the right thing to do? Because we all need each other to exist and maintain the balance? Didn't we?*

"For balance," I said. "We all have our roles to play in the balance—my father, my mother, the archangels, the humans."

Uriel nodded. "And you, my niece, you have a role to play in the balance that can easily tip the scales in either direction. Your decision will decide for us all."

"I don't understand," I said. "What do I have to do with it? I'm just a demon."

"You are so much more than that, Morena," he said. "You are the living embodiment of balance. It's why you feel remorse and pain for those you killed in haste. It's why you want to protect your loved ones. It's why you don't judge individuals as good or bad. You are the personification of the line that none of us can cross."

I grabbed my head against the dizziness taking me over.

Uriel's words jumbled in my head. My vision narrowed like entering a tunnel. My vision went black.

I came to in the lab laid out on a table like Alessia had been before she died. *Fuck. Am I dying?* I did a quick assessment and nothing hurt. My head was a little foggy, but there wasn't any pain. The scent of a fresh cup of Earl Grey tea wafted around me. I sat up and strong arms were around me.

"Jax," I rested my head against his chest.

"It's me," he said, his voice soft. "How are you feeling?"

"Fine," I said. "A little hazy but fine."

"Here." He handed me a cup of tea. "Drink this and see if it helps."

I inhaled the floral and green with a hint of orange and took a sip. "That's good."

"Is it still warm? I made it a few minutes ago."

"It is," I said. "Thank you, Jax."

Jax tucked loose hair behind my ear. "Are you sure you're okay?"

"I am. Where are the others?"

"If your mother wasn't with them, I'd say they were comparing dick sizes," Jax said.

I laughed. "They still might, and Mother probably has the biggest."

Jax laughed then. "You're right. She can be intimidating."

"Did I hit my head, or did Uriel really tell me I am the balance?"

"You didn't hit your head, and it wasn't a dream. He did say that," Jax said.

"What the fuck does that even mean?"

"Doesn't it make sense though?" Jax asked. "The way the air shifts in the room when you are there?"

The what? I stared at Jax in silence.

"I mean how everything changes when you are there." His face turned pale and his cheeks took on a pinkish tone. "You know what I mean."

I smiled. "I'm not entirely sure I do, but I like that you're flustered."

"Rena," he said. "Be serious. I think we should leave before they come back."

"Why?"

"Your mother was pissed at Uriel, and I expect her to come back with his head in her hands."

I laughed again. "Mother would never kill one of my uncles. It's like an unwritten agreement between the archangels. Besides, where would we go that they couldn't find us?"

Jax let out a long breath. "I guess that's true, but I'm worried about you."

"I want to understand what Uriel was telling me. I'm not going anywhere," I said.

The door opened. Mother walked in like the leader she was, followed by my uncles. However, I'd never seen two archangels look like scolded children, but that is exactly what Michael and Uriel looked like.

"It appears we may have overstepped, Rena," Michael said. "And we would like to offer our apologies."

Uriel said nothing and stood like a soldier with a stoic expression.

"I'm not sure how you overstepped, but I do want to

know what you meant." They were not getting off that easy. I leveled a gaze at all of them including my mother. *Answers would be given today.*

"It's complicated, Rena," Michael said.

Uriel's expression hardened. If I wasn't mistaken, his look said he wanted to talk. *So why didn't he?*

"Mother? Why are my uncles not sharing information as freely about me? And why do I get the feeling the reason has everything to do with you?"

"There are some things that must come in time, and you must trust me when I say this is one of them," she said.

"The things that were said cannot be taken back. I know there is more to what has been happening. I don't want it to be hidden from me any longer."

"I'll tell you the truth," Uriel said.

I nodded. "Proceed."

He cleared his throat and turned to my mother. "Lilith, forgive me for what I must do."

"I will not." She turned her back to him.

"When you were born, Rena, the conception was a mystery to us. Lucifer was an archangel, but Lilith was the original vampire. She could turn humans into vampires, but she couldn't have children," he said. "Or so we thought until she became pregnant with you."

I glanced in Mother's direction, but she still had her back to us and her head was lowered. I found Jax's gaze and received the support I needed. He moved closer to me.

"Your mother reached out to one of our own for guidance. Zadkiel obliged with little known knowledge of artifacts. While he couldn't give her the exact answer, it was within these artifacts that Lilith found an answer."

"And what was that answer?" *Breathe in. Breathe out.*

"She opened her womb with Lucifer's blade, and it allowed a seed to take root."

"Me," I whispered.

"Yes, you," Uriel said, his voice gentle.

"And that is why Father gifted me with that blade," I said. "It is as much a part of me as it is him."

"Yes," Uriel touched my shoulder. "That is why. And why your aunts and uncles are so connected to you even when you don't know we are. Why you are not Nephilim. Why you are much more than any of us."

"And why did you never tell me this, Mother?"

"I promised your father I wouldn't," she said.

"Why would you make such a promise, and why would father expect you to?"

"I wanted you to always see yourself as the miracle you are but without expectations attached to your life. Your father didn't want you to know angels had been involved with my pregnancy so that your choices were yours," she said.

And who am I? What does that make me?

CHAPTER 38

RENA

"So, what am I then? Are my parents still my parents?"

"Your parents will always be your parents," Uriel said. "You are still the daughter of Lilith and Lucifer. That does not change with the blade creating space for you."

"Would I have been born without it?"

"No," Uriel said. "Your mother's womb was frozen and a fetus could not form there."

"I don't have any siblings because I have the blade. Father gifted it to me?"

"No," Mother said. "We chose to only bring you into this world because we weren't sure if there were consequences we didn't know. We have always loved you. From the first day of conception to your birth and equally as much if not more today. We are proud of you. So very proud."

"We'll talk about your role later," I said to my mother. I was angry with her, but I still loved her. I didn't want her to think that had changed. "Michael, you've been quiet. Are you going to add anything to this story?"

He met my gaze. "Uriel speaks the truth. The blade is tied to you. It allowed your mother's womb to nourish a child but trust us when we say your parents are your parents."

"But how does that make me the balance? Can someone explain that for me?" My patience was spread thin, and I wanted answers.

"That is not as simple to explain," Uriel said. "But I will try. Any artifact of an archangel is infused with a certain amount of their power. In some cases, these artifacts have special significance, and in the case of Lucifer's blade, there is a very special circumstance."

"What kind of circumstance?"

"It was forged with angel fire in Hell and imbued with Lucifer's power. This was done before he fell from Grace, but after he had declared his love for Lilith."

"So, his love created a path across both sides of the equation," I said.

"Yes," Michael confirmed. "More or less."

Uriel let out a breath. "Your ability to sit on either side of the line of balance is important because those who follow you will follow you to either."

"Follow me where though? I'm not a general to lead them into battle," I said.

"Aren't you?" Michael arched a brow and pressed on. "Didn't we all follow you here and into a forest to fight an enemy we didn't know? We will not be the last to do so, Rena. We need to prepare you."

"But what about the battle my father is ready to wage with Azazel? It needs to be stopped, and I don't know how."

"Be careful with which side you choose. You might lead

those who follow you to their end only to find it was the wrong path," Uriel said.

"Do not respond to me if you only have cryptic shit to say. I understand the importance of this, and I will do the right thing," I said. "But I neither have the time nor the patience to listen to riddles."

"I wasn't talking in a riddle," Uriel said. "Any choice you make impacts the balance between worlds."

"You keep saying balance, but isn't it always tipped in your favor? Is that really balance?" I met Uriel's hardened gaze with my own.

Uriel snapped his mouth shut.

They gave me so little information about my situation. *Am I angel? Am I demon? Or both? Did I have a special angel power like they did?* The explanation from my uncles made it sound like both. Father's blade always found its way back to me. *Could it be part of the enchantment of the blade?*

"The third wave should be about halfway through, Rena," Jax said from his place by my side. "We should prepare for the battle to come."

"How do I do that when I don't understand the consequences or even if what I'm being told today is the truth?"

"You love your Father," Jax said. "And you want to save him from a terrible decision that could shift the balance. I believe that could happen regardless of where you stand on the situation."

"That is the first thing anyone has said on the subject that I can identify with or believe," I said. "Let's figure out how to move this battle to Hell."

"I have an idea about getting us close enough to your

father to shock him. That could release the influence of the Ascendant enough that we can free him," Jax said.

"And if it doesn't work?"

"We'll remove him from the equation by any means necessary. You can use me for it if you need to," Jax said, his expression firm.

I saw the pain in his eyes. He didn't like this any more than I did, and he was looking for a last-ditch effort to stop the war.

We didn't know who my father would be when we got close to him. The Ascendant could have permanently altered him. It would break my heart to find him that way. He'd always been such a loving and doting father in my child-hood. Today, that part of him was shut off, and he was a general commanding his army. The decisions he made were cold and calculated like many of those he punished.

"So, how do we shock my father's system enough?" I asked.

"Lightning would be the best, but it is unpredictable. Something else to shock his system like a defibrillator or some other mechanism like that but stronger than is used on humans," Michael said.

"Is it that simple?" I looked at Michael and Uriel.

"We cannot tell you how to facilitate this. It has to be your decision. "

"I guess we'll try this plan, then, and hope that it works," I said. "For all our sakes."

There was only one source I could think of to give me the power needed to free my father.

"Uriel, if I summon Barachiel, can I trust her?"

"She is a general for your father," Uriel said. "You know better than I where her loyalties are."

"If I knew I wouldn't ask."

Barachiel did things her own way. When she followed Father and made her fall from Heaven, she pledged her loyalty to him, but she'd been largely absent through the years. She showed up for events, and she supported Father.

"I cannot answer for you. You must decide for yourself," Uriel said.

"Fine," I turned away from him. "Barachiel, sister of my father, I summon thee to here and now."

The light in the room tinted to a shade of green like the color of spring grass. Barachiel materialized in front of me holding a white rose.

"Thank you for coming Aunt B." I hadn't seen her in some time, but I used the name I'd called her when I was a kid and couldn't pronounce her full name.

"It's not like I had a choice with a summons, Morena, but I would not have ignored you," she said, her voice gentle and kind. She looked over my shoulder. "Brothers, Lilith." My uncles nodded but didn't say a word. As far as I knew, they hadn't spoken more than two words in centuries. She paused. "I recognize you, but I don't know your name."

"Jax." He held out his hand.

"Oh, yes. I remember you now," she said. "Morena's friend."

"That's me." Jax met my gaze. His expression hardened a bit and his body stiffened. "The friend."

"Jax has been around for some time, Aunt B," I said.

"Of course," she said. "I meant no harm."

"I'm sure you didn't," I said and forced a smile. "I need your help."

"I assume this is about your father," she said.

"You assume correctly." If she returned to my father, this would be treason for sure, but we'd committed it already.

CHAPTER 39

RENA

Aunt B's face contorted into something between shock and amazement, and I wasn't sure which was better in this case.

"So, you want me to strike Lucifer, King of Hell, with a lightning bolt in the chest?" Her eyes widened.

"Yes, exactly," I said.

"Do you understand what you are asking?" She turned to face her brothers. "Did one of you put her up to this?"

"No, Sister, we did not," Michael said.

"You are aware we cannot, Barachiel," Uriel said.

"That doesn't mean you won't though," Barachiel quipped back with a smile that didn't reach her eyes. "And what of Gabriel?"

"He did not," Michael said. "He's been dealing with his own... struggles."

"Gabriel? That's a terrible sign," she said, her voice full of concern. "If the messenger is incapacitated, we are at a disadvantage."

"We are aware," Uriel said. "Very aware."

"Then we are all in agreement that this is the only way?" Barachiel asked her brothers.

"We are," Michael said.

"Yes." Uriel grimaced.

"If you are not, now would be the time to speak. Once this course is started, it cannot be undone," Barachiel said.

Both Michael and Uriel remained silent, and it wasn't the first time I'd observed this. They were two of the most powerful angels, but they did not assert themselves in front of her.

"Very well then," Barachiel said. "Since we know you have made the decision, I will strike Lucifer with a lightning bolt. We should discuss the possible outcomes so you are prepared."

Barachiel narrowed her eyes on Michael and Uriel. "And you will both be available to Morena if she needs you. Are you willing to do that?"

"Yes," they said in unison.

"Lilith, you will need to step back and allow her to do what she thinks is best."

"Understood." Mother's posture stiffened.

"And Jax." Brachial handed him the white rose she held. "She will need you by her side through it all. Are you able to support her in whatever decisions she makes?"

"As I have in our past and present, so will I in our future," he said.

I warmed on the inside, but my cheeks burned.

"Morena, if you are sure, let us begin," she said. "There are three possible outcomes that will happen. One option you must be aware of is that if I hit him with the wrong dose of lightning, he could die. Even an angel as strong as Lucifer is not able to withstand a full measure of lightning direct from Heaven. It is unlikely this will happen, but I must tell you to prepare yourself in case it does."

I swallowed, and it lodged in the knot in my throat. The point of this was to save my father, not kill him. If there was any risk of death for him...

"Morena, back to me," she said.

I snapped from my thoughts.

She continued. "The second option is he never recovers, and this is almost as bad as the first one. He could permanently be locked in a transient state between life and death, and for an angel, that is forever. Our bodies do not break down like a human's." She glanced at Mother and Jax. "Or a vampire."

Both options so far were terrible. Neither was what I wanted. Neither set him free from the Ascendant and the second was more like an eternal purgatory of a prison.

"What's the third option?" I asked, my voice trembling from the dread of how bad this one would be.

"The third and final option is that he is incapacitated but will make a full recovery. This is the one we want to achieve."

That was the only viable one in my mind. The other two scared the fire out of me. "How do we make sure we get that one?"

"There are no guarantees, Morena. You need to understand that the risks are real and while the first two options are not likely, they could happen. You must decide if the risks are worth it. Could you live with yourself if they were to occur? Could you live with yourself if you did nothing?"

Jax slipped a hand around my waist and pulled me to his side. I sank into him.

No child should have to decide this around their parent. Father had done everything to keep me safe for my entire life, and yet I stood here with his fate in my hands. The angel everyone feared most, and his existence seemed so fragile at the moment.

But the other option of the Ascendant consuming him and controlling him at someone else's will was worse. My father's free will was everything to him, and I knew he wouldn't want to live a life of servitude.

"And who will run Hell while he is incapacitated?" I asked.

"There is only one who can hold the throne in your father's absence," Barachiel said, her gaze focused on me. "That is you, Morena."

I sighed. Part of me knew this was coming. Father had groomed me for it from the day of my earliest memories. The hardest part would be for Jax because I wouldn't have time for him. I'd seen how Father and Mother had days where they barely saw each other when Mother was in Hell. There were days when I barely saw Father because of his commitments and duties.

Jax pulled me tighter to his side, and I looked into his eyes. I saw the same fear there. *Would this break us along with my Father? And if it did, what would happen to the balance?*

CHAPTER 40
JAX

I stared into Rena's eyes. The decision solidified in the darkness of her pupils. Her mind was firmly made up, and I knew what she was going to say before she said it. I loved her determination and perseverance, but real fear gripped my heart that this would be the end for us.

"I understand," she said. "We will move forward."

Hearing the words was like a weight landing on me... on my entire body. I stared down at the floor like a different answer would be written there.

"But I will not accept the first two options. The third one is the only one," Morena said, her voice commanding and strong.

I snapped my head back up toward her. Her eyes were locked with Barachiel's. *Did she just threaten a powerful angel?*

"The line is thin on how much power is enough and how much is too much," Barachiel said. "I cannot promise a specific outcome."

"I'm not asking for your promise," Rena said. "I'm telling you how it will be."

She threatened a fucking angel. A high-level angel. That was like threatening a general in Hell.

Something flashed across Barachiel's face that looked like anger, but she returned to her catlike smile. "I'll do my best, but we are all subject to situations, Morena. That is all I can say."

Rena narrowed her eyes on her and pinned her with her gaze. "Then your best better be enough, Aunt B."

Lilith cleared her throat. "How close do we need for you to get the most accurate shot at him?" Her voice shook as she said the words. Fear marred her face.

"The range is vast, but a hundred yards will give me the best shot. I need to be uninterrupted when I pull the lightning to me. The interruptions can cause fluctuations, and lightning is a moody business," she said.

"I'll be your buffer," Lilith said. "I'll protect your back."

"Lilith," Michael said. "You can't do it alone."

"This is for my husband, and I can," she said with so much conviction.

I looked at Rena, and it settled over me that I had the same devotion to her that Lilith did to Lucifer. Rena was the only thing that mattered to me, and I'd burn not only the Overworld but Heaven and Hell to protect her. She was everything that made sense in this world, and nothing would matter without her.

"I'll stand with Lilith and Barachiel," Uriel said.

Michael touched Uriel's arm. "Are you sure, Brother? I could do it."

"No, it needs to be me. I'm the most feared, the reason the Ascendant exists, and the others will not challenge me."

"What am I missing?" Rena focused on Uriel. My skin crawled at the intensity with which she looked at him.

"We are choosing a side, Rena." Uriel's tone was soft. "We are breaking our own rules."

She swallowed hard. "So, the angels who don't agree..."

"Will no doubt try to stop us." Uriel's brown eyes were full of sadness. If I didn't hate the way he looked at Rena, I'd feel bad for him.

"It will be a different kind of war," Michael said, his eyes distant. "One that hasn't happened in two thousand years."

"Since Lucifer chose me," Lilith said, her voice barely a whisper. The guilt in her tone was audible.

The same guilt in Lilith's expression was on Rena's face. It was the first time she visibly wavered, but I suspected she'd been wavering inside the whole time. The war she thought she was stopping revived an old one that didn't end well last time. Lucifer didn't speak to all his siblings, and the divide would be worse... for those who survived this time around.

"Who will side with us?" Rena asked.

"Obviously, those in this room. Zadkiel tends to stay neutral," Michael said. "But he might choose in this case. I'm not sure where Gabriel's head is after everything, so I would not count on him choosing either unless forced."

"Raphael will not stand with us. He believes in the old ways," Uriel said.

"I don't expect Raziel to side with us either," Michael said. "Or any of the others."

Rena sighed. I pulled her closer to me, sending my strength to her. She leaned into me.

"What if they outnumber us?" I asked. "What do we do?"

"The number does not matter," Barachiel said.

"Says the only one of us who can control lightning." I turned to see Gabriel enter the room.

"Brother, are you well?" Michael asked.

"I am much recovered." Gabriel's voice was tinged with remorse. "It is regrettable I was affected, but I'm in control of myself now."

"That is good to hear, Uncle," Rena said. He was closest to her, but she didn't go to hug him like she would have before he kidnapped Lilith.

"We're glad you're here, Brother." Uriel grasped Gabriel's arm. "I hope you brought your sword."

I stiffened at the memory of Gabriel's sword in my chest. Rena ran her hand up and down my back and squeezed my waist. Her touch soothed my anxiety.

"Others are on their way," Gabriel said.

Zadkiel appeared through a bright light. "Were you calling me, Brothers? And Sister, I haven't seen you in so long." Zadkiel embraced Barachiel like the long-lost siblings they were.

"It is good to see you, Zadkiel," Barachiel said, holding on tight to her. "I miss our chats."

"We will do those again," Zadkiel said.

Barachiel's expression tightened. "I hope we do."

"We should get moving," Uriel said. "I'm assuming we want to fly over the area."

"Yes," Barachiel said, pulling away from Zadkiel. "We should."

"I'll go with you," Rena said.

Lilith and I didn't have wings, so we wouldn't be able to fly with the angels. A pit formed in my stomach at the thought of Rena being out there alone with them. They might be her aunts and uncles, but they were far from trustworthy in my eyes.

"I'll be fine," Rena whispered to me. She pressed a kiss against my cheek. "They are here for us."

"They are here for you and only you," I said. It should have comforted me, but it didn't. Instead, I'd never wished for wings more in my life. "I know you need to go, but I wish I could go with you."

"I know," Rena said. "I wish you could, too, but we have to trust them. This is so much bigger than we thought."

"It is," I said. I wrapped her up in a hug and didn't care who was watching. "We will succeed, and your father will be restored to himself."

"Do you really think this is going to work?" Rena whispered to me.

"I'm not one to trust angels, Rena, but I think this is the best shot. No matter what happens, I'm here for you. I'll do whatever you need me to do."

"Thank you, Jax," she said. "You don't know how much that means to me."

"Is everyone ready to go scout?" Barachiel asked.

Rena pulled away from me and looked up in my eyes. She gave me a tiny smile. "I'll be back soon."

The angels and Rena left Lilith and me in the lab, and I

felt like I was picking up broken pieces of myself off the floor. My heart ached at the absence of Rena, and I wished again for wings.

I walked the length of the room and turned to walk back.

"Do not pace, Jax." Lilith held out a hand in my path. "Morena did the same thing when you were injured."

Her eyes held sorrow in them, and I understood it on a level I never would have a few days ago. She could lose her husband and daughter, and I could lose my only father figure and the woman I loved. The sheer idea of losing Rena gutted me and hollowed me out from the inside. There was no world, Over or Under, without her.

A sharp pain intruded into my gut. I grabbed my stomach. "Lilith?"

She hooked her arm under mine. "What's wrong?"

"My gut," I said. "Stabbing."

"I should have warned you, but I thought there would be more time," she said, her voice panicked.

"More time for what?" I ground out.

"When Rena needs you, the bond between you will reach out whether she wants it to or not. We need to go find her now." Lilith pulled me toward the door. "Breathe through the pain, and it will be manageable.

I inhaled as she pushed me forward. And again. I forced myself to power through it, and it did get easier. When I was in control, Lilith and I moved at full vampire speed toward the direction my body indicated... toward Rena.

CHAPTER 41

RENA

I perched on the edge of the cliff with Barachiel on one side and Uriel on the other. Michael, Zadkiel, and Gabriel were on the opposite side. Others showed up as the minutes passed. Some I knew, and others were distant relations I didn't know at all.

The fear grew inside me as we scoped out the battleground area and the camps. Father's final wave had arrived, and his generals were moving the army into the formation for battle. Similarly, Azazel's army was grouped up in preparation, although they were sloppy and didn't have tight ranks like Father's. Azazel's lack of organization surprised me given his fondest for warfare. This wasn't a scouting mission after all. The time was imminent for combat.

I wished Jax was here. It was a selfish thought when so many others were here to support me, but he was the only one I wanted by my side. He was my strength, and he had been for longer than I'd realized. I felt incomplete without him near. Looking at the vast numbers of soldiers below, I understood I might not return to him. My insides were crushed by the possibility. I wanted more time with him, but the odds did not appear to be in our favor.

There was a lightning-wielding angel on our side, though, and our hopes for surviving and saving my father hinged on her. Everything today would be about protecting her so that her aim would be true.

"Someone is approaching," Uriel whispered.

"Angel or demon?" I asked.

"Neither." He paused, concentration on his face. "It is your mother and Jax."

Panic seized my chest. "Are they okay?"

"It's hard to tell. They are moving so fast," he said.

I inhaled but didn't catch any scent. "Which direction?"

Uriel held his hand out to me. "Come. I'll take you to meet them."

I glanced down at the field and then to Barachiel.

"Go," she said. "We'll let Uriel know if the action starts."

"Thank you," I said to Aunt B and took Uriel's hand. I dropped his hand as soon as I was standing.

Uriel leaped into the air, and I followed him. He hadn't flown that far when he started a descent.

"I don't see them."

"We'll intercept them," he said. "Their speed would be hard to interrupt otherwise."

I landed next to him on the path he selected. "How long?"

"It should be less than a minute," he said.

A rustling noise came toward us, and I got a whiff of both

of them. The tension in body eased a smidge that they were near.

"Jax," I whispered into the air. A breeze blew my hair, and he stopped right in front of me.

"Are you okay?" His hands roamed over my arms and cradled my face.

I relaxed into his touch. "Yes, but I'm glad you are here."

It was bittersweet to have him here. The risk was great, but my strength multiplied with him near, almost like he was half of me.

"I should have insisted on coming with you," he said, pressing his lips to mine. "And you're not hurt?"

"No, I'm fine. The battle hasn't started."

"But we do need to get back. It will not be long now," Uriel said.

"Have you seen Lucifer?" Mother asked, glancing between Uriel and me.

"Only briefly, Mom," I said. "He's wearing his Devil face all the time according to reports. You know he's not himself doing that. He hates that face as much as it is scary to humans."

She nodded. "Jax and I can follow your scent on the ground."

I leaped into the sky, and Uriel followed me this time. I kept an eye on the ground to make sure Jax and Mother went in the right direction.

"We could have carried them," I said and glanced at Uriel. The tension Jax washed away returned. It was hard to flap my wings and forced them to move.

Uriel's movements were stiff, and his eyes looked vacant.

"It's starting, isn't it?" My voice trembled with fear.

He returned to the present. "Yes, we need to hurry. Barachiel is preparing to summon the lightning bolt."

"Mother and Jax are on the right track. I think we can go ahead."

Uriel increased his speed. I pumped my wings to keep up.

The group came into view, and Barachiel was already in position to perform her task. I landed next to her and drew my father's blade from the sheath.

"We have you, Sister," Uriel said to Barachiel as he took his fighting stance. Michael gave a signal that he, Zadkiel, and Gabriel were ready as well.

Mother and Jax cleared the trees and took protective places. Mother stood where she had line of sight of the field. Jax faced the woods. I took one last look around. Everything would change from this moment, either for good or ... I wouldn't allow myself to think of the alternative. We had to be successful.

I nodded to Barachiel. She locked onto Father's position. Her eyes closed for a moment and were an electric blue when she reopened them. Brachial extended her arms out with palms up at the same time as her wings. She lifted off the ground, her attention fully on my father.

She whispered, "I call the lightning to my command. Thy bring death, but thee also bring rebirth. I call thee to rebirth Lucifer tonight."

A halo the same color as her eyes glowed around her. Her features were strong. The ring of blue intensified as she powered up. It would be beautiful if its destination wasn't my father's chest.

A small group of the weird angels from before appeared over the field. I glanced toward the other cliff peak to Michael. He gave one nod, and he, Zadkiel, and Gabriel were in the air with swords drawn. They sliced the grey-winged angels from the sky. The sight of angels dueling in the sky was biblical.

Unfortunately, the dropping bodies gave us away. Michael led the others in maneuvers as distractions. Barachiel was glowing blue. There wasn't much that could distract from that.

A larger group of the grey-winged angels flew toward the distraction. *How many of them are there?*

"I'm ready." Barachiel's voice vibrated with power.

"Father is there." I pointed. My arm down to my finger was what she would use to align her aim.

A handful of grey-wings surrounded us.

"We've got them," Uriel said.

"Anytime, Barachiel," I said.

"Don't rush me," she hissed. "This is your father."

I held my breath.

She focused the energy into a stream and drew her arm back like a spear.

"Rena," Jax called my name. "Look out!"

I turned my head. A flash of grey passed in front of me, and a shove slammed me into Barachiel. She and I tumbled to the ground and skidded to the edge of the cliff. The bolt she'd built rocketed to the field and exploded in a crowd of Azazel's army. I peered over the cliff to see the others scramble. *Fuck.*

I found Father's position. He appeared unphased by the disturbance and mowed down handfuls of Azazel's soldiers.

I extended my hand to help Barachiel up.

"Unless you want to get electrified, I'll get up myself."

"Can we try again?" The others were still fighting the grey-wings, and I wondered which one had hit me. I held Father's dagger out, hoping the bastard would approach.

"Yes, but I'll need a minute to get enough power back," she said.

"Make it a fast minute," I said. "These new angels are multiplying up here."

"I'll hurry, but we have to get enough power for it to work."

"Understood. Let me know when you're ready, and I'll come line you up." I dove into the fight next to Jax. He had four of the assholes circling him.

"Are you okay?" he asked.

"You need to stop asking me that. I'll be okay when my father is back to himself." I planted a foot in the knee of one of the weird angels, and the snap of it was satisfying.

"Noted." His double-fighting swords whipped through the air, taking the head of one of our enemies.

"Morena," Barachiel called.

"Don't die," I said to Jax.

"Already dead," he said and laughed as he cut another grey-wing across the middle.

I ran to Barachiel. I repeated the position from earlier. "Ready."

She launched the lightning bolt at Father. I held my breath and looked down my extended arm like a scope. The bolt struck him square in the chest as planned. Blue sparks shot out all around him, blanketing his army.

Father dropped to his knees. His eyes rolled back in his head. He slumped to the side and landed on the ground.

"Mother," I shouted. The plan worked, but I wasn't prepared for what that looked like.

She broke free from the fight and stood at the edge of the cliff with me. "Take us to him, Rena." She wrapped an arm around my neck, and I gripped her waist. I jumped off the side of the cliff. Wings flapped around us, and I prepared for an attack. When I looked to my left and right, all I saw were our allies. Thankful for their support even when my father was neutralized.

The demons on the battlefield were going to be the opposite.

CHAPTER 42

RENA

Father's supporters formed a ring around his body. Some howled out, and my fear spiked that the bolt might have been too strong. Aunt B's concentration was good. She landed the lightning burst with perfection. *Father will be fine. I believe it.*

"Rena, this will require death to cut a path to him. Some you know may fall," Uriel said, his voice a warning. He'd released me from my burden of those I'd taken before, but this would be a new round of guilt to haunt me.

I touched Uriel's arm. Jax stepped to my side, so close he almost touched me. "I understand. This is the way it must be."

Sadness filled his eyes. He was thought to be the hardest of them all, but inside there was a depth to him he kept so hidden no one else saw. It was a layer to him made of love and a juxtaposition of his hard exterior.

Our group navigated the fight like an obstacle course. Each time I faced a demon, Uriel was there on one side to end them and Jax on the other. It was ridiculous the way they didn't let me fight. I'd been trained for this kind of battle my whole life. Frustration spiraled in me, and I felt like I might explode.

"Stop," I yelled. My voice boomed out, but it wasn't my demon voice. The sound was something else. I didn't recognize it.

The battle sounds tapered off until there were none. All the demons froze in place. I spun. The entire battle stopped.

Demons from both sides bowed their heads and took a knee. I glanced at Mother.

"What is happening?" I whispered.

She looked from Michael to Uriel, but Gabriel propelled himself to stand in front of me.

"They are bowing to the Queen of Hell," he said.

Grief permeated my insides and shredded me into a thousand ragged pieces of soul. I found Father's body on the field and ran to him.

I dropped down next to him and checked for breathing. He wasn't dead, but he was in some kind of stasis. A light, bluish sheen covered his body from the lightning bolt. I held my hand over him and lowered my palm down to the light.

Zzzp. "Fuck." I jerked my hand away and cradled it. Pain throbbed up my arm.

"It will dissipate," Barachiel said. "I can move him through a portal, so you can take him home."

"Lucifer?" Mother knelt beside him. Her hand hovered over him as mine had. Tears spilled down her cheeks.

"Mom." I touched her arm and pulled her hand into mine. "It's going to take some time for him to wake up. His body needs to heal from the voltage. We need to get him out of here."

"Let's go home," she said. "Jax?"

He squatted down next to me. His gaze filled with concern. "Portal?"

"Yes, please."

He went to work on it, and Barachiel guided Father toward where Jax manifested the portal.

"Rena, your people will need their orders," Uriel said. "They are waiting on their queen to give them the direction they need."

"I don't know what to say to them," I said. I'd been trained as a fighter and a leader, but I didn't know how to fill Father's role. He was the only king Hell had ever known.

"Send them home," Uriel said. "Tell them this battle is over."

"But is it?" I asked. "Have we really resolved it? We won't know until Father wakes up."

"The war might not be over, but this battle is," Uriel said. "The moment you commanded the battlefield, the fight was done."

The demons were still on bended knee. In the distance, I saw the grey-winged weirdos weren't.

"He's right, Rena." Jax placed his hand on my lower back. His touch bolstered my confidence. "End it and send them home. We'll do the same."

"All right," I said, unsure what I was supposed to do or how I conjured that massive voice the first time.

I cleared my throat and inhaled a deep breath. "This battle is done. This day is done. Lieutenants, call your portals. Return home as I will with my father." My voice boomed out like it did before, so I hadn't needed to worry. I started toward the portal Jax opened, but I paused and turned around.

The lieutenants called their portals, but the others remained on one knee. I realized it was out of respect for my father. The angels thought most of the demons lacked respect, but they didn't. They knew exactly what that kind of deep admiration was.

"I'll see you all in Hell," I said and moved to the portal to walk through with my father and Barachiel. Mother on the other side and Jax beside me.

When we came through the other side, I was surprised to see Uriel, Michael, Zadkiel, and Gabriel with us.

"He is our brother, Rena," Uriel said, answering my unspoken question.

I nodded.

"I'd like to take him to our bedroom," Mother said. "He'll be most comfortable in our sanctuary."

Barachiel looked at me, and I stared back, waiting for her to move him forward.

It hit me. She was waiting on me. "I agree with my mother. He'd want to be in his own bed."

"This way," my mother said, leading Barachiel to their inner sanctum few had seen. It must be strange for Mother to have this group here in a place where the angels usually avoided, let alone have angels in her most private space here. It had to feel like her world shifted off its axis— as if it hadn't already with Father's situation.

"Will he forgive me?" I whispered and looked up into Uriel's solemn brown eyes.

"My brother is not one who forgives easily, but he does forgive. Have faith in the path you chose."

My heart ached like it was shredded, and every nerve in it was alive to transmit the pain. Jax slipped his arm around my waist, and I turned into his body. My head rested in the crook of his neck. For the first time, I allowed my pain to bleed out with the affliction of my decisions. I sobbed against him until my knees buckled. He picked me up and held me close to him.

"Let it all out," he said. "I've got you."

CHAPTER 43
RENA

We took turns sitting with my father. *All of us.* I hated when my time ended, and I knew Mother did too. Many times, she'd ask others to pull up a chair instead of leaving when the next person came to visit.

I had to leave at the end of my turn because I'd assumed the role of ruler in my father's absence. More than anything, I wanted to do him proud.

Uriel relieved me of my spot by Father. "I'll read to him," he said.

"He'd love that."

Jax waited at the door. He'd stayed close to me since our return. There for the cry, I'd had the first night, and there to support me as I figured out what it meant to rule while my father healed.

Jax slipped his hand in mine and laced our fingers together. "No change?"

"None," I said, my voice defeated.

"It's only been a week, Rena. Barachiel said it would take time." He squeezed my hand.

"But he's a demon or an angel or whatever celestial being the Devil is supposed to be. He should heal at super speed," I said, my frustration pouring out of me.

"He was hit by a lightning bolt forged from Heaven. That's not normal energy, and you can't expect his body to heal so quickly," he said. "And you want him to be himself when he does wake up."

"Yes." The more time that passed, I worried he wouldn't wake up at all, and when that thought took over, I drifted into the valley of despair. I rubbed my eyes. "What's on the agenda today?"

"Michael and Gabriel have an update on the grey-wings and have been scouting for Azazel's whereabouts. They believe they know where he is hiding."

"I've never been so ready to kill as I am with him. He fetched the Ascendant and started this in motion. Now, the rest of us are left to clean up the disaster he created." My anger grew, and I shook.

"Remember the breathing technique," Jax said. "In for four, and out for four." He had me practice the exercise when my emotions got out of control, and for the most part, it worked. "One more time."

I inhaled. *One. Two. Three. Four.* And exhaled. *One. Two. Three. Four.*

My body relaxed and the tremors subsided.

"Better?" He asked.

"I'm always better when you are near," I said.

"You give me too much credit," Jax said. His cheeks turned a deep crimson, at least deep for a vampire.

"Jaxon, did I make you blush?" I smiled. One of the few I'd managed since we returned.

"No," he said, angling his head away from me.

"I like it when you're vulnerable, Jax," I said, my voice low like the heat building in my belly. "It does... things to me."

He met my stare, and I saw desire in his eyes. If we didn't have intel on Azazel and the grey-wings, I'd fulfill whatever desire he wanted. There was longing in his gaze. In the way his survey lingered on my lips. The constant heat I had in my belly whenever he was near grew every day and only got stronger as time passed. I had so much to do here, but I wasn't sure how much longer I could go without him inside me. A deep need in my most inner self to show him how much he meant, how much I loved him, ached in me.

Jax cleared his throat and gestured to the door of the room where Michael and Gabriel waited for us.

I sighed and opened it. Chairs scraped against the floor. They both stood when I entered. "You are not my subjects. I don't know why you stand like you are."

They exchanged looks and took their seats. What message passed between their angel minds was a mystery to me, but I suspected it was something about me being stubborn.

"Jax said you have news on Azazel and the grey-wings," I said. "What have you found?"

"They are hiding in the Eden mirror world," Gabriel said.

"Then we must go soon," I said.

"We—" Michael glanced at Gabriel, and I saw fear. "Gabriel and I and the others think we should deal the justice. Leave your hands clean."

I leaned over the table and pressed my hands onto it. "The punishment is mine to deal. It is my father lying in a demon-style coma, and it was my decision that put him there. A decision I wouldn't have had to make if Azazel hadn't stolen Uriel's artifact."

In one... two... three... four.

"You should not be tainted by this, Rena," Gabriel said. "There is still much work for you to do, and your focus should be on those tasks."

"What tasks, Gabriel? What else have I to do?"

He hesitated, exchanging the same scared look with Michael.

"Your mother for one," Michael said. "Each day she falls into a deeper state of depression, and she looks pale even for a vampire."

I'd noticed it, too, and tried to get her to drink some blood. She'd refused me. Mother looked weak, and I was sure it had more to do with her soulmate lying unconscious than it did with hunger. It was like a little piece of her died each day he didn't wake up. I glanced at Jax. If it were him, I'd feel the same way.

He met my gaze, and the recognition there told me he matched my intense anguish.

Jax broke away and took a seat. "I agree with Michael. Your mother needs some coaxing, and she needs to know she is loved."

When he met my eyes again, I wasn't sure if we were talking about my mother or us.

"I'm going with you to Eden, but I will see to my mother first." As the seated ruler, it was my duty to resolve this issue and punish Azazel, but I couldn't leave without checking on Mother.

"She's in the private study looking for any texts concerning your father's condition," Jax said.

"Thank you." I squeezed his hand. "I'll meet you all back here as soon as Mother is situated."

I hurried down the hall to the study. The door was cracked open, and I found Mother with her feet tucked under her in a chair. The book she held was old.

"Have you found anything?" I took the seat next to her. She placed the open book on the small table between our chairs.

"Nothing useful," she said. She held out her hand to me, and I took it. "I'm afraid we are going to lose him, Rena."

The sadness in her voice and on her face sheared away my confidence. "Aunt B said he would recover."

"Barachiel says a lot of things." She dropped my hand and stared at one of the bookcases. "What if he doesn't?"

"He will, Mother," I said, leaning forward. "He will be himself before we know it."

"I hope you're right." She paused. "I'm not sure I'll survive it if he doesn't, and I can't imagine leaving you here alone."

She was in a worse state than I'd realized. Her internal thoughts led her down a path of grief, and Father was still alive. She needed a reminder.

"Remember how distraught I was when Jax was injured?"

"This is different."

"No, I don't think it is," I said. "You told me the decision was mine, but there wasn't a choice in my mind. Just like there isn't a choice for you. You have to live for him and for me."

"You are so persuasive, Rena." She reached out for my hand.

I placed mine in hers. "I love you, Mom."

She squeezed my hand so tight I was sure the blood would be pushed out of it. "You have no idea how special you are. I love you, my daughter."

I studied her closely, and she looked a little more alert. "Maybe today is the day."

"Maybe so," she said, her voice a little lighter than before. "Go. I know you have things to do. You are the queen now."

"Just until Father wakes up," I said.

"Go." She shooed me out of the room.

I hurried back to the gathering room and froze in the doorway.

Raziel.

CHAPTER 44

JAX

Rena backed out the door, her eyes glued to Raziel. I stood up and moved in front of her. "He's here to help."

"Help who?" Her voice shook. "Jax, he is the one who gave my father no choice but to fall to Hell."

Her wings unfurled. Fire dripped in molten drops from them.

"Your father left of his own volition," Raziel said.

"Shut up, Brother," Michael said. He placed a hand on Raziel's shoulder and pushed him down into a chair.

Rena lunged for him. *She actually lunged for him.* Her breathing was erratic. She stopped on the opposite side of the table.

"Rena," I whispered and placed my hand on the small of her back. "Breathe."

She leaned back into my touch like I had power over her, but she had all the power over me. I'd kill Raziel myself if she deemed it so. I'd drink his blood and dismember his body so he couldn't heal if that would make her happy.

"Tell Rena what you told us," Michael said.

"Why should I tell this... I don't even know what to call her. She's not a Nephilim." He paused. A sneer marred his perfect face. "A half-breed."

Mother fucker. I leaped into the air toward him. Gabriel grabbed one of my arms and Rena with his other. Michael pinned Raziel to the chair.

"I will obliterate you, little vampire," Raziel said.

"Not if I drain you dry, you piece of shit," I growled at him.

Raziel laughed, a wicked, bone-chilling laugh. "Shall I share your secrets, little vampire? Like how your wretched self loves my niece."

This is an angel. I was disgusted by him. Rena gave me a little squeeze. She knew I loved her, and she loved me. This creature held no influence on me. I relaxed into Rena's side.

"I'm good," I said, control coming back to my voice. "You can let me go."

Gabriel returned to the other side of the table and stared down at Raziel. Michael didn't remove his hand.

"Release me, Michael," Raziel demanded.

"The tension in your body suggests you are still ready to fight, so I think not, little brother." He drew out the last two words the way Raziel had drawn out his slur for Rena and me.

This angel might be accepted by his brothers and sisters, but they knew he had a dark side. I didn't like Uriel, but I respected him. I neither liked nor respected Raziel. He was a fucking asshole.

I swallowed down the temptation to pummel his face as his brother held him. Rena laced her fingers through mine, and my anger subsided. Only she could relax me with a simple touch.

"Tell her," Michael said to Raziel, his voice so menacing it gave me chills.

"Fine," he said. "Lucifer will remain in stasis unless you use my obsidian ankh to draw out Uriel's power."

Rena's fingers tightened around my hand.

"I'm assuming you don't have it with you?" she asked.

"No." Raziel shook his head. "The same demon who stole Uriel's famous artifact took my ankh to protect himself from the power of the Ascendant."

"But he was controlled by it just like Lucifer," I said.

"Ah, little vampire, he was. Do you know why?" Raziel leaned forward, a manic smile on his lips, and clasped his hands together.

"Obviously we don't," Rena said. She narrowed her eyes on him, and if looks could kill, he'd be dead ten times over. "So tell us."

"The secret to the ankh is that it doesn't protect the user at all. It draws the power out, but as soon as the idiot used the Ascendant again —"

"The control of the amulet returned," Rena said. "We need to go to the Garden of Eden to retrieve it."

"Yes, we do." Raziel stood and walked toward her.

She turned her back to him. "He stays here."

I smirked a little more than I should have and took my place by her side.

"It can fix your little vampire too," Raziel said. "Return him to the half demon he was. The two half-breeds together."

I rolled my head on my shoulders and counted as I'd taught Rena. She touched my arm.

"He's not worth it, Jax. Leave him."

"You're right," I said, taking her hand and pressing my lips to them. "He's not... but you are."

I spun on my heels and planted my fist in his jaw. The distinct crack of bone satisfied me. Pleased with myself, I stood back and watched for his next move.

Raziel's eyes rolled back in his head, and he teetered toward the ground. None of us moved to catch him, and he smacked the ground hard.

"Will he be okay, Michael?" Rena asked.

"He's a healer," Michael said, his voice flat. "He'll be fine."

"It would be in our best interest to get out of here before he wakes up." Gabriel ushered us toward the door. "He's going to be pissed."

We walked to an open area where I could call the portal.

"Nice shot, Jax," Michael said. "We've all wanted to do that for years."

I chuckled to myself. It was nice to see this side of the angels. I formed the symbols to call our path.

The portal materialized in front of us, and I held Rena's hand as we walked through.

CHAPTER 45
RENA

Eden looked as beautiful as the first time we arrived. One day, Jax and I could come here to explore versus on a mission to try to stop a battle or save my father.

Jax led us to the door to the mirror world with ease. The empty space between what I called purgatory looked the same. When Jax opened the door on the other side, I inhaled a deep breath, glad to be through the in-between section.

"Which way?" Gabriel asked.

"Their scents are heavy here, but they lead off in that direction." Jax pointed to our left.

"And we're sure he has the ankh?" I asked. "And we're positive Raziel wasn't lying?"

"My little brother is many things, including a petty imbecile, but he is not a liar," Michael said.

"Raziel would not lie," Gabriel agreed.

"I didn't expect you two to be so passionate about the light Raziel is painted in." I stifled a yawn. My brain and my body were both exhausted, but this was our chance to save Father. Like Mother, I hadn't had much of an appetite, but Jax forced bacon in front of me every morning to keep my energy up. I pushed forward through my bone weariness.

Jax was intent on the ankh's scent as he eased around corners. He had no fear for himself. It was all reserved for me. He held up a hand to stop us.

"How will I know where he has the relic?" I whispered to Gabriel.

"The key of life will pull you to it," Michael answered for him.

Why would it pull me to it? Surely, he meant the artifact would pull all of us.

The scent of Azazel and his men was stronger as we rounded a corner. Jax paused and nodded his head to the opening ahead. The space was the clearing that mirrored the one in Eden.

A force slammed into me like a magnet. I gasped.

"You feel the draw?" Michael asked.

I nodded, not yet able to speak.

We inched closer in unison. I strained against the tug of the ankh. It was hard not to run toward it. I ground my teeth against the urge.

"Okay?" Jax asked from my side.

"Yes," I gritted out.

"I'm here," he said. "Tell me what you need."

I reached for his hand, and he locked his in mine. I gripped him like a life preserver.

"Michael, his forces are vast. There are more than on the field," Jax said, his voice strained.

"I feel them too," he said, his voice less than confident. For the first time, Michael sounded unsure.

Even with archangels, we didn't stand a chance against a thousand or more demons. *Plus, the grey-wings if they are here.*

The battlefield. The queenly voice. "I know what to do," I said. "The voice that came out of me when we stopped the battle."

"Can you find that tone?" Gabriel said. "Things don't always work the same on this side of Eden."

The ankh yanked on me, and I stopped. No way could I project the voice with this nagging at me. I focused deep inside myself. Used Jax's breathing exercises. *In...two...three... four. Out...two...three...four.* I repeated the drill a few times. The draw was still there, but the drain of it was manageable. I was in control.

"Yes, I'm sure," I said, my confidence restored.

Azazel lounged on a massive chair that resembled a throne as if he proclaimed himself king and these were his subjects. The grey-wings stood closest to him. He trusted them more than his demon followers. *How had he created them?* Chills skittered across my skin.

Michael and Gabriel stiffened beside me. They felt the power present too.

"Do you know where the ankh is, Rena?"

I did. He was wearing the symbol around his neck. It sat right over his heart. "Yes, he has the necklace on him."

"Whenever you're ready." He squeezed my hand and dropped it.

"Ready." I stepped forward into Azazel's view.

He whispered to one of the grey-wings. The grey-wing

whispered back and stood tall. Azazel's subjects looked at me.

"Kneel," I said, letting the voice echo out across the group. "Kneel to your queen."

They did. All of them. Even Azazel. But the grey-wings did not. They were not demons and not bound to the rules of Hell. They would not take my command.

"I don't like this." Michael turned to me. "I don't think you should be the one to take the ankh from him."

"It has to be me," I said.

"Very well," Michael said, his voice strained.

I approached Azazel with my small crew surrounding me.

"No harm to us. No harm to you," the grey-wing Azazel had whispered to said.

"I agree to the terms." I held the grey-wing's stare.

He nodded once.

I reached around Azazel's neck and lifted the ankh over him.

"Don't hold it in your hand," Michael said, a warning in his tone.

I wrapped the leather cord in my fingers without touching the ankh and backed away from Azazel.

"This isn't over," Azazel said. He raised his head and met my gaze.

"No, it's not." I narrowed my eyes on him, pinning him in place, and released my demon face. "You can be assured of it."

I turned my back to Azazel, knowing my crew would

protect me if he tried anything. As we traveled down the maze back to the door, I thought of how remarkable we were. The daughter of Lucifer and Lilith, a former demon who was now a vampire, and two archangels working together as a team. I'm pretty sure that wasn't what was happening two thousand years ago when Father chose Mother. When he chose love. Because what do we have in this life, whether it is long like ours or short like the humans if we don't have love surrounding us?

Jax opened the door and ushered me through with his hand on my back.

"What's to stop them from following us?" I asked, staring at the door.

"Nothing," Jax said.

A broad smile crossed Gabriel's gentle face. "We can lock the door," he said.

"How?" I asked.

"I have the key." Gabriel retrieved the Ascendant from the bag.

"Gabriel, you shouldn't have that in your hands," Michael admonished him.

"Tsk tsk. Oh ye of little faith, Brother." Gabriel held the Ascendant to the door of the Eden mirror world. There were clicking sounds similar to doors latching. "They will remain here until you choose to set them free."

"We can't just leave them here," I said.

"Yes, we can," Michael said. "And you have the key when you choose to set them free."

"What key? The Ascendant? The ankh?"

"You are the key, Rena," Gabriel gestured toward me. "If

you touch the door, it will open for you and you alone. That is the message I used when I locked it."

"And they will be safe in there until I return?"

"Yes," Michael said. "No harm will come to them as long as they are there."

"You can be sure of that?" I stared at the door like it was an artifact, but it wasn't. *I had to make a decision and trust those who stood by me and advised me. This is the right place to leave them for now.*

"Yes, no one will be able to enter until you unlock the door," he said. "Correct, Gabriel?"

"That is correct." Gabriel touched my shoulder.

"Then back to Hell we go," I said. "Jax, do us the honor?"

Jax spun up a portal to return us home, and I was ready to go see my father. I ran down the corridor to his room. Footsteps trailed behind me as the others followed.

Mother's head was on her hand, her face turned in my direction. She was sleeping. I'd rarely seen her sleep or look so peaceful. Part of me wanted to let her sleep, but the time lost with Father grew. She'd want to be awake for this.

"Mom, wake up." I shook her shoulder. "I have something to show you."

She stirred awake. "Rena, you're home. And you are safe? No wounds?"

"None," I said. "But I do have this." I pulled the ankh out for her inspection.

"Why do you have an ankh?"

"It's Raziel's obsidian ankh," I said. "It will pull Uriel's power out of Father."

"Raziel is here?" Mother stiffened.

"He's a jerk," I said. "And he was in my meeting room when we left."

She blinked several times, but her focus came back to me. "I'm shocked he showed his face here or even helped you."

"Jax punched him if it makes you feel better." I smiled at her.

She smirked. "It does."

"Are we ready to try this on Father?"

"Yes, I hope it works," she said, her anticipation audible. "I need him here. By my side. By yours. Supporting our family."

"Let's suck out all of Uriel's power from Father," I said. "I'm ready to give him his throne back. It's not as comfortable as one might think."

"He might not want it back." She meant it as a joke, but dread hit me like Jax's punch landed against Raziel's jaw.

Michael and Gabriel stood on the other side of the bed. Jax took his position beside me and placed his hand on my lower back. I leaned into the pressure, relishing his touch. The comfort from that casual placement gave me more strength than I could have hoped for.

"What do I do? How do I work it?" I looked at Michael and Gabriel.

"Place it over his heart," Gabriel said. "And his hands over it.

I laid the ankh on Father's chest. It was off-center, and I pushed it with my finger. *Zzzp.* I jerked my hand away. A small charge like low voltage electricity stung my fingertip.

"That's why I told you not to touch it," Michael said, admonishing me the way he had Gabriel.

"Noted." I adjusted Father's hands so that they covered the ankh. "How will we know it's working?" It didn't look like it was doing anything.

"Just watch," Gabriel said.

A low hum vibrated the air. It was almost like someone humming a sound.

"It's tuning to Lucifer's vibration to separate the Ascendant's power," Michael whispered like our words would break the ankh's concentration.

"And it can tell the difference?"

"It knows what belongs and what does not," Gabriel said.

The hum grew louder, and a soft green light sprouted through the spaces between Father's fingers. *Green. A healing light.* The light expanded around him and ate up the residual blue from Barachiel's lightning bolt. The soft green haze filled the room, and the hum turned into a soft and sweet wordless song. My soul welcomed the music like a friend. The light snapped back like a rubber band, and the music abruptly stopped.

CHAPTER 46
RENA

Father didn't move. He didn't appear any different except for the absence of the blue light. Mother grabbed his hand in hers.

"Why isn't anything happening? Nothing changed." Panic shook me from the inside out. I'd been so sure, so confident this would work.

"Patience," Gabriel said. "He has to find his way back. It will happen."

Jax slipped his hand from my back to my waist and pulled me closer. I leaned into him.

Mother held Father's massive hand between both of hers and lifted it to her lips. "Come back to me, husband. I need you."

I laid my hand on top of Mother's. "We both need you."

Father moved his hand in Mother's. I stared at it and looked up at his face for signs.

"Yes, we're here waiting for you, my love," Mother said, her voice shaking.

Father's mouth opened. His lips moved, but no sound came out. Mother and I leaned closer. I couldn't hear anything.

Mother kissed his cheek. "I know you are there. I know you can hear us. Open your eyes and be present with us."

Father's lids fluttered like Mother's words commanded him. Relief waved over me. I closed my eyes and let out a sigh.

Mother gasped.

I looked back at Father. His eyes were a crystal blue like the ice in Antarctica and not the brownish-red they had been. I'd never seen them so clear. But he was awake.

"Lucifer?" Mother said his name like she wasn't sure it was him. "How do you feel?"

"I'm happy to see you, Lilith," he said, his voice a little rough but otherwise his natural one. He lifted his hand and caressed Mother's cheek. "And you." He turned to me and patted my cheek. "I'm happy to see you too, daughter."

"Do you remember what happened?" Mother asked.

"It's like a haze is over it. Like someone else was living it, but I do remember," Father said, his voice guilt-ridden. "And I'm sorry. To both of you."

"The blame is on Azazel," I said. "And he will pay. We will see to it."

Father gazed up into Mother's eyes with love like it would burn the world down, and I supposed he almost did for her. He lit the angelic rules on fire to be with her two thousand years ago, and he never regretted it that I could see.

My gaze traveled around the room. "Why don't we give Mother and Father some time to catch up."

Father looked over at his brothers. "Thank you for guiding my family to bring me back. You could have left me there, but you didn't."

"That's what brothers are for, Lucifer," Michael said. "We will always be your brothers." Michael patted my father's leg and glanced at Gabriel. "Speaking of. We need to go deal with our little brother."

"That we do," Gabriel said. "Be well, Brother. We missed you."

"Welcome back, Lucifer," Jax said with a formal bow.

"You do not need to be formal with me, Jax," he said, glancing between us. "You are family too."

Jax smiled.

"Get some rest, and we'll meet you in the study whenever you are ready." I kissed his cheek and then Mother's. "I love you both."

"You are so loved, Rena," Father said.

I took Jax's hand and led him into the hall.

CHAPTER 47

RENA

After we saw to the pressing matters for Hell and checked on Father again, Jax and I ended up in front of the door to my room.

"It's late." He lifted one of my arms and placed it around his neck. "I should let you rest."

"I don't want to rest," I said, opening the door and leading him into the room. "I want you to stay." I caressed Jax's cheek. His eyes darted to the bed and back to me.

"I need to tell you something." He licked his lips.

"If it's because I've never been with a man, Jax, I'm ready. I've been ready for a while. I mean I've done stuff. Not intercourse but other stuff. Just waiting for the one person I wanted to realize I was here." I babbled like an idiot in the most unsexy way. *Sweet angel's ass. I'm an idiot.* My cheeks burned.

"Rena..." His voice was rough with desire. He plunged his hands into my hair and devoured my mouth. He broke the kiss and looked into my eyes. His thumbs stroked my cheeks.

"I've always known you were here. I was waiting to be worthy of you, and I'll spend every hour of every day proving my worth to you."

"There's only one thing I need you to do to prove anything to me." I looked at his parted lips and back up to his intense gaze. "Make love to me, Jax."

His hand found the zipper on my jacket and slid it down. He bent forward and sucked on my neck. His fangs brushed over my skin without breaking it. My core clenched. I shuffled out of the jacket and dropped it on the floor. He ran his hands over my bare arms and grasped the hem of my tank top. He skimmed up over my torso until he reached my breasts. His thumbs swiped back and forth over my nipples. My mouth found his and urged him on. The need in me grew with every touch. I wanted him with all of me.

He broke the kiss long enough to pull the tank over my head. I took hold of the collar of his T-shirt and yanked it free of him.

"Hey, I liked that shirt." He chuckled against my lips.

"Oops," I dropped the shredded fabric.

He worked the clasp of my bra until it was free. The red lace dropped to the ground, exposing my breasts. *This is really happening.* I slid my arms around his neck. He pulled me to him and our torsos were pressed skin to skin. My nipples hardened with the contact. He trailed a line of kisses down to my chest and circled my peaks with his tongue.

I pushed him back and shimmied out of my pants. He watched until I remained in my red lace panties. His heated stare ignited an inferno in me that rivaled the fires of Hell. I reached for the button of his jeans. "You're overdressed, Jaxon."

"Am I?" he asked, his voice husky and low. "Can you help me with that?"

I unsnapped the button and worked the zipper down. He toed his shoes off and tugged his jeans to the ground, kicking them to the side.

"No patience." I tsked at him.

"I've been very patient," he said, slipping a thumb under each side of my panties. He ripped them off like they were paper.

"Damn..." I said, practically dripping for him.

I wound my hand into the waistband of his white briefs.

"Rena," he warned.

"I don't take orders." I tore them away, freeing his massive erection. His cock hit my stomach, and I dropped my eyes. My mouth went dry. It was huge. Much bigger than the guys in the pornos I watched. I'd touched myself and knew exactly what I was working with. If the dicks in the pornos fit those women, then surely his would fit in me. I took a step back.

He pulled me close, pressing his hard length into my stomach.

I swallowed against my anxiety. This was Jax. Here with me, and I'd wanted this for so long. The pressure to be perfect for him clamped down on my heart.

"Don't be nervous." He glided his lips over my shoulder. "I'll show you."

His simple but perfect words eased my worry. Jax

scooped me up and set me on the edge of the bed. He pushed my legs apart.

I looked into his eyes. "I trust you."

He smiled and ran his tongue over my clit.

The bundle of nerves radiated out through my body in massive quivering spikes of pleasure.

"Jax," I murmured, my voice breathy. I tangled my fingers into his hair.

He slipped two fingers inside me and moved them around.

Arousal coiled in my belly, but the sensation was unlike my other experiences. Stronger.

"You are so wet. Are you always like this for me?"

"Yes, every day," I said.

"Then I will worship you like this just as often." He added a third finger and moved faster. He alternated between licking and sucking my clit. Every nerve in my core crackled with electricity. My breath came in pants.

"Come for me, Rena."

"I told you I don't..." My center clenched and warmth spread out over my body. My head fell back. I shattered on his fingers. "Jax."

My eyes fluttered open.

Jax sucked on his fingers. "You taste so good."

My core tightened again. *Fuck. That turned me on.* My arms and legs shook as I tried to sit up.

Jax hooked his arm around my waist and moved me back on the bed. The tip of his dick rubbed against my mound, and I almost came undone again.

His tongue ran over my shoulder and up my neck. He

paused to look into my eyes. "I've wanted this for so long. You are my world, Rena."

"You are mine." I ran my hands down his back. "I want you, Jax. All of you."

"You're sure you are ready?" He positioned himself at my opening.

"Yes," I said. Scared but ready.

He dipped in with the head and entered me. My pussy stretched at his girth. He held still, allowing my body to adjust to his size. He raised high up on his arms and positioned himself over me. His movements were slow as he ground his cock in circles against my clit until stars formed in my vision, and I closed my eyes.

"I'm going to explode," I gasped out.

He stroked deep into me and every punishing stroke drove me higher. The sensations rocketed like fireworks igniting inside me.

"Come with me, Rena." His voice was rough with passion.

"Now?" I moaned out.

"Now." He nipped at my neck. "Rena."

His fangs sunk into my throat. The pleasure intensified, and my body convulsed around him. His release filled me. His forehead rested against me. He raised his head and brushed the damp hair from my face. He smiled, and it was brighter than any light the angels could bring.

"Was that okay?" I asked, acutely aware of how timid my voice sounded. My cheeks heated.

"No," he looked into my eyes.

My heart dropped, and I squirmed to get away.

Jax pinned me to the bed. "It was much more than okay. It was like my own personal paradise, and I will never get enough of you."

I relaxed. "I can't imagine it being any better, but I'm all for trying again."

He chuckled and pressed his lips to my forehead. "I love you, Rena."

"I love you." I smiled up at him.

Jax rolled off of me and pulled me to his chest. "How long do you think we'll have to cuddle before they come to find you for Hell business?"

I giggled. "Did you just say cuddle?"

He pulled me closer. "I did, and I plan to do a lot of it with you. Hell can wait."

CHAPTER 48
RENA

"We could have stayed in the shower longer." Jax wagged his eyebrows.

I laughed as I pulled my boots on. The shower was good and so was the bed and so was bent over the counter in the bathroom. *Why had I waited so long?* "I'm afraid angels will start appearing in our room if we don't show up soon."

He pulled me to him and covered my mouth with his. "Our room? You don't want to send me back to my quarters?"

A nervous twinge worked around my stomach. "I assumed you would stay with me. But you don't have to. I mean, I want you to but only if you want to."

He placed a finger over my lips. "Of course I do."

A knock rapped on the door. "My queen, Uriel is in the study."

"And so it begins." I sighed.

"I'm sure your father will be back on the throne soon." Jax pushed my hair over my shoulders. "You've got this."

I slipped my hand into his. "We've got this."

"Always." Jax pulled my hand to his mouth and pressed a kiss to my knuckles.

I called through the door. "Please let him know Jax and I will be there in a moment."

"Yes, my queen," the voice said from the other side.

"Shall we?" I met Jax's gaze. His eyes were full of love, and it reminded me of how Father looked at Mother.

"I still don't like him," Jax said. "Uriel, that is. But I trust you."

"Let's go see what he has to say." I turned and pulled him toward the door.

He tugged me back to him and devoured my mouth, leaving me breathless.

"Now, we can go." He winked at me.

Uriel sat at the large table with his head in his hands. The archangel looked exhausted. White light blinded me, and Jax tucked me against his side. Gabriel and Michael appeared on either side of him.

"What's going on?"

"Barachiel is missing," Uriel said into his hands.

A knot formed in my gut. "Aunt B? What happened?"

"We're not sure," Gabriel said, his tone grim. "But we found a trail of angel blood in Eden."

"But Azazel can't get us, right? Not until I let him out.

Isn't that what you said?" Nausea waved over me. My chest tightened, and I struggled for air.

"They can't unless you unlock the door," Michael said.

"We think it is Raziel who took Barachiel," Uriel said, finally meeting my gaze. His eyes were haunted. "And that's worse than Azazel."

"What about Raziel?" Father's voice came from behind me.

I turned to see him with Mother at his side. "You're up. How are you feeling?"

"Like myself today." His focus leveled on the archangels. "Now, what were you saying about our little brother?"

"We believe he has taken Barachiel," Gabriel said.

"Why?" Father's face contorted in confusion.

Gabriel and Michael exchanged glances. "We don't know, but we think it might have something to do with the bolt she conjured and threw at you."

"Ahh. Yes," Father said. "And you think she was taken why?"

"She is nowhere to be found, and there was angel blood in the garden," Michael said.

"Do not fret, my brothers. She is working for me and tracking Raziel," Father said. "But since you are all here, I want to share a decision."

My hands shook. Jax placed a hand on my lower back, and the familiar warmth spread from his touch.

"Lilith and I need some time, and I'm going to take a vacation from Hell," Father continued. "Morena will sit the throne in my absence, but I would like all of you to serve as her advisors while I'm gone."

"None of us can stay here full time with her, Lucifer," Uriel said, his eyes on Jax.

"No, but I trust you will check in with her daily." He removed the ankh from around his neck and laid it on the table. His gaze fell on Jax. "And maybe one of you will be able to stay with her soon."

I hugged my father and mother. "Thank you," I whispered.

"You are the best thing to happen to Hell, Morena," Father said. "I'm proud of you."

"As am I," Mother said. "Be kind to yourself and your advisors."

They nodded to the angels and left.

"I think Rena and Jax might need a few minutes," Uriel said. "Shall we, brothers?"

A bright light flashed, and Jax and I were completely alone.

I lifted the ankh off the table by the leather cord. "Would you even want this? You make a pretty damn good vampire."

"Being a vampire has some perks, but I'd rather be able to stay here with you full-time. You are everything I've wanted and all I will ever need."

I brushed away the tears from the corners of my eyes. My heart was full, and regardless of where we were, I wanted to be with him. "Jax, it has only ever been you for me. If this is what you want, then we can do it whenever you decide."

He lifted the ankh from my hand. "Now," he said. "I want it now. I'm ready to be me again and to be here with you permanently. You are my world. It's time for us to be free to share our love anytime and anywhere we choose."

My heart fluttered. The love I had for him deepened like our souls entwined. "I'm ready for that too," I said and pressed my lips to his. "I'm ready to love you for eternity."

Eternity with Jax wouldn't be long enough, but we would live it together.

To be continued...
In Book 2 of the Falling From Hell series: *Reverie*
Scan the QR code to find out more

Acknowledgments

To my beta readers, ARC readers, and fans, it is the love you have shown me that keeps me writing on my dark days. Thank you for your support, and a special thank you to those that seek out indie authors to support.

To my family, thank you for being there through cover and blurb decisions and celebrating the wins with me. Special thanks to my sister who surprised me with a celebration when I hit the bestsellers list. Your support is everything to me. Thank you!

My developmental editor always calls me out on my shit, and I know she'll know what I mean by that. Dawn Alexander, you challenge me and make me a better writer even when I'm in that space where I hate the book before I fall in love with the story again. Thank you for not being afraid to say "I've never seen you do this before" when I try something that doesn't quite work and for telling me when I take a chance that does!

And to my new proofreader, Fenley Grant, who is an amazing author on top of proofreading. Thank you for taking this project on for me and helping to make it a better book for my readers. I appreciate you!

About the Author

Susan Person is a multi-contest finalist in the paranormal and dark paranormal romance categories. Recently, she returned to college to pursue a degree in anthropology and graduated in 2021. Susan enjoys meeting writers and readers alike at conferences. She knew at an early age she wanted to write powerful heroines and fulfilled that dream by writing badass empowered heroines who take charge in their paranormal worlds.

Susan grew up on a thoroughbred horse farm before moving to the big city of Dallas. She considers herself a Texan but is loyal to her home state of Arkansas. A lover of travel, she has visited several countries with many more to go on her list. She particularly loved dowsing at Stonehenge. The outdoors are a place Susan finds inspiration and can often be found in a park, at the lake, or on a road trip. She especially loves the mountains. Furry animals hold a special place in her heart, and dogs tend to seek her out as a friend.

Connect with her at susanperson.com

instagram.com/susanwritespnr

tiktok.com/@susanwritespnr

facebook.com/susanwritespnr

goodreads.com/susanperson

bookbub.com/authors/susan-person